Flash Baby

VERONICA SCHREIBER

© Copyright 2006 Veronica Schreiber.
All rights reserved. No part of this publication may be reproduced, stored in a retrieval system, or transmitted, in any form or by any means, electronic, mechanical, photocopying, recording, or otherwise, without the written prior permission of the author.

Note for Librarians: A cataloguing record for this book is available from Library and Archives Canada at www.collectionscanada.ca/amicus/index-e.html
ISBN 1-4251-0381-2

Printed in Victoria, BC, Canada. Printed on paper with minimum 30% recycled fibre. Trafford's print shop runs on "green energy" from solar, wind and other environmentally-friendly power sources.

TRAFFORD
PUBLISHING

Offices in Canada, USA, Ireland and UK

Book sales for North America and international:
Trafford Publishing, 6E–2333 Government St.,
Victoria, BC V8T 4P4 CANADA
phone 250 383 6864 (toll-free 1 888 232 4444)
fax 250 383 6804; email to orders@trafford.com
Book sales in Europe:
Trafford Publishing (UK) Limited, 9 Park End Street, 2nd Floor
Oxford, UK OX1 1HH UNITED KINGDOM
phone +44 (0)1865 722 113 (local rate 0845 230 9601)
facsimile +44 (0)1865 722 868; info.uk@trafford.com
Order online at:
trafford.com/06-2138
10 9 8 7 6 5 4

Prologue

I went down the aisle labelled, *New Baby*. My eyes fell on the bright fleshy colours of the Anne Geddes section. Big pink-toned babies, nude and giggling at the camera's flash caught in their podgy eyes. The babies were in costumes—chubby honeybees or stubby buds or the sun itself and you couldn't forget the cherubs.

I looked at the vast selection of cards and my fingers selected one: a nude baby girl giggling at the cardholder. Her little body was neatly tied with a pink bow. The card inside read, "What a Surprise! A baby girl! Congratulations!"

Holding the card, I glanced at the old store clerk who was arranging guardian angel pins and fuzzy beanie babies near the cash register. I looked back at the photo to make sure that the dumpy smiling girl with the pink bow covering her tiny genitals was what I wanted to give as a congratulation.

I handed the card to the clerk and she smiled at my selection and carefully placed the card in a small brown bag and rested it on the counter. She gently tapped and slid the bag to me.

"Do you want to buy a beanie baby maybe?" She gave me her old grin trying to be kind underneath her clucking plastic teeth.

She picked and squeezed one baby to show how plush it was to the touch.

"No thanks." I jingled my coins in my pocket.

"Alright." She tapped three digits into the cash register and pressing with all her might the big total button. "Ah. One seventy eight, please." She glanced back at me with a smile.

I gave her the exact amount.

"Thank you. Bye-bye."

"Bye."

I left, ringing the little bell which hung above the door.

Starting

My father sat there holding his cards and shaking his head as he drank down his beer. If he was a little boy he'd be screaming with excitement, hoping this time he'd win. My father "the breadwinner" would gamble with his five Shabbies as he called them. This time they were playing a newcomer to the sport. Robert Malt lived in Wicklow Forest but hung out at Port's Pub. He had long hair, was thin and always wore tight pants and baggy sweaters. He was The Freak if you were to ask my father. Robert asked the Shabbies to play and at first they laughed. But I swear my father saw four big bright letters spelling EASY over Robert's head. It was one of my father's enlightened moments, so he replied to God's grace, "Take up a seat Robbie-boy."

That night I was sitting behind my father colouring in my colouring book. My mother was out with the girls so he got stuck with me. My father placed the weekly bread on the table, losing all of it to Robert. Each time Robert won my father grumbled, "Pure Luck, pure luck."

The next hand my father believed was his winning lot, but

you see, he had no more to bet cause Robert and his numerous lucky hands had it all. So he tried to convince Robert of something to bet. Unfortunately, the Shabbies were broke, Robert had all their cash. Then Robert, Robert looked over at me trying to help my father find his lucky bet. I looked up at Robert. I didn't know what the girlie-boy wanted. I went back to colouring. Colouring my magical purple horse.

"Twinkle, twinkle little star." I decided to make a night scene with stars all around her. "How I wonder where you are?" I stopped singing cause I heard my name being called. I didn't bother to look up. If it was important they would've shouted or screamed it out as my mother did.

I was scrubbing the crayon onto the paper to give that shiny, wax effected sky with a few big white stars so the magical horsy could find her way to the magical palace.

"Na, na I'm in," my father said.

I imagined the magical horsy walking in the dark as I mimicked my father's favourite tune, "Na, na I'm in. Na, na I'm in." Turning into: "Na, na, na, na." My picture was done and I looked up to the sounds of the cards being played. It was instinct after awhile to see who took the centre pot.

I saw Robert's face grow into a smile and my father's big body sank into the chair. The deep silence came, followed by everyone watching me. When I looked up into my father's face it was horribly sad. His big blue eyes were watery, like two big sinking boats. I wondered staring at my father, did I do something? Was I bad? It came together as my father finished his beer and shook Robert's hand. I knew he must've lost big time cause he was shaking the winner's hand who had the pile of money on his side. My father looked at me trying hard to smile and cover up the loss. I went back to my next picture. I thought I would try to draw a red dragon.

"Eliza, come here my dear, come here." He stretched out his arm and his hand beckoned me.

I dropped the red crayon and placed my hand in my father's big hand. "What is it, Daddy?"

"Eliza, I want you to meet Robert Malt."

Robert Malt held out his hand and I shook it. Shook it sternly like I was making a deal.

"Hello, Mister Robert Malt." I just got better behaved.

"Hello there, Miss Eliza."

I saw my father's lips move but I couldn't help thinking of the fire-breathing red dragon. How was I going to draw it? Maybe I should make it purple.

"Eliza, Eliza?"

"Yes, Daddy?"

"Just like when your Auntie takes care of you, alright?"

"Yes." I shook my head horse-like. Right then I was pretending to be the magical purple horsy.

"Tomorrow at noon," Robert said as he got up with his thick wallet. Leaving my father to the oohs and ahs of the situation.

My father sat there for a few moments staring at nothing it seemed. He watched me as I gathered up all of my colouring activity. I got my coat on and struggled with the big buttons; they were too big.

On the ride home everything was silent; usually he had some sort of story to tell about the Shabbies. But nothing. Just like what he won, nothing.

When we got home my mother was standing in the living room, her slender cheeks sucking on a strong cigarette. She saw my father's lowered head and his eyes that were avoiding hers. He could try as hard as he wanted to but her eyes always caught them and stared them down as if they were dirt.

My mother took me aside and kissed me with her smoky breath and walked me to bed as my father stood in the refrigerator's light grabbing, let's take a guess—a beer. No, his lucky beer at that. Once I was in bed, she'd shut the door and I would watch the wasted smoke disappear. Then I'd pop out of bed and press my ear to the door.

My mother's footsteps entered the TV room. "So, did you lose it all?"

"What, my sugar plum?"

"Don't give me that, Morris. You lost it all even with your only child sitting there, an you bet it all. Didn't you?"

"Maril, I had a beautiful hand—"

"I'm sure you did. But Morris, you fucking lost. Now how much?"

"What is it to you? We'll be fine for the week."

"You're one fine fucking loser Morris, one fine one. An look at you, you can't even admit to yourself you lost an we lost it all didn't we? Didn't we? You're a fucking loser! An your daughter sitting—"

The slap. It seemed like thunder coming out of nowhere like his big EASY signs. Her delicate body, she called it, smacked the linoleum.

"You fucking Bitch. Tell me, what would you do if I fucking won? Would you still be a fucking bitch to me? Bitch to me what a fucking loser I am, Maril? Na, I don't think you would."

"You know Morris, you'll never fucking win that's why we live here. We'll be here to the day we die cause you're a fucking loser. I don't see a winner. I see a fucking loser. A loser. A loser Morris!"

He bolted her twice and I never heard her cry. I waited and waited.

"Maril, if you ever say, I'm a fucking loser or the G word again, I'll bolt you one straight to hell. Now, tell me what do you think of that?"

She didn't answer.

"Answer me or I'll bolt you one! That's right, act all fucking sweet. Answer me an be the bitch you are, Maril! Come on! Let's hear it!" He screamed, that's when I raced under the covers and I held my head tight and plugged my ears. Under the covers I hoped to dear God that she'd answer him.

Later, I woke up to footsteps. I tightly held my eyes shut and my head was revealed and kissed. I knew I was forgiven cause she answered. Now I could sleep and dream about all that rainbow shit you're supposed to: A little pony perhaps and a field of flowers to bounce here and there, and maybe another boy or girl to play house with. One dream I kept bolting this boy, Bobbie from school. At the end of the dream I bolted him to hell for sheer fun of it. He really did go to hell. I guess I was tired of picking flowers and noses. You can only pick so much till it bleeds.

Feeling Me

The next morning my mother got me ready in my little pink dress that I got for my birthday. Well, it was for my birthday party. In that dress I used to stand on my tippy toes and pretend I was a ballerina. Even then I knew what I wanted.

My mother put on my coat and hugged me tightly. Tightly always. Then I was left in my father's hands. I knew well enough never to look at her face the next morning cause that's when she would cry. I learned that my mother had feelings too. One morning, after my parents fought, my mother was dressing me, my father was singing heavily and I was giggling cause he was happy. I was young so I forgot. My eyes wondered onto my mother's green eyes that were black and I knew they were white when she tucked me in. My mother's hair that was usually in pink or blue curlers was all over the place. Her eyes caught mine and she frowned as she saw them. She knew that I knew. Knew it all.

"Mummy, your eyes are black!" I told her like she was unaware of the fact.

I saw tears form in her eyes and run down her bruised cheeks. She squeezed me and patted my head. I felt like a baby chick when she did this. The only thing that she didn't do was coo and she didn't feed me worms.

She said under her deep breaths, "You're a good girl, Eliza."

Hugging and crying on me, I cried too. What was I supposed to do?

I lied there in her arms listening to her breathe; I wondered if someone had died. Did daddy die? But I thought I heard him singing. Was he an Angel? My father came in doing up his tie.

He looked at us, knotting the tie up to his neck. "What's this, what's this? Maril? Maril, honey?"

My mother let go of me. She stared at my father with hate as she wiped her tears away with that ragged pink kimono.

She stood up and glared at him. "What's this, Morris? It's you, Morris." She took my hand.

"What do you mean?"

"I mean you, fool, that she's crying, crying cause I'm crying."

"Then why are you crying?"

"I'm crying over you. An now she sees an knows."

"Knows what?"

The yelling always turned into screaming until the first slap. I was knocked down. I ran to the corner of my room. I didn't want to be hit for holding my mother's hand. Now look who's shameful. Saving myself and leaving my mother to have it in. At the same time, that's when I discovered hiding my face and ears made everything disappear. So I disappeared. Not till I opened my hands and eyelids did I return.

I heard my father shouting, "So, Maril, what do you think now? You bloody bitch that won't die."

I covered my face and ears again hoping to disappear. I kept remembering my father's bolts and I never forgot, never forgot them. I knew sitting there curled up that it was my fault for my mother's sores and bruises. It was mine. That I never forgot. Never did.

Eliza Fellows

The freak's house was way off in the boonies. He lived near Wicklow Forest a provincial park now. My father kept looking over as if he wanted to say something but all he did was smile and look away. I stared outside hoping to see a deer or a bear. I never saw anything. Nature was as still as the wallpaper forest in the dentist's office. It was never meant to move. It stood still and picturesque. How many times did I want to shake it up and find those deers and bears. It drove me insane sitting, staring and waiting. Waiting, staring and sitting. It seemed stiller than ever.

The road up to his house was gravel. My father carefully drove up; he didn't want to crack the windows or chip off his rust. He was particular about gravel roads, cause that rust was priceless. He ground his teeth always, when he heard each new stone hit his car with that TING! TING! TING! There were always two more to follow the one. I held in my laughter by holding my mouth; the complete opposite when I had to tinkle. But it was pain holding it in. My stomach ready to burst.

He'd curl up his shoulders and grind his teeth and swear under his breath. He drove so slow. Each TING! became louder and bigger. Once we came to a stop and he relaxed. It was funny to see him scared. Scared of two things—gravel roads and mother's eyes.

I looked at the big wooden house. My father took me out and carried me to the door. "Now Eliza, you behave an be a good girl. Do as you're told an nothing bad. Okay?"

He placed me down.

"Yes, Daddy." I still didn't know where I was, where I was going. I just thought it was a new babysitter and I couldn't figure out, why it was way out here. All the way out in the boonies.

He knocked on the door's window. Robert Malt appeared.

"Hello, Morris an Eliza. How are you?" He smiled like a big cherry.

"Good."

"Pick her up at four."

"Alright."

Robert took my hand and waved to my father. "See ya."

"Bye, Daddy."

Robert locked the door.

"Okay, Eliza." He paused and grinned at me. "Let me show you around, an then we'll get started. First, did your parents feed you?"

"Yes."

"Amazing, but good."

The house was huge and covered in nude photos of all sorts. I hid, laughed and giggled at the sight of the many nude grownup men photos and then I stopped when I came across the little boy photos. They were even funnier because they were sitting in school desks like when I went to school, but they were all nude. They looked stupid just sitting, nude with that trunk-thing hanging there. It was such a funny playing object because it was attached to them. It was all just too much for me to take. First my father, then the nude boys playing with themselves as they took their lessons down. So I burst. Each thought being unbearable. Just tickling and exploding in my stomach.

"I'm happy you find amusement in them." He had a girlie laugh that made me laugh even more. My favourite photo that made me think: This bald man lying down all relaxed, looking at the viewer as he felt his hairy stomach. I just couldn't believe it at the time, that he had hair down below but no hair on top; that didn't make any sense. I looked over to the little boys, and I decided that it was better to have hair on the head than hair down below because who was going to see it. That made more sense to me. What the hell was that guy thinking to be bald? What a freak. I learned that word from my father when he talked of Robert behind his back. But looking at this bald and hairy man, I thought who was the real freak? That's when I thought Robert wasn't much of a freak.

"Okay Eliza." I turned around to look at him. "Now tell me, do you want to be a star?"

"Yup, I wanna-be a star." When he said star, I just jumped up at it. I'm sure my eyes must've popped.

"Good. Now, let's get you on the box. It's pretty isn't it?"

"Yes." I responded, getting on the red velvet box that was in the other photos.

"Okay, make any pose you want."

So I did. I kicked off my shoes and stood on my tippy toes and raised my arms and hands to meet in a semicircle and I smiled like one of those beautiful ballerinas. My head was held high for I was being a star for the first time for someone else. For someone else who wanted to see me as a star, instead of me standing in front of the mirror doing twirls and bows for myself.

FLASH! the camera went. My eyes squinted. Then I saw those dark-bright-white-blue circles blotting everywhere.

"Good, very good. Eliza, I want you to sit an place your hands on your lap an show me, what a good girl you are."

I did and I smiled. Showing that sweet goodness that I was taught.

FLASH! Squint. FLASH! Squint.

"Okay, now Eliza, remember those other photos?"

"Yes." I really didn't know what to think but I liked when the camera went FLASH! cause I saw those little circles all around. Like the little stars and birds you see when you get hit on the head.

"Alright, now let's see." He loaded the camera. "Alright, almost ready. Are your eyes okay?"

"I guess so."

"Very good, you see Eliza, you're a natural. A natural born star." He fiddled with the camera again. "Now, I want to make you into a beautiful star. Tell me, do you want to be beautiful?"

"Yes." I smiled. I felt then he should've known that I wanted to be everything a star was.

"Okay, let's start. I want you—" The phone rang. He ran to get it. I just sat there staring out to the sky watching the leaves blow. He came back and checked the camera. "Alright Eliza, or Eliza of the stars. I would very much like you to take off your clothes. Do you think you can do that?"

He looked up at me. I was already struggling with the zipper of my dress. "Yes," I responded catching his glance. I wanted to show him I was a good girl but a big girl. It was important to be a big girl when you're a little girl.

"Good."

It was hot under those spotlights. Finally, I zippered down my pink dress ending in a nest around my feet. I struggled once again with my hated leotards and my underwear just slid off. Thinking nothing.

"Good. Now, sit the same way you were sitting before. Do you remember?"

I shook my head. And I did it. I sat with my hands on my lap and stared at the camera with a big smile. FLASH! Squint. FLASH! Squint.

"Good."

From all the "goods" he said, it went to a new pose and a new FLASH! A squint. I never saw so many circles flying around and sometimes they would block Robert's face.

After posing tirelessly with a now aching smile, this little star was tired. Robert being the girlie-boy sensed it. Since he was my new babysitter, he made me lunch—peanut butter and jam sandwiches. I munched them down quickly. Robert watched me. I'm sure he was amazed with how fast I ate.

After hearing so many goods, that's all that went through my mind with the continuous flashes. As I ate the sandwich, my eyes stood still gazing on that picnic tablecloth where that shining white plate lay echoing the lights from above. There I saw his reflection, older-looking upside down and I kept hearing good, good. You could say I had a lifetime of goods and flashes.

"That's good, eat up. It seems to me your mummy an daddy don't feed you enough."

He was always imposing. Of course, when I was young I

didn't understand that. All I did was smile. It is a given being a girl. I made sure I swallowed before I talked, cause I didn't know whether he would smack me if I spoke with my mouth full.

"Mister Malt, they feed me." Very polite, very polite.

"Good." His girlie pink lips replied. They seemed a lot like mine. I touched mine to make sure I still had them. They were there.

He handed me some carrots and I ate those quickly trying to see my lips.

The next activity he gave me was paper and he told me to colour, which I did. He watched and drew me. I drew little pink ballerinas and I was in the centre with a red tutu and a big crown. I kept seeing those bright circles all over the page. So I tried to catch them with my yellow and blue crayon making them into stars. The picture was alive with flashing stars and tippy-toeing ballerinas. I remember it being my best picture ever, because it moved and seemed so real to me. I looked over to Robert; he was smoking and checking his watch.

"Are you done?"

"Yeah," I replied already handing him the page with a big accomplished smile on my face.

He gazed at it with his eyebrow crocking over each image like he was seeing something else on the page. Then his eyes crocked on me. Right then, I'm sure my smile left my face and I waited for an answer. Is it good? Is it good? I wanted so badly for it to be good. As his little lips curled into words as they held that smoke. I was already trying to feel it out.

Then it came. "Very good Eliza, very good. Now tell me Eliza, what do you want to be?"

"A ballerina."

"I'm sure you'll be one," he replied half smiling, smashing the smoke in the ashtray.

My smile grew bigger. I was so happy, so happy he thought so too. He actually believed in me. That I, Eliza Fellows, would be a ballerina. And somebody saw the talent in my toes, in my hands, legs and rosy cheeks.

Then my father's harsh knock came. Everything he did was harsh and heavy. Robert held my hand and I grabbed my coat.

"Hi, Morris."

"Eliza, come here." I came struggling with those buttons.

Robert handed me my drawing. My father stood there with my hand in his, waiting for a command, what else.

"Bye, Morris."

That's when we left. I waved back to Robert.

My father placed me in the car, quickly buckling me up, but never looking at me. He walked over to the other side quickly. It was as if he couldn't move fast enough.

"Bastard," my father said once inside. "One filthy bastard." He handed me a red sucker; it was my favourite.

We drove back home. Silence again. I stared out still seeing those circles. At times I tried to touch them but they popped away from me.

"So, Eliza, how are you?"

I looked up.

Originated

A perfect house, the sun setting behind the house with the perfect couple standing and smiling. One day on a very, very late stormy night, the husband helped his dear wife, pushing her gently and carrying the suitcase out of their home, tentatively rearing his wife into the passenger seat in his VW. Once he had her tightly in, he slammed the door followed by a quick frantic run around the car. He whipped the door open and jumped in.

Up above two engulfing clouds collided, sending their deep ripple through the transparent air. The rain spouted out and he rolled up his window. With his seat belt snapped, he zoomed into reverse and roared out of the neighbourhood.

The rain exploded into hard smacking raindrops. He kept looking over to her, forgetting about the road and the car's blinking light in the rear-view mirror.

The car steamed up with her breathing and the rain outside pounded down like it was breaking through that tin roof. The wipers didn't help much, but they were still kept on, spreading the thick water.

The husband rolled down the window. One hand on the steering wheel, the other wiping the window clean of the steam, only to be covered up again. And his pants were soaked by the forgotten open window.

The neon Emergency sign filled the wet car window with big blobs of electric red. He pulled in and raced out of the car, grabbing a vacant wheelchair.

A nurse came darting out for his wife.

"She's having a baby." He wheeled his wife to the nurse.

"You can't park here," her fuchsia lips demanded. "Park over there." She pointed to the parking lot as she rolled his wife into the hospital. He watched his wife, hearing her wheezing away and holding their unborn child.

Soon enough, trying to keep it perfectly planned, the husband came in carrying the orange suitcase she had packed months ago, as he had read to do in the pregnancy magazines. Both of them had tried to come to an agreement on their child's name. From a long list of names, they finally agreed upon Christopher or Justine.

After running all over the seventh floor trying to find room 732, 732 came out of nowhere after he passed it twice in his urgent search. Before he entered the room, he carefully patted down his thinning hair and wiped his brow of the sweat mixed with sticky rain.

There she was sitting up in bed. Ready to deliver. She smiled slightly under all the pain and he kissed her hot head.

"How are you feeling?" Not the smartest of his sex but this was his first time.

"Bloody pain." She continued wheezing. "I can't do this, I need the drugs. Go and get the nurse." She touched his face.

A new stroke of sweat broke out on her forehead. He wiped away her sweaty blond bangs from her brow. "I thought we decided." They had decided to take no drugs. That's when they were all smiles and remembered the breathing routine. Doing it together like it was some sort of dance step.

"Get the fucking nurse!" She went back to wheezing.

He left, not loving his wife's decision to take drugs. She yelled and swore and that concluded that she definitely needed it. The nurse came back and gave the spinal shot and relaxation kicked in. Her face eased and he remembered the breathing routine. So the drugs did help.

At exactly 9:13 PM or hospital time 21:13 on April 3rd, 1976, Christopher Jamison was born whining under the doctor's bright lights. Clipped, knotted and neatly wrapped, he was placed into his mother's arms. She held her restless son close to her breast, providing him with that familiar warmth. The father poked at his newborn son.

Expressions plastered with smiles at the complete wonderment of new life. As soon as the husband found a comfortable position to be fitted into the picture, the nurse snapped and the Jamison family was complete. The smiling nurse said, "Congratulations."

It was their first family photograph, they all had shining red eyes with the dated orange paint of the mid-seventies in the background.

Once at home with the new baby, they would take me shopping and point out various frames for their first photo. Me being too young for sophisticated communications of yes or no or even a nod of my head, all I could manage was googoo and gaga.

I discovered that I could use my face to communicate, giving them a pout if it was plastic and a little smile if it was wood. In the end, they picked what matched the heavy wood carving in their home, a rosette design of mahogany. They placed it beside their wedding picture on what would be the family wall. Once in a while my daddy or mummy would stop and stare at the orange hospital photo. They would gaze at their picturesque son, and give a longing glance at my advancements of building another square with four blocks. I would look up at them and smile and sometimes drool in my cotton jumper because I would be so excited by their caring smiles.

They took lots of photos of me and my building blocks.

When I was older the building blocks were replaced by Lego. There is only one photo of me and this boy, Henry, who was the neighbours' child. Both parents thought it was a good idea for us to play together, maybe in the end be best friends. I could see them planning it out—warming their fingers against my mum's pottery teacups as they talked to the neighbours with everyone smiling and nodding their heads to a good idea.

So I'm there playing with my Lego, building some building, and my mother is pushing Henry into my room. I looked from my mother's familiar white weekender shoes to Henry's big rain boots. At first I thought he was going to piss in them because they seemed so huge, they were like firemen's boots.

She left Henry who being a big retard tried sitting down in them. The rubbers rubbed together. Twice he couldn't sit down. Finally, on the third try, he figured it out and smiled as his ass met the carpet. Not the brightest, but he was a fast learning retard.

Once he was completely settled and the rubber stopped kissing, he looked up at me and he was ready. Making sure that my mother wasn't looming around, I asked, "What the fuck are you supposed to be?"

"I'm a boy."

"Right, but what's with those boots?"

"Spaceman."

"I see." At least he knew he was a boy and I decided to give him a chance with my Lego. "Want to make a building?"

"Yeah."

He crawled on his fours to get closer to me which was smart of him because standing up and sitting would be another trial. He sat beside me and we started building under my design which I had to simplify into a square boxed building.

I told him, making sure that he understood the concept of Lego, "You take one piece and another." I held a blue and a red rectangle. "And you click them together like this." I clicked them together.

"Yeah," was his response.

We used up all my Lego for a massive squared building. He listened to my directions and he got the hang of what a square looked like.

My mum came in with the camera and the congratulations of a big beautiful box.

Click. After a cheerful pat on each of our heads, we followed her for cookies and milk for a job well done.

All three of us soaked our cookies in milk. Most of Henry's cookie floated and sunk to the bottom of his glass or landed on his green and yellow striped polo-shirt.

"Whose idea was it to build a box?"

"Mine."

"Did you know Henry, that Chris's father owns a boxing company? That's where they make boxes. What does your dad do?"

"He owns land."

"What about your mum?"

"A nurse and she takes care of me."

"Did you two enjoy playing together?"

"Alright."

"Yeah. At home I'm not allowed to play with blocks."

"It's Lego."

"Why is that, Henry?"

He shook his head in response as he wiped the crumbs off his face.

I drank my milk and told Henry to come back to my room. I sat down and was about to ask him what to do next. Instead his little yeah voice spoke up.

"Now for Godzilla!" he said getting up and almost tripping over me because one of his rubber boots slipped off. He retraced his steps and pulled the black boot on. "Now for Godzilla!"

I sat there not knowing what he meant because he hardly spoke at all. His boots said more than he did. And with one booted foot he kicked the wall in.

"Stop it!" I screamed because the Lego went flying all around. "Fucking stop it!" I tried grabbing him.

"Ahhhhhh!" He did some Godzilla sound and pushed me down with his mouth wide open. His saliva drooling all over me.

I grabbed him and we rolled over the fallen bits of Lego. I pinned his arms down with my knees. I found a piece of Lego. It was a little blue piece. I shoved it into his mouth and I held his mouth shut. He squirmed but he couldn't move.

"Die you fucking Godzilla! Die!" I pinched his nostrils shut. "Die you fucking Godzilla!" I enjoyed how the little retard struggled with his boots squealing away, calling for his mummy.

My mum came and pulled me off, throwing me onto the bed. She picked the choking little Godzilla man and slapped him hard on the back. The blue piece of Lego came flying out past my head, hitting the wall and landing on my bed.

"Chris, what did you do?" she screamed out as she held the crying Henry. His face was all red and wet and he continued on gagging.

"I didn't do it!" I sat there screaming at her.

"Are you alright?"

"Can I—" he said between sobs, "Go home?" Big cry baby. "I don't feel too well." That's right, cry it all out.

"Yes." She held Henry's hand and watched me.

"I didn't do it!" I said shaking my head. With those tears building up in my eyes.

They left. I sat there on the bed, being more scared of when she would return. I put the Lego into the box. I placed the big box at the foot of my bed. I took the wet piece with chocolate chip cookie crumbs stuck to it and I used my bed sheets to clean it off. I threw it in the box. I crawled on my bed and tried hard to look like a wounded soldier.

The wooden carved door opened and closed. Her rubber feet came closer to my room. She peeked in. Her eyes looked deep like the corners of her mouth. "What happened, Chris?" She folded her arms.

I got up and wiped my eyes with the sheet. "Nothing, we were just playing."

"Don't lie to me. What happened?" she said raising her voice.

I looked about because it was my first time lying. I didn't know where to stare. Everything flashed back at me: my eyes moved from the striped blue wall to my mother's eyes and back to the striped wall.

"Chris, what happened?"

"Nothing."

"Come here." She pulled her arms together.

I reluctantly let the blanket go and came to her. My eyes raced around my mother's because she looked so ugly and battered. I had always thought till then that she was beautiful.

"What happened?" Her lips tightened up under each asked word.

I peered into her blue eyes that became a cold grey tone. "Nothing, Mum." I shook my head trying to be that cute little boy that would make her smile.

She slapped me hard before I could add that we were only playing.

"Don't ever lie to me! Chris——" She grabbed my arms and shook me. "Chris, he almost died. That's not playing! Now tell me the truth." She tightly held my arms.

"Mum, we—"

She pushed me aside and grabbed my Lego box.

"When you decide to tell me the truth!" Glaring at me. "You'll get your Lego back!"

I grabbed her arm. "Mummy, Mummy!"

She turned around. "Are you going to tell me?"

I stood there frozen in thought and all I could think about was my Lego box she held. She twitched her arm from my hand and walked away. Shutting the door. I stood there hearing the Lego pieces call out and go silent.

"Mummy, Mummy!" I kept shouting out her name. My Lego was gone and I sat there on the bed. How could I tell her that I tried to kill Godzilla? It wouldn't sound right. The retard Henry thought he was Godzilla. I was only trying to do the right action. He kicked my Lego. He kicked my bloody Lego and I knew I was right. That was the pain of it all.

Plan B came up with more tears and shouting out her name in between the gobs of almost choking on the tears.

She never came and I fell asleep under the covers with the lights on.

"Chris?" My dad's voice entered my head. I woke up. I found my dad in the doorway waiting for me with crossed arms.

"Hello, Dad." I wiped my eyes.

"Come on."

He put his hand on my shoulder and led me into his den. My mother was sitting on the couch having a cigarette—she usually smoked at funerals. My father sat beside my mother. Both of them stared at me.

"What happened today?" he asked sitting in a perfect position of cross-legged entertainment.

"Henry from next door came down and we played with my Lego."

My mother took a long exhale on the smoke. She was as ugly as before but her mouth was puffing smoke instead of shouting.

"And what happened to Henry?"

"Mum took him home."

"Why?"

"Because he wasn't feeling well."

"Why wasn't he feeling well?" my mother asked crushing the smoke.

I stood there knowing all these questions were trick questions. "He kicked my Lego building. And I tried to stop him, but he pushed me down. And I was only trying to stop him from breaking my stuff."

"Is that the truth?"

"Yes." Because it was. He was Godzilla. He wasn't the friendly spaceman with oversized black boots.

"Why did you lie to me before?" Her eyes were puffy.

"I was scared."

"Do you know what almost happened to Henry?" she said leaning forward. Now she was concerned.

"I didn't mean to hurt him as badly as I did. I just wanted him to stop. He was wrecking my stuff."

"Chris, that is no reason to hurt someone. You know what happened?"

"Yes." I looked down because they weren't seeing the fact that he was wrecking my Lego. They both took turns lecturing the dangers of how I played earlier that day. I blanked out after awhile and just watched their faces, while they both observed mine for an agreeable yes to life and death situations. Their moving mouths and lecture tones didn't interest me, not until the word, "your Lego."

My ears popped open and I saw my mum place the box on the floor so gently that not one single Lego made its light plastic sound. I almost made a run for the box.

"Chris, we both decided." There was a long pause and stare as they shook their heads to show me that they had both decided. "We got rid of your Lego." The magical word Lego hung in the air. And disappeared. Out of some sick-loving parental guidance, they replaced it with wooden building blocks. My father picked up the box and shook it to show that there was a new sound. Heavy and knocking against each other.

"We both know that you like building so we got you—" He shook the box advertising their responsible parenting. "Building blocks."

I didn't say anything. I got building blocks for fuck sakes. I had those when I was a baby. I stood there as they shook and opened the box to show that they were building blocks, big and woody.

Having that big dumb hollow sound. Revealing their colourful tones of the alphabet and numbers.

"Where's my Lego?"

"We got rid of it," my mum responded being absolutely disgusted with my answer not being a right away thank you.

"Oh."

My father placed the box in my arms. He smiled, nodding his head for me to do the same towards my mother. I nodded and gave them a smile. My mother kissed me to show me that I was being good and once again Chris was loved.

I was so pissed because they took my Lego away. Building blocks fall down so easy while the Lego stays connected. That's the brilliance of Lego. And they couldn't understand that. I held the box silently and I went back to my room. As I passed the windows in the house I wanted to break them all with these alphabetical-numerical blocks, wanting to show them that these were more dangerous for their son.

I went to my room and placed the box with blocks where the Lego was once. I sat there hearing my parents in the kitchen, both making dinner. I wanted to cry out, scream out and make them feel guilty for taking my Lego. Instead, I sat there looking at the blocks.

The Usual

My father carried me into the house like an airplane. He vroomed me right into my mother's arms. She pinched me with her long nails until I safely crashed into her body. She squeezed me.

"My Eliza," she said softly patting my head.

"Mummy," I shrieked hugging her tightly back. I wanted to squeeze the life out of her too.

"Maril, where's my love's tender kiss?" He smiled, gently caressing the silent television's light.

My mother's eyes rankled over his and he loved it. He loved it always. His smile always grew along with his widening eyes. She would walk over holding me tightly against her chest. As she came toward him, he'd grab her, and both their chests would crush into me. Squeezing me like a lemon. Being crushed between their chests I could hear their different beats. Boom, Boom, Boom, Boom. Their chests became a world of stereophonic sounds. But it only lasted for one kiss, that's four Booms, one swallow, one kiss.

After, my mother carried me to the washroom where I was scrubbed to death. At least it was warm water not her spit.

"Lord, I was kissed by an Angel. An Angel came down an kissed me. Kissed me right on my lips."

My mother was an Angel. An Angel.

She would look up disgusted outside the washroom's door. Still scrubbing the red sucker's stains off.

"By an Angel."

She gazed in that youthful way to him. "Ah, Morris." The scrubbing would not stop till the only redness left was the scrub's scar. "Don't you know Eliza that it is supposed to stay in your mouth, not on it, or in your hands." She'd look at my father who was already getting a beer. "Morris, what are you teaching her?"

He'd always flick his hand and pick up his big, sagging pants all dusted with his work.

As I dried myself off I watched my mother enter the television room. "Morris, go an change. I don't need all that filth you work in all over here."

"Maril, I pay for this. If I want it to be filthy so be it."

"Morris, change."

He'd get up and shake the dust in front of her. She stared at him with that angelic spite. Looking down at him. Down. He would storm into his bedroom and change. He came into the kitchen with his new clothes on. "Is this better?"

She shook her head. "Eliza, come an help mummy."

I'd come and hold the plates as she placed the toasted bread with butter and poured the thick stew. "Take this to your father." I gave it to him and went back and took mine and we sat with our own golden TV tables. We'd watch these strange shows. Comedy shows.

They would both sit there laughing at the tube; I could never understand it. Then the commercials would come on. This was the time for great discussions.

"Morris, what are you doing tonight?"

"Jimmy an I are going out."

"Where?"

"Pub."

The show would come on and they'd lapse into humour. My father would ruffle my hair when it must've been a good one. My mother, like a lady, would always touch her lips as she bellowed and swallowed her food.

"Damn, that's bloody well funny."

"Morris."

They bellowed and my hair would be ruffled and I would smile.

"So, Morris, was Eliza okay when you picked her up?"

"She was good."

"Did Robert say anything?"

"Na."

"So then she was okay?"

"Yes, she was, now shut up. Damn, Maril, sometimes I just want to belt you."

"Morris!"

"Yes, Daddy wants to belt Mummy sometimes, isn't that right Eliza?" He asked ruffling my hair and I didn't know. I thought daddy was making a funny. So I shook my head to answer yes.

"Morris! Morris you're impossible an Eliza you behave!" Did I get the eyes there! And I just kept on grinning.

"Ah, don't listen to her, Eliza, she's just being an old witch. Don't you think Mummy needs a good wallop?"

"Morris!"

I remember looking back and forth and giggling at each word they said. My father's white teeth gleaming and my mother puffing her lips in anger as her tongue lashed out his name. At that point, I saw the old green witch snarling at my father with his blue eyes sparkling and the music from the commercials in the back, toot-to-toot-to-toot-too.

My father would take me in his arms and whisper secretly, "Go an get Daddy a beer before that old witch snaps off your head, too."

I went into the fridge and took out a beer. As usual, my father would explain to my mother the reasons for his behaviour. But the whole time his big blue eyes would be wide open admiring my mother with that great smile he always wore, when he knew he had upset her and she'd be yelling or explaining to him. But I never bothered to listen I just liked watching their movements. My mother would sadly stare at me as my father rambled off jokes. Now I wish I knew what he was saying. It's always like that.

"Eliza, Eliza go an wash yourself off."

"Yes."

"Wait, Eliza, rise, rise against her. Tell her, 'no Mummy, you go an wash'."

"Eliza, don't listen to that useless ogre go an wash."

"Eliza, rise, rise before it's too late, too late I tell ya."

"Wash!"

"Rise!"

"Leave me alone." I ran out laughing into the washroom.

My father got up and stretched. "I best be going an Maril, don't wait up."

"Don't worry Morris, I won't. Your sister is coming down."

"Doris, that fat bitch, what does she want?"

"The usual."

"Well, I tell you right now she's not staying here. If that no-good man threw her out that's where she best belong. Don't look at me like that, Maril. I've put out plenty of times before, an you know love, I don't have that much an that you know. An besides, we have told her before."

"Yes, Morris, I know, I know. What are you doing with Jimmy?"

"The usual."

Fat Bitch Aunt Doris

My father left with his usual words to the usual night of drinking and gambling. I came out of the washroom and my mother was madly cleaning up for Aunt Doris. Aunt Doris was fat, big, huge, large or extra but she was fat. So my mother had to make room for her. My mother set the kettle on high and got the chipped dynasty set out. Once she arrived, I was already colouring and she came in crying. And it starts not with hello but he:

"He comes home an he's all pissed an what do I see after pouring my heart out to him, is lipstick on that fat chest of his. I ask him, 'what's this?' an he slaps me. Trust me, I try to be all calm, all loving an then he starts hitting me. Hitting me hard like I deserved it. I swear to you, I get punished for the love I give. But he's worthless, spent all that dough on sluts. Sluts, freaking sluts as I'm at home talking to his dear-old mother saying how sweet an caring her bloody son is. Then he comes home pissed, penniless an with that slut's lipstick still on him. An he beats me an throws me out, only God knows. God must know. An I'm starting to think that there is no man out there for me. They're a bunch of bastards. Bastards an look at you, Maril, you've got Morris, perhaps one of the last good men on earth. I feel sorry for Eliza cause all that's left are bastards."

What would be funny about it is, that I'd be there drawing, drawing big ships that you would see docking on Docker's Row where Doris's sluts would catch her juicy man. Then came a big boom at the door. Doris got up as my mother caught her breath after spilling the hot tea on her blouse.

"Damn bloody pig is at the door. Fucking leave me alone, I'm with family!"

"Doris, you fucking bitch, get out here!"

"Leave me alone!"

"Fucking bitch, get out here!"

"Leave her alone or I'll call the fucking cops! Get off my property!"

"Hear that you fucking pig, you can't touch me here!"

"Doris!"

"Fucking leave her alone! I'm dialling!"

The whole time my mother swore, I swear my ears must have perked up with my green eyes looking at my mother who seemed more than ready to fight. And I tell you, she wasn't even near that phone. I was freaking out. I was terrified more of my mother than that fucking bloody pig that Doris called her man. Another big bang came from the door.

"Doris, where do you fucking find these pieces of dirt?" my mother whispered more to herself as she got up. I remember hoping she would reach for that yellow phone in the kitchen. Instead she headed for the door. Doris picked me up and held me between her fat breasts. I dug my head into them as she patted me. I was too afraid to look up.

"You fucking bitch!"

"Get the fuck off my property, you fucking pussy!"

"I want Doris!"

"The cops are coming for you, you fucking bloody pig! Now, GET OFF MY PROPERTY!"

My mother came in smiling.

"Well, Doris, that was nice of him to drop by. Really, Doris, where do you find them?"

"I tell you, Maril, I'm cursed, cursed with falling in love with pigs."

"Well get off it." Now, my supermum was pissed at Doris. Doris just shook her head and let go of me. I went back to colouring those big blue boats.

"Doris, come an help me in the kitchen. An Eliza, dear, beddy time." I took my mother's hand. My mother stood there as she watched Doris enter the small kitchen. She washed me and sent me my good night kisses. That night as my mother left the room, I faked sleeping for the moment so I could hear them talk.

"Doris, I really don't want to hear it."

"I just wanted to thank you."

"Let me tell you, he's a small fish compared to the rest."

"I know, I know."

"Then listen."

"I will, but I was wondering if tonight, just tonight, if I can spend the night?"

"No, Doris, an for one thing Morris will fucking piss me around."

"Well, fuck Morris, an fuck you."

She left, but in a month's time she'd be back. That's how it always was with Aunt Doris, that fat bitch. At least, at least I thought. Standing there and listening to the door slam. I went to bed thinking of her.

Father came home and headed for the fridge as he told my mother of his winnings. But every time she heard it, it was like she wasn't listening. I could see her sitting there and waiting for him to shut up. She'd be staring at the cross hoping on that stale faith my father called it. He'd be standing there maybe under it gleaming brightly like any well-deserved bastard talking about his winnings. Winnings that you couldn't do anything with except buy bread and beer. My mother would come to a point of realization and just spit out but always starting with, "Well that's the lot of it, Morris."

"Damn right an it's about time that God blessed me with a little salvation. An that's when I said Amen after that lucky round."

"Yes, an Doris was down."

"What was that fat bitch trying to do, blow out my luck? Why was she down this time?"

"She was running away from Roger. She said he was beating her again. You've heard the same story before, Morris. I told her to listen."

"You tell me, Maril, what's the point of telling her that?"

"I don't know, she was getting on my nerves. But she wanted to stay here an I sent her home."

"Damn right an it's about time that fat bitch takes all that medicine. I bet you anything love, she drives those fucking bastards to beat her. Damn, I would've fucking killed her."

"Well, that's what I thought an we'll see her again an this time you can tell her."

"We'll see if we'll let her in this time."

He would retire in front of the television and my mother would join him. Both doing what together I never knew. Cause all I saw was that warm glow flashing to different blues and no sounds were made. I'd fall asleep knowing everything was alright.

The next morning before my mother could drive me to school, a police officer stood at the screen door. My mother answered as I slurped the milk from the cereal bowl leaving the soggy cereal. Cereal is just gross, the only thing good about it is the sweetened milk.

"Hello, are you Mrs. Fellows?"

"Yes, what's this about?"

"Is Mr. Fellows home?"

"No. What's this about?"

"Yes, I'm sorry Mrs. Fellows, but Miss Fellows was found dead this morning?"

"Who do you mean?"

"Doris Fellows."

"She's dead?"

"I'm sorry."

"How? Who found her?"

"Roger Clunk, her live-in."

"Thank you, Officer."

"Will you be alright?"

"Yes, I will be."

He left my mother. She stood there for a moment. She stared at me and gained her colour back and lit her happy smoke.

"Eliza, let's go before you're late."

Fat Bitch Aunt Doris 2

When I came home, mother was on the phone. Father was getting a beer and shouting at my mother to say whatever to the other person on the phone.

"Ah, Eliza, so how is my lucky girl?"

"Good, Daddy." I paused there throwing down my light school bag. I was curious about Aunt Doris, that fat bitch, I kept thinking. It just seemed to rhyme. I wanted to know, really know, if my father heard anything and what he thought. I was too curious to wait and listen in on their conversations. That became a pain. And anyways, this was big. Her death, like her, was big. "Daddy, what happened to Aunt Doris?"

He took a quick sip of his beer. "I'll tell you, me an your mum warned her, warned her an look where she lies now. That's a lesson for you. See, we could all say we feel sorry for Aunt Doris, that sounds weird of me to say, doesn't it Maril? Aunt Doris. Damn, she must be laughing, hearing me call her that. That Fat Bitch, pardon my French, Eliza."

"Morris, shut up! An your mum wants to talk to you."

Father got up and took the phone. "Hello Mum ... Yes, we'll be there ... Yes all of us ... At what time again? ... Six? ... Alright, alright love you Mum ... Yes, yes I know ... Bye. Maril, at six tomorrow at Saint John's Church off Simon Street."

"There's only one here, Morris."

"Well, I'll save my tears for tomorrow then. No point being a baby, right Eliza?"

"Daddy, I'm not a baby."

"That's my girl."

"Morris, for Christ-sakes stop it!"

"Ah Maril, my sweet Marilyn an does she hold daddy a kiss?"

They kissed as she finished cutting up the carrots. She caught me staring. "Eliza, go an wash up."

As I washed, I could hear my father's fat lips hit my mother's lips. The funny thing was they didn't even seem bothered by my aunt's death. As I tried scrubbing off the marker's ink on my hands, I kept thinking of Kenny, a boy who I hated and who hated me. We tortured each other every day at elementary school. Kenny came from a wrecked family, his mother died giving birth to him. So I used to always call him a son of a bitch. He was. One day, I found out that Kenny's dad was dating my Aunt Doris. Like usual they shacked up. No surprise, it didn't work out. I remember she used to come to our house bleeding with a smashed up nose and puffy eyes. She'd be there, smoking and drinking as my mother cleaned her up, and my father would be arguing with Aunt Doris and my mother shouting at them to shut up. Then she left him. Kenny was always my enemy. That dirty son of a bitch I used to call him because he always smelled really bad.

Aunt Doris's funeral was small. My father's friend Jimmy was there. The whole time I stayed at my mother's side as she talked to Doris's friends. They were all fat and I could see my father pointing to them as he laughed with Jimmy. Jimmy had a cackle that could not be missed. My father's mum, my grandmother, sat earnestly by the small urn (surprisingly) praying. That was the last time I saw her. A week later she died. Because she forgot to take the urn home. So my father went over to the hospital where she resided and delivered it. At that moment, or at least my father told us, that she must've mistaken his shadow for Doris's and she screamed under her raspy voice, "Dor—" Unfortunately, she had a fatal heart attack.

"You know, Marilyn, she was very, very happy," said one of Doris's fat friends blowing her wet nose into a tissue. "I don't know if she told you, she was gonna marry, marry him. I was more than surprised when she told me this the first time they met."

"At one of those bars?"

"At Pinky's that night. It was ladies' night out of all that. An I truly believed her. She loved Roger an Roger seemed to love her. So when I found out, well, really, I knew something was up when she didn't come into work. But I'd never have thought Roger was capable. Roger, thin as a rod killing Doris. Poor, poor Doris. God knows I'll miss her. An I see that brother over there doesn't seem so teary eyed." Her fat finger pointed towards my father as he chugged back the wine, tipping the glass at her.

"Morris, has grieved an trust me, he misses her. He's just too upset, that's all. I've never found out how she died, though."

"Well, Roger being thin an all, took the damn frying pan an hit her over the head. That's what the Officer said. But I still find it amazing how she just went. She used to get really smacked around with all those other bastards an the frying pan gets her in the end. You heard Roger turned himself in?"

"Yes."

My father came over chuckling.

"Maril, it's getting late, an I'm sure Eliza is ready for bed, ain't that right?"

"Yes, Daddy." I was standing there listening to this fat woman blab and she looked disgustingly at my father's grinning mouth.

She darted her big blue eyes at him as that pink-lipstick produced a couple of spitted up words. "So, how are you, Morris?" she asked licking the spit off her lips, missing a good gob in the corner.

"Quite well, an how about you?"

"Alright, mind you."

"Good. Maril, shall we be off?"

"Bye."

We left, leaving her to grieve as she burst out with a wet sneeze. That night driving home I watched my father.

"Thank God, thank God it's over. I thought it would never end."

My mother didn't respond, she just stared out, out in silence.

Aunt Doris's funeral wasn't much. Roger, I found out much later got released and is living in Saber and working at one of the factories. At least that's what my father told me for he ran into him. Now, I wonder how that would've went. I always imagined it: My father at lunch would see him and it would click. The thin, bony form of Roger with his blond hair buzzed off. Roger would be sitting down on the other side of the room, probably. My father would look at his buddies and say, "That's my sister's bastard who killed her." They would all respond questioning, maybe wanting to see a fight more than likely, and make a couple of bets out of it. Like who would hit first and who would cry. Right there my father would've laughed and said drinking his apple juice, "Hey, Roger's a good man. Trust me, he did me a favour, he did himself a favour an for that matter, he did the world a favour." And he'd burst out laughing and finish drinking his apple juice maybe wishing it was beer right then.

Beginning

The time I started ballet school was out of my father's winnings. Like my mother, I would never have guessed he was capable of winning.

I was ten and cleaning up the dinner dishes as my mother was in the television room with her friend Linda who she worked with. My mother just started working at Hives Grocer on Strait Street. Note the yellow and black uniform she wore. She worked to help pay the bills because my father spent his hard earned money on his gambling. It was his money, if you were to ask him. His stakes always got higher and higher. Like the bills that grew. So my mother dealt with it by working. Using her money, if you were to ask her.

After work, my mother and her new friend Linda spent time drinking beers and lighting cigarettes. As the night drew on their laughter got louder and louder. Linda had a particular laugh that was very high and sounded like a bird twittering. Sometimes when I went to bed I would dream of little birds twittering. Those dreams were very boring.

But that night my father came home early. In other words, I was still up. Watching the comedies as my mother and Linda had just opened their beers.

"Hello, Morris an Jimmy."

"What are you doing home?"

My father looked unusually happy. I just took it like my

mother, he was a happy drunk. Red and Jolly. You would have mistaken him for Santa Claus if he was holding milk and nibbling on cookies.

Jimmy was going balder and his pot belly was overlapping his thin waist he saved for the ladies. He ogled Linda as she patted her sprayed bleached-breaking-hair and smoked. She tried to make her little lips look as sexy as they could for the belly-balding Jimmy. My mother sat there blowing her smoke to the ceiling. I'm sure she was thinking I've seen it all. No more surprises for me, Morris. My father smiled wildly and brought his hands forward holding chocolates and roses.

"This is for you, Maril. It is for believing in me. You're my lady of luck."

"Would never have guessed it," she said taking the treats.

Jimmy, who was eyeing Linda, made a drum sound by tapping the canned beers he held.

"Ten-thousand!" my father shouted.

All attention was made in excitement of "Wooooo!" We all jumped up and down and ended in singing screaming harmony. "He's a jolly good fellow, he's a jolly good fellow."

"He really is a jolly good fellow, my Morris." My mother hugged and kissed him. He held onto her and taking one of the beers shook it up and cracked it open spraying everyone. Jimmy handed out the beers while Linda lit everyone's smoke.

"So love, how does it feel to be married to a ten thousand dollar winner?" He pulled my mother close to him.

She kissed him again. This time longer.

"Wooooo!"

"Eliza, my dear have a beer. I don't think your mother will mind."

I had my first beer. My mother was so enthralled she didn't even stop my father's bad decisions. It was complete heaven to them all that night.

"You have to celebrate too," Linda said, lighting my first

cigarette and patting my cheek.

Of course, I coughed and everyone laughed, remarking how sweet it was.

Soon like the taste of the beer, I became a natural at puffing that smoke. My father turned on the radio to the old tunes and they all danced together as I finished my beer and sank into the corner of the sofa. I stole another cigarette. I sat there silently watching the slow dancers. The song ended. My mother let go of my father and crushed her smoke. She looked up at me as my father held her tightly. She got the mother concerned look on her face.

"Eliza, time for bed." I placed the empty beer can and crushed my second smoke. Like my mother crushing the whole butt.

"Eliza, we'll talk about your share tomorrow."

I went to bed, tired from the beer and the two cigarettes that were still burning in my throat as the beer like the sandman pounded on my head. With the pounding I thought of my share. I glanced around my dark room with a little light sneaking in from the outside over my ballet poster, I got for my birthday. I wanted to be a ballerina.

"Get up Eliza, breakfast." My mother screamed followed by her vibrating knock on the door to really get me up.

I walked into the morning atmosphere of the kitchen and sank into the chair. Falling asleep at the table.

"Good morning, love," she said with a kiss.

I looked up. To my surprise my father was kissing my mother. My father was here. Usually he left for work or would be sleeping. He sat across from me smiling.

"Good morning, Eliza. I see you're a sleepy head this morning."

My mother and my father were still in their pyjamas.

"Eliza, I made you a cheddar cheese omelette. Yes, the French are dining here. Wake up."

I ate as my father dipped his toast in the coffee and flipped the page over.

"What do you think of the French?"

"Good." I said almost choking on the hot melted cheese.

"Good."

When I was finished, she took my plate and placed it in the sink. She drank more coffee. My father placed down the paper.

"Eliza, what do you want to be most in the world?"

"A ballerina."

"What the hell is a ballerina? Maril, do you know?"

"You know. The girl in the poster."

"I see, you want her. I don't know about that. I don't know if that ballerina will be so agreeable."

"No." I said shaking my matted hair. "I want to take lessons. So I can stand on my toes. That's what I want. I want to stand on my toes."

"I see, you want to be a twinkler toe-er. Well, I think we can see to that. Don't you agree, Maril?"

"Yes."

That day my mother looked for it. I was signed up to take my lessons at the St. Maurice Theatre. That's the day I became a ballerina. Well, at least I thought. Sitting there eager in my seat, laughing at my father who kept repeating, "She didn't want a doll, jewels or bubble gum she wanted to be a twinkler toe-er."

My father's winnings actually did something good for the all of us. After a week, my toes were in soft-toe ballet slippers and I was learning to become that girl in the poster. At the St. Maurice Theatre, which was out of Saber and in one of the middle class neighbourhoods of Wolston, I was the only dancer from Saber. I worked twice as hard, every night I practised to be the best in the class. Because ballet was mine. I felt I owned it. And I did. I would practice in my room with the slit of a mirror to watch my little body mould into a dancer.

After the winnings were spent, life became pretty much the same at home except with new items looming around. My mother's new clothes and styled haircut, hair that was no longer tied in a white knot, but curled into a voluptuous red.

My father would say, "She was the hottest bimbo in Wolston."

My father got a new tube and traded in the car for a better one. One that didn't chug a chug on the way. He got one that just vroomed. So from there on I was vroomed to dance school and sometimes school. But my mother still wore her busy honeybee uniform and my father still worked at the factory. Linda and Jimmy married, two months after they married they had a baby girl named Sharon May. Linda stopped working at the Grocer. Still Jimmy and my father gambled—that was just a given. My mother and Linda still got together and talked about their husbands. The topic became, maybe to both of their relief, their husbands' gambling.

Older

When we, by we I mean to introduce my two best friends Kelly (Kel) and Andrew (Drew), when we got older partying is what we did best. Drew was the one with the parents who travelled to the tropics on self rediscovery. Thus, Drew's home became the party house.

After school, me and Kel would meet Drew at his parents' fancy silver Mercedes. The discussion of the party would take place with a couple of shots and then, we'd ring up the people who knew people and created the domino effect. Drew would get the dealer to deliver the sweet weed. After the dealer came, we'd blast the music and give the night's party a little blessing of the weed.

After the house filled, me and Kel would be in the corner watching the scene unfold with the numerous pretty girls screaming with each drop of liquor and dancing wildly. We chugged back ours, gazing intensely at the girls sexy moves. But when you're drunk, hearing the beats and peering at the girls bouncing back and forth with their tits trying to keep up with each beat is very assuring, followed by the screams for more liquor.

Kel had his eye on this one. She had short blond hair that was permed and sprayed into cement format because when she'd shake her head, her hair wouldn't move. I thought at first he was just kidding, this true blonde with a red face but the direction of Kel's eyes ignored the red puffy face and all he saw was those massive tits in a thin white cotton shirt which had printed on it: a black outlined girlie white face written below SLUT. It wasn't the word SLUT that attracted him, it was what was underneath and it was bouncing up and down and his love and fascination with blond hair was a definite bonus. The one who I fancied was her friend, she had long dark brown hair pulled back in a ponytail. Her tits might not have been as big as the blonde's, but she had a beautiful face with big luscious pink lips. Every time she took a sip of beer she'd lick her lips and glance over in my direction.

Both of them looked over and giggled in that school girl way. Knowing that we were surveying them and maybe even undressing them in our minds. Kel nodded at them, and like girls, they turned away but very slowly, so we'd catch that open smile and their lovely glare before they got back to that entrancing sexy bounce.

Kel went up to both of them and asked them with his arm around them. "How are you two doing? Are you enjoying yourselves because I personally had a hand in making this party and let me tell you, I had you in mind. What do you say, are you enjoying yourselves?" Screaming it out as he nodded to that slow West Coast Snoop Doggy Dogg's beats.

"Yeah we are. Is that your other friend over there?" The blonde asked looking at me with her heavy black lashes falling over and pointing as she tittered and touched Kel's arm to gain balance because that shy little titter of hers knocked her off.

Kel obviously didn't follow the finger, he followed each beat that rotated off her mighty tits. He took a sip of his beer and gave me a quick look. "Hey, come with me." They walked over with loving arms around each other. "What about some more beer, girls?"

"Yeah."

I passed the beers to them and gave one to Kel and myself.

"Cheers to a fucking great night!" I shouted it out and I drank it down watching that cute ponytail chick give me a smile of excitement, oh yes.

"Girls, I'm Kel, and this is my right-hand man, Chris."

"Hello there." I gave them a smile, especially the ponytail chick, and then, I took a long hard suck on my smoke as I ogled her. She was sweet with her head bopping away and her backside slowly swaying to the music.

"Amanda," she said wiping away the drops of melted ice that slipped down into her shy cleavage. Kel examined the wet cleavage while Amanda was eyeing me up and down and her face only got redder when she caught my eyes.

"Nadine." She held out her hand and I shook it. I stared her right down with my smoke in my mouth and she picked up on it. She gave me one of her open smiles of approval. That open smile. Fuck, I thought she was like one of Drew's smiling nudes on the wall, letting you know that they were wide open for game.

"Why don't we dance?" Kel asked being all gentleman-like with Amanda and I took Nadine's hand. We got into the crowd swaying to Snoop Doggy Dogg's "Who Am I?" We danced as her body inched forward into mine and that cute little ass of hers rubbed against me making me hard underneath the drunkenness. I quickly tried to down that beer so I could have both of my hands on her and keep her in my hot spot. She was perfect. I placed my arms around her where she moved up and down like a perfect fucking dog. My hands steadily went over that curved downing back to that little ass where I set them in place. I glanced over at Kel who was resting his playful head on Amanda's tits as he told her jokes that she laughed at.

In between the yelling of "yo" and whispering to her "yo, babie" she smiled and giggled like a good girl as she moved her tiny ass against my dick. The first girl to do that and she was incredible. She gently hit it and not too hard to let it go flying. With my hands holding onto her, she'd shake her body and move it down where my hands got a little side feel for her tits. Watching her lick her lips into a open smile. Nice and wide as she sipped her beer. That mouth of hers heaving back so much beer and then, that last lick. Complete fucking ah.

Kel slapped the back of my head. "Come on." He had Amanda underneath his arm.

I took Nadine, who quickly slipped underneath my arm. We moved out of the dancing circle and followed the laughing Amanda back to one of the bedrooms. We opened the guest bedroom door and Drew had his bong going with a new-found girl. Both of them sat in the chairs by the window. We sat on the bed and he passed the bong to us.

"I, I put rum in it." Drew told us in his high voice as he blew the smoke out.

I took the first hit. Sucking it back. Feeling that long dark smoke cloud in and out. I passed it to Nadine and I did it for her. It was her first time doing a bong. She took a good long suck and held it in and blew out one exhausted grey cloud. It was passed onto Amanda. Kel did the honours and then took his hit. All of us sitting there. I could hear Drew's expanding laughter in the back.

"How are the ladies feeling?" asked Kel as he hugged Amanda and looked over to Nadine who had a permanent grin.

"Good."

"Really good," Nadine replied, looking up at me. "This is really a good party. I haven't been to one like this in a long time."

"I know. Remember the last one, Na? Both of us just sat around. We just got pissed on the limited amount of beer, and then, we left early because they stopped playing the music. No one was dancing because they weren't playing the music loud enough because they were scared of the coppers." She fell off the bed as she reached for the bong.

"Plop!" I glared down at her and gave her a long hard laugh. I took the bong.

"Way to go, Amanda!" Nadine shouted.

Kel then pushed her off the bed and I pushed Kel off the bed. Drew quickly took the bong seeing that this was not a good idea for the ceramic bong.

Nadine grabbed a pillow and bashed Kel with it, so he couldn't get back on. As a result, a playful fight broke out. All four of us pillow-hitting each other. Kel held Amanda by the waist and pulled her down onto the floor where they started kissing. Nadine got up, pulling me to the washroom. I grabbed her by the waist and we walked in there together as I kissed her neck, nibbling at her earlobe. She pulled away but she was enjoying it. I pulled her back in and held onto her, biting at her lobe. I was using moves on her from this porno-video when it turned into a regular gang bang.

I locked the door first. I brought her lips to mine. Kissing her hard and grabbing her tongue with my teeth as I squeezed her ass and she squeezed mine in return. My other hand wondered up and squeezed her tit and she threw back her head and moaned under it. Her ponytail swaying back and forth.

Her tit was soft and hardening against my hand.

I kissed down her neck, sucking in the skin to give a couple of hickeys—that was a big thing to do. Stamp her with her own pressured blood.

I undid her little black buttons as her hands moved under my shirt. I felt around for the bra-strap's clasps, they were located in the front. I undid it and her tits bounced out meeting my eyes. There they were, her white tits with her small nipples looking up at me. I pinched and teased them. Finally, I sucked the life out of them, pulling at them with my teeth and she moaned. I put my hand down under her pants, under her panties and felt the moisture coming as my finger poked around it. I felt her pussy all around and located that wet hole. She moaned more as she grabbed at my hard dick a little bit too hard. I pulled her back not even thinking twice. She took off her clothes; I took mine off taking out a condom. She grabbed the towels that were hanging around and threw them onto the floor and waited for me to put the condom on. I pinched it on. I went inside her as I took a mouthful of her tit and played with her moist pussy. She kept on moaning and I just ripped right inside her. Feeling that hot rush between her legs and her hands kept pulling at my head wanting me to kiss her.

It was over. My first time was fucking fantastic. It felt like it wasn't going to stop. So I lingered for a bit in there. Until the hardness turned into a flop and I automatically came out. I sat beside her as she lay down with her hands on her stomach. I admired her beautiful naked relaxed body. Feeling the sensation tingle through me.

Kel knocked on the door. "Hurry up, Man!" He ended it in an explosive laughter with Amanda's voice trailing off.

Both of us rushed to put on our clothes and clean up. Before opening the door she held my arm and we kissed.

I opened the door and Kel and Amanda entered with the extreme urges of laughter. Drew was sitting by the window sucking on the bong.

"Come here." I sat down and she sat down.

Drew passed me the bong; I sucked long and hard and blew out as I passed it to her.

"Where did your little friend go?"

"I don't know. She told me that she loved me and I asked what? A bit high at the time and she told me again and I was silent and started thinking of my mother and she was always saying that I'm too young to know what love is, so I couldn't love. It was one of my mother's drunken nights, that's before they started going to the tropics."

"What for?" She passed it back to Drew, rolling her eyes at me.

He took another hit and replied in his high voice. "To, to

rediscover their love. But it's great." He gave Nadine a reassuring smile. She smiled back and he turned his head to the sheer white curtains as he tried to poke his fingers through them to get to the windowpane.

"Yeah."

Talking about love, although feeling good, I didn't feel like talking about it because Nadine was right there. I just screwed her and she might start thinking that she was special or that we now became us.

"Oh, fuck Man." Drew cracked out laughing. "Got a smoke, Chris?"

I threw him the pack.

The washroom made noises of a real hard banging that Kel was giving to Amanda. I walked over to the washroom's door. "Fucking keep it down!" I pounded on the door.

Nadine came up from nowhere and pulled me away and gave me a new beer. I placed my arm around her. "You're great!" I shouted at her, I wanted her to remember something good.

She danced in my arms and the washroom's door popped open. Kel came out drinking a beer as Amanda gave Nadine a wink. Everyone rested on the bed. Conversations passed by as fast as the bong's smoke filled the air. Amanda and Nadine went on about the stories of their friendship. Drew tried poking his way through the curtains and I just sat back with Nadine glancing at me. I made sure to laugh back, so she wouldn't think I just used her for my first encounter with the female body.

The music in the background, I could hear and feel it vibrating off the walls as my head rested there. I watched Nadine's big smiling eyes observe me; she was like a big Bambi. She'd place her arm around me and whispered something because she'd giggle and I would giggle back hoping to God that sounded right. I didn't want her to be offended that I just screwed her and that's all. Amanda got up and took her forever-friend Nadine. Nadine gave me a quick secure happy kiss on the cheek.

I watched Kel get up and I got up following Kel and the girls outside.

Amanda wrote on a piece of paper and gave it to Kel. He folded it delicately and placed it into his pocket and Nadine came over.

"Here Chris, give me a call and we'll go out, okay?" Always smiling.

"Yeah." I gave her a kiss and a grin.

And like a flash a taxi pulled up. Kel and me giving each of them a wave and they were gone. I still had the piece of paper.

"That Amanda loves to fuck. She was on top of me at one point and God did her tits just move. It was the fucking eighth wonder of the world. I never did a pussy like that before. What about Nadine? She's cute."

"Good." I didn't feel like saying anything else. It was my first time. It was definitely a lot better than my hand. I felt I had that secret power of fucking the whole lot of them. Nadine was beautiful, I mean, I felt, I could still get some more beautiful girls. Explore other pussies with no commitments of gifts and chocolates. I was finally initiated into the beautiful world. Hopefully Nadine, being a bit drunk, would forget. Philosophizing in my mind the numbers on the paper. That ended with me admiring the extremely bright lights of the street and I looked at Kel and I thought, did I just say all of that out loud.

"You're fucking gone."

"Right, yeah, let's go back in."

Kel turned around, and me still having the paranoia on strong, I flicked the piece of paper into the bushes hoping that it would rain and wash it away.

The party still boomed on as I crashed in the back with Drew who was getting it on in the washroom. Unfortunately, for privacy's sake, they forgot to shut the door but I just sat there having a smoke, staring outside, hearing the groans and the beats. Soon enough my head gave up on me and I fell asleep. Nice and deeply.

16

Hives Grocer became my full-time summer job to pay for my ballet lessons. My mother got me the job right before she took the option to quit. I became the next Fellows to wear the honeybee uniform. From there, without choice, I paid for my dance lessons.

My dance teacher, Mrs. Lynn, helped me to get into the Royal Wolston Ballet School. In the fall, I'd start my first lessons at the new school for professional dancers. So I had to save up. Also, it was my last year in high school and Mrs. Lynn registered me at St. Maurice High School. Her husband was one of the teachers there. So I got in pretty easy. I switched schools to be closer to the Royal Wolston Ballet School. And it gave me a chance to get out of Saber.

Working and working is what I did that summer. That's when I picked up the habit of having a smoke during my breaks. My job was the checkout girl in a honeybee uniform, where men who were trying to be cute were always asking me or the other girls, "Are you having a buzzing day" or "A buzzy day." They really wanted to put that buzz in every word. The only two girls who didn't get the buzzing words were the Checkout Twins—July and June who were weird in every way for they wouldn't date any guy unless he had a twin. Besides wanting twins, they chewed their tongue constantly because they weren't allowed to chew gum. It was rumoured that if they did chew gum, preferably Hubba Bubba, they'd blow big bubbles and their curly pig tails would get tangled in the snapping bubble. Supposedly, that explained why one pig tail was bigger than the other. The older ladies who came in entertained them with buzzing jokes. The only problem was that they would repeat them to the other checkout girls. But out of good mannered faith, everyone gave them a laugh to make them feel good and normal. To show them we understood their lingo. They were like us. Only challenged.

"Men-tal-ly chal-leng-ed," my boss Robert Kates would say. He paid less for the retarded twins, that's why he hired them. Two challenged twins challenging their brain capacity to package groceries so nothing got squished or bloodied with meat.

Working hard, I learned like the rest to find more time for breaks, heading out sometimes with a stolen pack, meeting the others out there. The other dopes I worked with, really. I stood in the corner against the wall avoiding them. They were true Saber progeny. Most of them went to my high school. Lori was a bleached-blond-better-be dating Chuck who worked in the meat department. She was pregnant with his baby, a big surprise for a Saber girl. That was the big show. The staff room was the backdrop of Lori being pregnant. I still insisted that it was the meat packing department because a whole week customers were returning their meat saying it was spoiled. That only made sense.

The other two checkout girls Christine and Cal were dating Jon and Todd both from the packing department. They were all doing each other. One afternoon in the staff room, Jon was patting down his hair and Christine was puffing and spraying hers with a good stolen Hives product. Jon was doing up his shirt. He was the sporty masculine sort. He was always the type to catch any of the checkout girls in the fruit section. He was always trying to squeeze a little juice. Except for the retarded twins. They brought peanut butter and jelly sandwiches.

He winked, showing he was a good sport for the ladies. For the Hives checkout girls. He was the big king bee if there was one.

"What are you looking at E-LI-ZA?" hissed Christine.

"Nothing much."

"That's what I thought." They both left lighting a smoke. I laughed out loud after that. I'm sure they must have heard. I waited for Christine to come back and we would get into some sort of spastic cat fight. Never happened. I pushed it though. She always hissed like she wanted to. So I thought why not.

After work I changed into my usual clothes in the staff room. I met up with my only friend, Frankie. Like a good Saber girl, I gave a pack of stolen smokes to my best friend. We walked around till we sat on a bench. Smoking the cigarettes, talking about shit and watching the traffic. Hoping to be taken away, at least I was. Being stolen was a high point for me after work.

At the time she was seeing Carl Cain.

"So, how are you an Carl?"

"Alright." She never seemed great about it. It was always alright. Shrugging her shoulders out of inevitable love for him. "What do you want to do tonight?"

"Flank Turn." Flank Turn was where the old factories were and now it was used for raves. It was one of the few affordable opportunities for a Saber kid. She looked with that question which was always burning, just burning. She couldn't even think until she had to ask it. Then she could function. Function as the Frankie I knew or rather liked.

"What do you think of Carl?"

"Let's go to Flank Turn tonight. Now, if I was saying let's go to Simon Street, I'd say think about Carl. Otherwise, Flank is the answer to that always nasty question. Alright?" Lighting a smoke. Sick of it all. "It's Friday for fuck sakes, Frankie."

"Right, fuck it."

We went to my place so I could change into danceable goods. My parents were both out at the pubs that night. It was Friday for fuck sakes. I wore my black tights with a short sheer skirt and a black t-shirt tight with this black ribbon choker I made. I was a real homemaker at heart. My hair was short and slightly wavy. I was trying to give that sharp twenties flapper. But my hair was auburn not black. Frankie cut her real curly dark-brown hair short so she was always like a puff ball if she didn't straighten it out, but she had beautiful blue eyes that were always stealing other people's eyes. That night she was wearing her dark purple jeans with a black holey sweater and a white t-shirt underneath. She thought she was very dramatic. She liked to catch the vibrations of the black lights.

We bussed our way up to Firth Street where all the factories were. Living in Saber, your father was a fisherman or a factory worker or did both just to get better beer. So we walked our way to Flank Turn Road. The windows were all blacked out and looked dead just like the rest of the factories. Except cars jutted out here and there around the streets like it was home for them all. So we got in and paid a sum, but tonight I thought it was worth the money wasted as my father would say.

We entered the loud place with lights hitting each corner of the complex. The music was beating hard as the sweating bodies jerked roughly to catch each beat while some bodies floated through them feeling the harsh beats like a bedtime tune. We smothered in nicely through the cramped space and it felt good seeing different faces and nothing seemed to resemble home.

We got into the groove of dancing. We received those beats and soon became the music itself. This was better than any stale club playing slashed radio tunes. The stale club was filled with off beat girls trying to dance those reggae moves as the hungry-bastard men of Saber watched with great appreciation. But here people were in the groove of dancing. There was none of that other shit that would get nowhere.

The passing of drugs came easy to us and we popped them, waiting, waiting hard for a change. To give all your senses that hypnotic feel. Sometimes feeling like two bodies were in you or being superhuman. The twinkling, more like throbbing lights, added to the super confusion. Losing it all. I was losing it all in Frankie's stark blue colours shooting from her chest. It was really fucking unreal.

My eyes didn't know what to do at one point but they dropped into a pair that seemed deadly as he stared at me. He was gorgeous with his bleached out hair driving every colour of the lights. He stared at me with that cryptic grin and I stared at him smiling slightly. Thinking nothing of it. Only it felt too good because right there and then I loved him.

Everything became dark, darker until we were the only ones. Standing there. It seemed like a bad romance flick mixed with that indecent urge just to fuck it up. Back to standing there together, together dancing into the beat, feeling it out like the beats were in us.

There, it went back to the lights and bodies. But we were still dancing, smiling like two dead people feeling each other out. His face was gorgeous with all the curves I wanted to touch and sink into. Sink into his pores and feel him out. Wanting to feel out those enhanced blue eyes and dip into his pupils, go deep down. After the blue colours and deep pupils I wanted his lips. Only thing that stopped that deep complicated exploration was his hands like mine slamming each beat. I had to get control. I broke past his hands and landed into him. I remember the beats going really wild, completely gone. We both laughed hysterically as we held each other.

It happened—his mouth, his lips became a reality. We kissed and I felt it all under the deep laughter. His prissy lips held and crushed mine perfectly as his tongue dipped into me. The sudden feeling of hot liquid filtered through. Mixing, mixing.

From there, I landed somehow outside with him. Both of us

laughing. He held me tightly and kissed me behind my ear and bit it.

We moved towards a car and fell in. I was laughing madly and he got on top of me laughing too. He bit at me like a vicious pig, nibbling and numbing my skin. I couldn't stop laughing. I thought he was snorting but I think I was only thinking that. Until I noticed the streetlight framing his naked body and face. His face I held with all that slow motion of the drug and kissed him. This is where I discovered the passion of sex. Or better yet the consciousness of screwing him. Really took hold. I was completely in love.

My breast being touched and thrust under his hand, made me lose it all. With the drug, laughter and my breast, I felt the first surges of a good bang. I wanted it hard and not knowing what to do under this spastic movement. I felt every impulse of it. The liquids hard and sticky moving against his hand that became harder. Until I exploded like a popped red Popsicle. And I lay there not knowing what hit me. Except trying to become aware that this was my first time. It felt good with that reddened sore. Feeling the body and remembering each touch and not believing it was that possible. Possible for me.

We dressed quickly, quietly like it was normal. I gazed at him like any good done-in virgin. I wanted to feel that little virgin power that seemed big as I stood there. Folding my arms against myself. We got into polite introductions, "Eliza" and "Ashley." Traded phone numbers. Said no to the ride home. We ended with a kiss.

We left separately. Me noting, noting in the back of my head my home.

I walked home not wanting the bus or any bright lit area. I just wanted to feel myself out that night and to get out as I headed home.

Truce

The next day, a Saturday, came with a big bang because my bedroom door always got stuck. Thus, a big bang. My mother came in my room wearing a green dress and red-lipstick.

"Eliza, are you alright?"

"Yeah."

"Me an your father are going out to the pub."

"What? What time is it?"

"Six. Are you alright?"

"I just got in late."

"We'll be back sometime after." After meant, after it was all over, the gambling and the money spent on beer.

"Alright."

Words were few on very late mornings like that. I lay back down, feeling the urges of hunger and the excessive blinding pain. Everything ached with accuracy. My body was still moving with the invisible beats. I lay there for a minute hearing the beats that were not really there. BOOM BOOM BOOM.

The phone rang its cordial cord and interrupted the chaotic trance of chasing beats.

"Hello."

"Eliza, what are you doing?"

"I'm at home in bed."

"I'm coming down."

The phone went dead. Fuck. Now I had to wake up. She was pissed at me, more than likely for leaving her at the rave. I took a shower and woke up a tad more.

A knock came on the door and she came in.

"Where the bloody hell were you last night?"

"I was there, an I left you trying to grab the lights. Tell me, what was I supposed to do?"

"Where the fuck were you?"

"Okay, Frankie."

We both sat down.

"We were dancing. It was good. An I saw this guy, Ashley an we went off. Well, I mean, we did it." I had to respond casually to it. I was too trashed to get over-excited.

"Holy fuck, I can't believe this, you found someone. Who more than I would have thought."

"I know."

"Holy fuck! Where's he from?"

"Not from here. I don't know. He gave me his number."

"Did you call him?"

"No."

"No, why not?"

"I just woke up for you. I'm not much in the mood for giving him a call. At least not right now."

"Eliza, I just can't believe it."

"I still can't."

"What does he look like?"

"He was." Stopping to gather words and a memory from last night. "He was gorgeous an good." Now the excitement was entering me. "It was really great an magical."

"Cause you were drugged up. I was having a great an magical time, too, until I realized you were gone."

"Not the whole time."

"I know, but still that's when I freaked out. Where did you fuck him?"

"In the car. An after we traded numbers an he drove me home. So, you don't have to worry about him ringing me." I'd say it was a nice picture. It was lovely for her ear. "So, tell me what happened to you?"

"I found my own way home an by complete accident, I saw Carl. I was waiting for the bus an he gave me a lift home. But the whole time, I was thinking about you. I was so fucking worried. You won't believe this. I was sitting in the car trying hard to get reality back, an of course, thanking Carl. He accused me of being with someone else. I'm drugged out of my mind, an basically coming down an he wants to know who I was with. The whole ride I was just still-like, in a trance. When I got home I crashed. Today, I woke up an I called him up. I dumped that little bitch that he was. I called you. It was just crazy, completely."

"I'm happy for you, too."

"I knew you'd be. It just sucks, that you're not going to be at school this year."

"It's not like I'm moving. I'll be here."

"Let's go to Lenny's right now. Have a drink to celebrate all that new stuff before going back to school on Tuesday."

Lenny's was a bar on Strait Street where most of Saber's high-schoolers hung out. Once we got there, it was only starting to get packed. Frankie, the poor loser, spotted Carl. We both saw Todd Stock beside Carl. He was one of Carl's friends. He waved. Frankie looked at me, knowing he was waving only at me.

We ordered two pints and sat at a table at the other end. But Carl and Todd came up and took the other seats. Frankie looked up and smiled. And it clicked—she wasn't over Carl. I felt stupid, really stupid thinking that Frankie would've gotten over Carl. He and Todd made themselves comfortable at our table.

"Hello." Carl leaned over to Frankie's ear. Unfortunately, that left me and Todd. He sat across from me, winking. He has been doing this for a year or so now. He tries so hard to get under me that I can't feel sorry for him.

"Yeah, Carl." Carl kissed her cheek as she looked up at me, in that puppy-girl way that was all too familiar. What am I to do?

What was she to do but get back with Carl. I knew I had my lot of everything. I was pissed at Frankie.

"So, are you two back together?" asked Todd. "Because my man Carl was pissing his pants over you Frankie. An that reminds me, I've been holding my breath out for you, Eliza. So, what do you say about us then?"

"Us, I really don't know, but I do know, if you hold your breath any longer you'll be dead."

"Frankie, talk some sense into her."

"What am I to do, Todd? When she already has sense."

"Carl, I don't know, I just don't know, man."

Carl ignored the whole situation and concentrated on Frankie's hair, the twirling affect. The whole situation disgusted me. Too many elongated grins and avoiding eyes. I had to get out. It was a nightmare.

I tapped Frankie's shoulder. "Frankie, I'm going."

"Why? It's your party. Eliza, come on." She swayed her head.

"I know." It all clicked into the word satisfaction. "I'm going to go home an talk to Ashley."

She gave me a hug. "Take care."

I left with Todd following right behind me.

"Hey, Eliza."

I responded with civil coldness. "What is it?"

Todd stood there for a moment. Although he always talked with his boys about girls, I never or anyone else ever saw any of these girls. I think these girls he ragged about were on his walls. He was a loser. He tried hard to fit in, but a loser like Todd, with fucked-up blond hair and a red face, was not going to cut it.

"So, Eliza, what do you want to do?"

"I'm going home."

I walked up to the bus stop. He followed.

"Look, Eliza, I know you have nobody an I'm free, so why don't I drive you home an we can make that summer romance come true."

"True for who?"

"For us."

"Ah."

"Come on."

The bus pulled up and I got on. Saving the last words for him to make up.

Ashley, he filled my head. Memories of last night and seeing him again. The idea of meeting him possessed my head with numerous over-plotted fantasies. When I got home, I was the only one there. It was dark, the way I had left it. I sat down on the couch and lit a smoke. I sat there in the dark, thinking of Frankie's misfortunate heart.

After killing the smoke I went to bed and dreamed of Ashley

in mixed situations of sex and denial.

My parents came home with a big bang. My father was singing some unknown tune.

"Just take him to bed, Paul."

I sat up in bed, knowing I wouldn't get to sleep till they went to bed.

"Thanks, Paul. Do you want some tea?"

"Yeah. That was pretty wild tonight, wasn't it?"

"Yeah."

"I've had an even game for weeks now. I mean, it just won't let up or get any better."

"I wish Morris would be the same. Instead of being the butt of it all the time. Here you go. So, how's Lisa?"

"Ah, she's alright you know. These straight games have been helping lots, ever since she's gotten sick. To be honest, Maril, I think she's pregnant. But she thinks it's some bad flu. Who am I to tell her?"

"Yeah. God, I've never been this pissed for a long time."

"Maril, that's what I like about you. You're such a saint on this day. An you make all of us Shabbies remember God."

"I'm sure I do. Paul—"

"Maril!"

"What?"

"I need water."

"It's beside you."

"Thanks lo-vffe."

"I miss you, Maril."

"I've been missing you too, Paulie."

The deep silence of the house came to rest. I lay back down and fell asleep. Nights like that felt like a dream more than reality. Colours and sounds were over emphasized. Concentrate. That's really the goal. Especially when you're hung-over, that's all I can think of is trying to fuse my brain back together.

Father and Son

It was our father and son outing. We drove with the radio announcers and guest-speakers, having a heated debate over one issue followed by a series of upbeat morning commercials. Otherwise, the interior of the vehicle was silent.

As for the scenery, Wolston, the big city passed on the left side. Tall cylinder chimneys to my right filled the landscape against the small apartments. We drove into the desolate factory district. The area was filled with new factories enclosed by the yellow painted parking lots fortified by metal gates with scattered, 'No Trespassing' signs. Imperial Boxing painted in blue on the side of my father's boxed brick building.

He pulled into the reserved spot that was closest to the entrance.

"You see that gate," my father said pointing at the glass door's metal gate before shifting the gear to park. "What I've been talking about—"

"It's so that the hooligans don't get in and have a party at your expense."

"Our expense, Christopher."

We got out of the car as he took out the keys to unlock the gate. The sign of Imperial Boxing pasted in thick blue letters on the glass door.

The beeping of the new alarm system went off and my father rushed to click in the secret code. The room was tidy and white. Family photographs in charming metal frames decorated the receptionist's desk.

"Tell me this." He flicked on the lights. "Do you and your friends go to any of those raves up here?" The fluorescent lights did their epileptic fit.

"No, unless we walked."

"Oh right, Drew was in that accident. How is he doing?" The lights recovered.

"Good."

"Alright, you've been here before, but I want you to get a real feel for the place because once you graduate, you'll be working here."

"Right," I told him. Another decision of my life where I had no part. He assumed that I would be him.

"Working here." Swallow and continue. "And taking your business classes. Just look around, that's all I want you to do."

"Well Dad, I'm looking—"

"Look Chris, look around and shut up! I'm sick of that smart mouth. Right now, let me tell you, you're the only one who appreciates it."

"Right, padre."

My mother was always trying to bring me and my father closer together instead of the telecast hockey games.

I stepped into the quiet work area where the smell of glue and grease were strong. Numerous machines hung from the ceiling or were bolted into the cement ground.

Next, I headed to the staff room. The fluorescent lights took a minute or two to get to the right shade of brightness and only half of the tubes lit up.

The room was made up of lockers, hard orange booths, snack machines and two payphones. 'No Smoking' signs were the only literature on the four walls. There were ashtrays on the tables. I sat down taking out my pack and lighting a cigarette. I turned on the radio and it was on an oldies station.

I hated this place. I built buildings, and my dad thought I must've been building boxes the whole time. My grades weren't good this year; I tortured both of them with that. Before I had top grades, they thought that business school was right at my feet but I'd sit there and argue with them that I didn't want any part of the factory. But they wouldn't hear of it. That's when I stopped paying attention in school. I was passing enough to get out. My mum thought it was drugs for a while.

I sat there in the staff room, puffing away, waiting for my dad to call my name and him never saying anything about me smoking. All he cared about was implanting that factory into me. I knew he was hoping to give me a lecture on each machine and maybe add in more statistics about input and output. I did ruin it. I didn't want to hear it. Hear the old man piss all over me. Both of us pissing on each other.

Saturday
The early afternoon sun slapped my eyes open and then I saw my mum leave the room. The blinds were opened—this was her way of waking me up on a sunny afternoon. I tugged the string to the wooden blinds and they came crashing down on me.

"Chris, wake up!" my mum yelled from someplace in the house.

"I am!" I yelled back as I threw the blinds on the floor.

I reached for the phone on my night-table and gave Kel a wake up call. It rang three times before he picked it up. I could hear him grunting out a form of hello that seemed more like a gasp. Instead of him trying to finish that hello, I screamed out, "KEL!"

"What the fuck? What the fuck was that?" He drawled out.

"Did you get tickets for the game?"

"Yeah, I did. And Amanda—" He yawned into the phone. "She's coming too."

"What?"

"Amanda sh—"

"What, she likes hockey?"

"She says she does and she'd be good after. Look, I'll pick you up in an hour."

In an hour he came with that shining red faced Amanda glowing in the front seat and Drew was in the back. Me and Drew both nodded our heads over at Amanda, neither of us really sure what to make of Kel's decision in bringing Amanda. We both understood the eager need to get off and it was better to be guaranteed of that.

Amanda turned around. "Nadine, was wondering when you're going to call?"

"I'll call her." I didn't like her prying.

"You have her number?"

"Yeah."

"Make sure you call her because she's asking me. She really likes you, Chris, and I think you two would make a cute couple."

"Right."

"A—"

All she could get in was an "A," before Kel noticed my rolling eyes.

"How was your dad's?" Kel asked with a smile, watching me in the rear-view mirror.

"Fine. He was asking if we've been raving out there."

"What did you say?"

"No."

Out of the blue, Amanda's voice broke through. "One day you'll own it." Now her voice was becoming too frequent.

"Right." At the time I couldn't insult her because I knew Kel cared about her in some way, or he was just screwing her and I didn't want to fuck up his opportunities.

"Kel, did you call in our bets?" I asked to make sure he didn't forget.

"Yeah, I did and I have a feeling Bury is going to pull through this time. Foxton said that they've been really practising."

Foxton was our bookie at the time. All the bets were handled through Kel who talked to Foxton.

"I swear this is the last hundred I bet on them. If they lose I'm going, going onto Main Line."

"Why not Saber?"

"I'll bet on how many teammates get called out for penalties, that's fucking why. I don't even know why they bother giving them a chance. They're the worst team. Guaran-fucking-teed."

"Except that one time."

"Right, but there's no question it was paid off. There's no fucking way they could have won. No bloody way, even Foxy agrees there."

"Drew, man, you're a traitor to Bury's blue jersey. What happened to that pride, Bury's going to bury you!"

Both of us got distracted by the red Main Line fans outside the arena's gates. It was all too obvious. A couple of Wolston pride porky girls walking up to join the line, both wearing the alarming red. I rolled down the window and grabbed Drew.

"Hey GIRLS!" They looked over at us. I took out some coins from my pocket. "What about giving Bury boys their winning suck off!" I threw the coins as Drew did the honoured gesture of his tongue poking against his cheek to add to the drama.

"Cocksuckers, we'll kill you yet!"

"Go and get a hotdog and start practising, baby!"

Drew's last words caused Kel to speed through the parking lot because he could see those Wolston red knights coming in for a save.

We got out wearing our blue attire and walked up to the

arena. Kel held Amanda underneath his arm, and both me and Drew minded out for the insulted Lines. We gave our tickets and headed up the stairs. Our section was filled with the atmospheric blue.

Amanda turned over to me. "Chris, I want you to know that Nadine is like a sister to me." She touched her heart and flung her stiff hair.

Drew rolled his eyes and lit a smoke, whispering, "Poison, brother."

"If you don't intend to call her, tell me now, but don't tell me that you are and you're not going to do it. So, are you going to call her?"

"I'm going to call her. Anyways, it's between me and Nadine and not you, but thanks for your shared interest." I gave her a smile. I basically told her to go fuck herself and she caught on.

"You're a pig!"

"Right, right!" I gave myself the satisfaction of snorting at her.

Drew followed me with the snorting.

"Fuck off!"

And with that Kel returned with the cups of beer and we all took ours, giving a quick, "Cheers!" and gulped it down.

The fan warm-ups started: The stomping of the floor followed by, "Bury's going to bury you." Once the teams circulated the rink, the fans quickly thumped back into their seats and the game began.

Smokes were being smoked down to the butt with Main Line's star Alex Owen delivering the first couple of goals. The whispers of fuck going already and five hundred dollars going down the tube and straight into the fucking hands of Main Line fans.

I got up to get the next round of beers. I got in line with the other sorry bastards who were glowering at the game on the suspended monitors.

"Come on." I whispered into the air as my armpits were

sweating out hope.

"Four beers." I passed her the money as she placed the plastic blue cups on a paper tray.

The game was severe, the puck was up there in Main Line's goal crease. Bury kept it strong and there it was like a lightning bolt sent from God——Bury's Jamie Brewster scored. The fans cheered and settled back, hoping to see a lot more of that play and hoping Brewster was going to be blessed.

Four minutes later Brewster, blessed with another slap shot, tied the game. Now it was a matter of Bury getting one more point. A nice simple game. 3-2. One more point.

I was demolishing my fingernails, my lungs were getting blacker and I had to go to the washroom to take a massive beer piss. But I couldn't take my eyes off that ricocheting puck that went from one goal crease to the other. "Are you worried?" I asked Kel as I spat out a shaving of my thumb's nail.

"No fucking way. Those bastards aren't going to win this time."

"They already let two slip by them."

"Exactly, last time they only let one and we were down. I've never seen Main Line play like that for a long time. But today, today two for them is all they're going to get and all we need is one more."

"Kel, can I have a smoke?" asked Amanda as she eyed Kel to remind him that she came with him.

"Get that fucking out of there Samuels!" Drew screamed.

With a defensive shot of Bury, the puck flew past Main Line to Brewster. Main Line's enforcer Jacob Steels cross-checked Brewster and a small fight broke out. Bury's star player was down.

The crowd screamed, "Get the fuck out Main Line!"

The referee took the advice of the Bury fans and awarded a penalty shot to Brewster. The crowd hushed down. Across from us, we saw the group of Main Line fans waving their red flags with white taped letters spelling Main Line.

Brewster shot the puck, the puck flew right through the

goalie's lock and into the net.

The crowd broke into: "Bury's going to bury you! Bury's going to bury you!"

We were on the edge of our seats hoping to the Mother of God that there were no more goals. One minute left. And thank God the puck went back to pussy sliding all over the rink, and then the buzzer ended the game.

"Wooooo!" The cheers escalated for Bury. This was Bury's night and it felt fantastic to watch Main Line walk off with their heads down as Bury's fans threw-smacked their blue cups in Main Line's direction.

The authorities started to make their presence known because they were afraid that Bury being drunk and stupid might tear apart their own arena.

Out of pure winning tradition, we drove down to the local pub where there would be other Bury fans bringing in Bury's happiness by quick gulps of Bury's own fresh brew.

At the pub everyone was standing up shocked that Bury had won. Luck was on our side again as we got a booth in the back, but unfortunately Amanda sat between me and Kel.

"This is for our winnings. Cheers!"

We all crashed our pints together and drank them down. Kel held Amanda underneath his arm.

"I told you, Bury's been practising. Today those boys gave it all they got and we got the money to prove it."

"Amanda, do you like hockey?"

"Yeah, I do. I used to play ringette."

"That's the stick the donut game, right?" asked Drew.

"Ha, ha, ha."

"Come on." Kel said as he picked up his beer. "Cheers to Bury."

After the cheers, Kel and Amanda talked excitedly close to each other, as me and Drew examined Kel's ogling eyes on her thick cleavage. From there me and Drew had an inspired conversation of tits.

Kel got up to get more beers.

"What are you talking about?" she asked placing her arm around me and taking a sip, dripping drops of beer on her blue shirt and breast. "Look at that." She said looking down at her breast. "Not even drunk yet and I'm getting wet. Oops!" She hushed her lips and fell over me tittering.

I watched her, waiting for Kel to see this red faced slut.

"I'm so pissed, Chris." She said it dreamlike to me.

I came towards her. "Get the fuck up," I told her. I was trying to be nice about it.

She held onto my neck. I took her hands and pulled her up. She rested her head on my shoulder. "I can see why Nadine likes you so much." I bumped her head with my shoulder. I guess I bumped her too hard because she rubbed her cement-hair head as she scrunched up her piggy nose.

Kel came back to the booth and handed out the pints.

"I think that girl over there likes me," said Drew. "She keeps looking at me. Chris, go over there."

I took my beer and I walked over to her.

"Hey," she said taking a long drag on her cigarette.

"Hi. My old pal Drew over there wants to meet you, but he's a little shy. Now, I can vouch that he's a real gentleman—" Her eyes went off me to someone who was standing behind me. I turned around and it was Drew.

"Thanks, Chris."

"He said you were a bit shy. Is that true?"

"Just a bit," he said indicating with his fingers.

"Why, do I make you feel shy?"

"Yeah," he said coming in closer to her.

"Why?" she asked tilting her head.

"You're a goddess."

She giggled and he kissed her. I took my cue and went back to the booth. I believe for now Drew's formulated pick-up words for the night were done. All he had to do now was listen, kiss and touch in the appropriate places.

Kel looked over towards me. "Chris, now it's your turn to pick out one of these girls."

Amanda being drunk fell over me. I thought at first she was going to remind me of Nadine. Instead, she twinkled her thick eyelashes. "Who do you want, Chris?"

Kel grabbed her back.

I sat back and scrutinized the scene and Amanda swung back, but Kel kept her steady. "Why don't you call Nadine so you're not so sad and lonely. She really, really likes you." Kel was nipping at her ear. "Stop it. I'm talking to Chris." She tried keeping her head straight and serious, and her eyes shone back on me. "Chris, you have to call her. I mean, there's no other way around it."

"Don't piss your panties over it, but I'm not going to call her."

"Why?"

Kel tried again to distract her, but she pushed him away. "Why aren't you going to call her? Is it because you already fucked her and she's just a notch!"

I was ready to hit her but I took a gulp of beer. "You can tell her that. I just don't care. I don't want a girlfriend."

"Fucking pussy!"

"Shut up, you fucking cow. With a mouth like that, you'd think you could put it to use on Kel's dick."

Kel burst out laughing and I caught her hand before she smacked me. He pulled her out of the booth.

"Pussy!" she shouted.

I sat there for a bit and Drew came over with the new girl.

"Where did they go?"

"He took her outside. She was making a scene."

Drew whispered something in her ear and we headed out. Kel and Amanda were leaning against the car. Kel had settled her down because his clothes were every which way while Amanda's hair stood on one side.

"Kel, can you drive?"

"Yeah."

Everyone was tired and didn't know what time it was except that it was dark with an edge of light coming through in the far off distance.

Drew's girl sat in the centre and they were cuddling. Kel drove with the window open to stay awake.

Amanda was the first to get dropped off.

She gave us her cheerful, "goodbye." Next was Drew. Drew and the girl left under each other's arms. We watched him silently unlock the door as she waited by his window. Then he opened the window and she crawled inside.

The sky was already cracking into the colour of blue as Kel drove up to my house. I stumbled out of Kel's car and I could hear his faint laughter as he drove off.

Fledged

I was on the train to St. Maurice High School for my first day at school. Already, the wool kilt made the back of my knees itch.

Once I got out, I followed the other uniformed students through St. Maurice. The neighbourhood was made up of old brick homes and old trees which aligned the streets. The school matched the neighbourhood, an old brick building with massive maple trees leading up to the school's entrance.

In the classroom, I sat down in the far corner of the room. The girl who was sitting in front of me turned around.

"So you're new. I'm Valerie."

"Eliza."

"Eliza, did you notice that I'm the only normal one. Well, both of us are normal but the rest are completely retarded. Right?"

"Yeah, I noticed that outside when I was coming in. So you're saying we're cool?" I wasn't too sure if she was being sarcastic about it. Because really I didn't notice anything.

"Hey, you know it. I'll show you the others later."

At lunch she took me to the others, who were behind the

school in a dark corner. There were three boys and two other girls. They were all smoking and they handed us one. I met the whole gang. They all lived around St. Maurice. When the big question came up about where I lived, I told them flat out that I lived on Wicklow Street.

After school, I took the train up to Union Street and there was my new ballet school, Royal Wolston Ballet glinting in the afternoon sun. I felt the hot sun on my back as I entered the cool air of the ballet school.

I changed with the other stretched out ballerinas. I went to the assigned classroom and joined the other girls and boys doing warm-up exercises. Once the instructor came in, we all stopped and watched her. I swallowed hard as my nervous stomach grumbled.

"Hello class. I'm Miss Clarbet. Now, the rules are to make sure that all you did just what?"

"Come to class fifteen minutes early to do exercises."

"Fifteen minutes at the very least and no later. The reason for this is?"

"So that you don't get injured."

"That's one reason, and the other reason is that I don't have to spend the whole class doing warm-ups. This class is not about warm-ups. I want you to remember this simple rule, come fifteen minutes before the class and no later. If you come later don't even bother stepping one foot in this room. Okay, in first position."

The whole class started in first position. From there I had my confidence back and I performed each instruction she gave.

After class, I stretched out my sore over-used body and wrapped my blistered toes. I painfully changed into my normal clothes and staggered out onto the street.

"Hey, wait up."

I turned around. It was one of the male dancers from class.

"I'm Matthew."

"Eliza."

"You're new here, right?"

"Yeah. How long have you been here?" I was getting tired of being new to everyone.

"A year."

We walked out together.

"Are you going on the train?"

"Yeah."

"Have you had Miss Clarbet before?"

"No. I've never been worked over like that before. I feel I was just stretched all over."

"That's how I felt. I couldn't believe it. I thought this was normal for this school to kill your body. So you're telling me that this isn't normal?"

"The other instructors I had would give you a chance to breathe, or at least you had the chance. But she just keeps you going."

"Do you think the other classes will be like this?"

"I don't know, but I have a feeling that it could slow its pace because I don't know how she's going to keep up with us. At least, I hope."

Matthew and I took the train. He told me the low down of the school and the other ballerinas. I was so charged up by him. The way he smiled with each exact point and how his green eyes would grow bigger with excitement. I wanted to grab him and kiss him. Instead, he got up, we hugged as long lost parting friends and the train's doors opened at Shepherd Lane. From there I was on my way home with throbbing feet and feeling good. Good because I was amazed. Today and especially with Matthew, I was laughing and looking from above at everything that was happening to me. Today came and formed the words good, great and fantastic on my tongue.

Fancy

It all happened quicker than I had imagined. I was sitting with the others, the other cool St. Maurice friends, when completely out of the shadows a new boy with darting blue eyes and a black sailors toque entered our group. His name was shouted out with cheers, "Ashley." I was taken in, completely taken aback by it. Ashley was standing right in front of me. The already foreseen problem popped up in my head. I felt like a comic character with all my words bubbled out before me: Do I act like he knows me?

The group of cool friends wanted to introduce me like all good friends wanting to show their new player. His blue eyes already noticed me, calculating the remembrance of my face.

"Hi, Ashley." I stepped right into it.

"Eliza, right?" he asked.

"Yes."

"Wait, you two know each other?" Paul seemed thrilled by the coincidence.

"Yeah, it was at one of those raves. A couple of nights ago."

"Six degrees just kills me man. Really, it does. So this whole time, whole two days that we have all been waiting for you, man, she knew you. It fucking blows me, that six degrees."

"So, tell me Eliza, what happened to you two at the rave?" asked Valerie.

"We just met each other, that's all, Val."

"Ah, is that so?"

"No, Val, I'll tell you." He came up and placed his arm around me. "Eliza and I fucked each other silly. Basically, on the physical level we got to know each other quite well."

I laughed, it was too much for me.

"Or better yet, Ash, we made respectful an caring love. Isn't that right, Ash?"

"Yeah E, that's right. Love is what provoked us that night."

"E was more like it."

We broke out the smokes and soon the girls and boys separated. I was pronged with all the sexual curiosity questions, but all I could think of was the snorting and biting.

Once the bell rang, we left in an orderly fashion. I purposely lingered behind, until Ashley caught up. It was perfect timing. I turned around and there he was. The cool group was already walking up the stairs as they forgot about us. He put his arm around me playfully as we rocked together.

"Tell me, Eliza, are you stalking me by any chance?"

I placed my arm around him. "I think you're stalking me."

We both nodded our heads, smiling the same way as the night before except in school clothes. It fell into a kiss. With the coolness of autumn, we kissed and made it last because this time we were somewhat grounded. The bell rang again. We ran hand in hand into the school. It was really sensationally romantic for my school girl years.

After school I met him at his speedy little black car. He zoomed me to the dance school. We made plans again to meet after dance class. We did our soon-to-be traditional kiss goodbye. It came to be that I was forming a boyfriend. A boyfriend that I didn't know how to start. That's what I remember thinking the moment I slammed the door to his car after class. We zoomed back to his place.

"So, are your parents going to be there?"

"My parents died when I was too young to remember anything. Lately, I've been dreaming about my mother's shoes. That's the closest I got. My uncle took me in. I used to go to Clover Academy. I was kicked out for drug use. My uncle decided and bargained with me. I suppose then I was acting like my mother because I put up a fight and he bought me off with my own place. All he does now is leave messages."

Ashley's story went on for a while. He lived in Clover Park, the rich area.

His apartment was bigger than my house and colour co-ordinated. In my parents house, colour co-ordination was found in the flower patterns or in the newer patterns of blue stripes. Ashley's colours were blues and blacks and mahogany floors.

I stood in the centre of it all. Ashley took off his toque and ran his fingers through his hair. He dimmed the lights. I hugged myself because it was cold. The window was open and the blinds kept smashing against the windowpane.

He looked sublime as he stood in the dimness of the lights. I'm sure he must've done this before because it played out in steps. I could almost see the numbers: 3. *He placed on a slow cat shrieking record. In between that number I dropped my bag.* 4. *He took off his blazer.* 4.5. *Tie.* 5. *shirt.*

As I stood there staring at him, he banged me against the wall and then the floor, carefully at first and then harder. I couldn't believe it. Any of it.

Fancy 2

My new life happened a lot sooner than I thought.

I got on the train and I met Matthew on Shepherd Lane. He came over smiling—that's what he did best.

"Hey, Matthew."

"How are you?"

"Good an you?"

"Today is another long, long lesson. But you know I don't mind it."

"I would never have guessed that you enjoyed it." We both teased and teased.

"But."

"I know already. You better watch it. I think Brooke is catching on. She's sort of the jealous type."

"You're fucking brilliant Eliza. Yesterday, when I got home, she left me a message and I called her. She starts pissing on me about all of these long lessons we are having. And she didn't believe me when I told her. In other words, she doesn't think these lessons exist. So last night I went over to talk to her and I accidentally stayed over. Always a bad move when it's really sex. But in the morning I was leaving for my lesson and she kicked me out. I actually put on this lovely scene. 'Brooke, Brooke I love you. Let me in. I love you.' It was brilliant. I'm now officially single."

"I never would've figured it out."

"How's that Ashley doing?"

"Very good."

The train came to our stop and we got off.

In class Matthew was already flirting with Julie. I started doing my exercises as I listened to him talk to Julie. I could hear her saying, "Oh stop it, Matthew," as she giggled under each word. That must've drove Matthew insane, that little giggle.

When it was time for me and Matthew to perform together, I watched the mirror to see what the viewers would see. Matthew and I performed well together; we echoed the moves onto each other. We were like two long lost lovers.

After class, I got dressed and met up with Matthew and Julie.

"Eliza, you want to come with us for a little drink?"

My eyes perked up at Matthew while he purposely ogled me. I grinned at him.

"Na, I think I'll go home."

"Ah, come on Eliza, it's Saturday."

"Alright."

Playing hard to get for Matthew was good for him.

We went to The Shank, it was near the school. We took up a big red booth and ordered shots and tossed them back. We lit cigarettes to give that foggy feel to the whole place. Matthew sat in the centre for attention.

"You know you two." I downed the shot. "That waitress, I think she's flirting with me."

"You're fucking gone."

"Na, I'm serious." I puffed the smoke and blew it out. "Every time she comes here, her big, fuzzy eyebrows perk up at me. I mean, they're really perking at me." They both laughed at me. "Fucking rude you two, fucking rude."

Matthew hugged me. "Don't worry, I'll take care of you." His remedy was to order three more shots.

The waitress came back with the drinks and they both observed me. I waited for that unknown move from the waitress or maybe from me. She placed down the drinks and looked right at me. Her eyes blue, really blue and big.

Matthew's green eyes stared at me as if he wanted to kiss me and forget about Julie. Julie went to the washroom. Matthew examined me intensely like he always did with those adoring green eyes and soft pink lips that I just wanted to kiss. He resembled a big fuzzy bear sitting there gazing at me.

"Are you coming home with me?" he asked, gently touching my face.

I shook my head instead of answering. He was just too cute for an answer. My voice came up, "I thought you were going home with Julie?"

"I am. I just want both of you. But you more. You know that, don't you?"

He wanted to kiss me as my lips stood still and reachable, but Julie came back and broke the physical thought.

"There's a dance floor back there."

"Does it look good?"

"Yeah, there's more people there than here. And it sounds pretty good. They're not playing this sappy music."

As soon as we opened the red doors, the loud music hit us and we danced our way through the crowded dance floor. I realized that Matthew was dancing with both of us. He was in the centre holding us as we moved anxiously up and down. Right there, he had both of us and he knew it, the cute little shit. As I shimmied to the fast beats, Matthew held onto my waist and I rested my head on his chest. I slipped out of him into the free space. He took my hands and held me there as we both swayed drunkenly. At that moment, we both forgot about Julie. All I saw was Matthew and feeling Matthew hold me up as I moved. I was so pissed and the beats all sounded the same and they seemed to jump all around at the same time. I just couldn't grasp anything. We both slowed down. I let myself rest on him to stop from gagging.

My eyes tried to find something to grip onto in the spinning maze. I found it in the corner with the blue eyes and bright blond hair. I'm sure it was Ashley. I stopped moving as Matthew kissed my neck. I moved away from Matthew and Julie. I looked in the same direction and Ashley noticed me. He came through the crowd to me. We kissed each other.

"What are you doing here?"

"I went out after ballet with those two," I shouted as I pointed with my finger.

"You look good." He went on about how good I looked.

"What the fuck are you on?"

"I'll show you soon. Come and dance with me."

We danced to the rhythmic beats. His violent blue eyes glared at me, and they were ready to tear me apart. I wanted him to tear me into two Elizas.

"Come on." He took me in the back room where this other group was all dressed in black and glittery. One of the guys winked at him. I giggled at this—this wink was like my waitress. Ashley handed me a little white tablet. I placed it in my mouth before big, bad Ashley could tell me anything. It dissolved and everything started to feel really good, again. Like everything had this new fucking sensation. My whole body was like it was fucking itself. Everything around me felt really real and I moved my body in this new way that made my body come alive.

After the dancing, we went to the back again and the same, smug winking guy was nibbling at some overdone make-up guy.

"Georgie, this is Eliza."

"The great Eliza. And how does the great Eliza feel?"

"Fucking great, Georgie Boy." I just had to spit it out. He was asking for it.

He smirked and kissed his powdered friend. "I have to agree

with you. Fucking great explains everything, doesn't it Ashley?"

"Ash." I tested. "Let's go to your place."

We left. At his place that's when the time hit me, it was past two, but I could have sworn it was only twelve. As he went to the washroom I went into his bedroom, threw my bag on the floor, stripped down and sunk under the covers.

I woke up with a ray of the morning's bright light slicing each eye into two. I opened them carefully, feeling the hard liquor nailing into my head.

I remembered as quickly as I forgot about my home. I slept the whole night—morning through at Ashley's. Home disappeared. I tried to swallow; my mouth was too dry and filled with the stench of stale sticky liquor. I could still feel its solid stickiness through my veins, keeping me on the bed. Keeping me still and squinting at the sun. I drew my eyes away with all the little power I had. I watched the half-open bedroom door and wondered how far the washroom was. The idea of the washroom consumed me. I tried imagining the easy flow of the refreshing cold water tearing through my torn sore throat.

The sun ate at my eyes. Back again to thinking of the few paces that lead up to the washroom. I could do it. Get up. Just need cold water. I tried to convince myself in bed that I wouldn't throw up, even though I could feel the sickness filling and burning with complete anticipation to gun out of me. I took one deep breath and got up feeling the pain of everything.

It came down, down to running to the washroom. I had no choice. I slammed the door out of assurance that I would try to be as quiet as possible.

The white clean toilet called to my stomach and I sat down beside it. I opened my mouth to my new-found friend. I rested my head, feeling my stomach punch me and it came up and filled my mouth. I knocked off the drooling saliva, I felt like the exorcist only my head hung in the toilet, and I was praying to God that I wouldn't do this again if only he let this stop.

...

It seemed to stop for a moment. I closed my eyes, feeling the ceramic coolness of the toilet take my fever away. I flushed the toilet with the little bit of strength that I had. And there I felt the heavenly breeze of the cool swirl of the toilet water.

I tried to swallow and I tasted the remnants of the stale saturated liquor mixed with the active stench of vomit. I held onto the corners of the sink for balance. Then it hit me again. My head on its own went for the toilet. I threw up absolutely nothing, which kills more. I sat there with my mouth propped open and the clear bile came up as spit.

I spat out the last drop of saliva and flushed the toilet. Cautiously, I got up holding onto the corners of the sink. I washed my sweating face and swallowed as much water as I could. After awhile, the cool rush of water brought me down. I saw myself in the mirror and my eyes were puffy and red. I sat down on the washroom's fluffy rug and rested my head against the drooping towels and fell asleep. Everything seemed to pass as I opened my eyes after the small rest.

All that was left to do was shower. I peeled off my panties and little tank top.

The shower was warm, and the reassuring soap cleansed me and my numerous body pains.

I went to the bedroom and Ashley was awake. He grinned when he saw me.

"Feel better?"

"A bit. How bout you?"

"I'm fine. I was wondering if you want to live with me?"

"What?" I was amazed as I stood there in the towel. My lips and eyes hung in a state of confusion.

"Don't you want to live with me?"

I didn't know what to think, except my voice answered "yes" followed by a friendly morning grin. I automatically crawled up and gave him a kiss. I was excited but didn't know if it was true or not.

We both lay there arm in arm. Like a live-in couple. Arm in arm in love but really we fell asleep. I woke up and he was gone. He was in the shower because I could hear the water dripping. I got up and dressed and went to the phone.

"Hello?" my mum's voice asked wondering who it was.

"Mum."

"Eliza, where the hell are you?"

"Mum, I'm at Ashley's, but don't worry I'm fine."

"Yeah, that's what your father kept telling me. I told you to call! What happened to that?"

"I know an that's why I called."

"Eliza, don't get smart. I don't need that from you, too. What are you doing at Ashley's?"

"Leave her alone! She's fine!" shouted my father in the back.

"Shut up, Morris! Answer me Eliza, what are you doing at Ashley's?"

"I spent the night, what was I supposed to do? Anyways, Mum, I don't want to fight about it. I'm fine an I want to tell you I'm moving out."

"Oh. An why are you moving out? Are you already pregnant an is this a way out of it?"

"No, I'm not. I'm moving out because it's easier."

"Yeah, that's right, it's easier to get pregnant that way. I suppose I will pack up your old baby clothes. Is that what you want? An is that why you're calling?"

"No, Mum, listen—"

"Eliza, you listen to me now! You know I married your father about the same age as you an I was already out, you know? So it's no surprise to me. But tell me you're not pregnant, are you?"

"How many times do you want me to tell you? I swear to God, I'm not, I'm moving out because it is closer to everything."

"God, if you were pregnant, I'd have taken you to the doctor or something because there's no way you're going to have a baby.

No bloody way. You're not going to end your life that way."

It was like she was talking to my father. Almost saying it was his fault for ruining her life. I'm sure she must've been staring at him as she said it. Giving him that won't-you-just-die look.

"Mum, I'm not pregnant. Don't worry."

"I didn't raise you to be some sort of baby-making machine. Just remember that Eliza."

"No worries, please."

"Remember?"

"Yeah."

"Are you in love, is that why?"

"No—"

"Cause if you are, it's not going to last."

"Mum—"

"Eliza, I'll see you later."

Future

The heavy wooden door vibrated the walls and windows which told the rest of the household that my dad had left for work. I lay there with my eyes shut trying to remember some dream that only gave me various images of me driving.

"Chris," my mum whispered followed by a steady handshake on my shoulder.

I opened one eye and saw my mum in a bright tropical flower dress that caused the other eye to pop open.

She bent over and shook me. "Chris, I'm going now."

I sat up.

"Come on. I need your help. I'll be at the door."

She walked out and carefully shut the door. I got up and placed on my pants and runners. I rushed to open the door and slammed it into my face. "Fuck." I held my smashed face and banged the door shut.

I held my thumping forehead and I was about to go to the washroom when my mum gave her morning shout, "Hurry up Chris, the taxi's here!" She was letting me know that I had no time to take a long morning piss.

I walked into the room and saw her ready with two bags by her side. She was going far away from the Atlantic to the Greek Islands to see a client.

She held the door open for me and I picked up the two bags and headed out into the pissy windy weather. The trunk flew open and I threw the two bags in.

"Bye. I'll call you," she whispered into my ear giving me one last kiss on the cheek.

"Bon Voyage."

Another kiss and one last tap under the chin and she ran into the cab. From the back window, she gave me a small quick wave as the taxi drove off.

I went back inside and answered the phone.

"Hello."

"Chris, is Mum there?"

"She left."

"Oh, are you going to be home tonight?"

"I'm going out, why?"

"No reason. Bye."

From there I got ready for half a day of school with a headache and my morning piss just burning to come out.

Kel picked me up and he drove towards the private girls' school. We were looking for those bad girls wanting to join two guys, but we drove right past seeing too many bags and armfuls of books.

Our high school was the posh high school. The entire school, except for the gymnasium, was constructed of glass. It was nice, but still the students spent most of their time outside except when it was raining hard.

And there was Drew guarding our parking lot.

"Do you have the shit, bro?" I asked Drew.

"Do you even have to ask?" He patted his bag.

Our crowd was seen as the hard-partiers. People from other

crowds always wanted to be asked to our parties. Nobody at school fucked with us.

The girls, unfortunately, were nothing to scream about. They all thought that they were the next screaming sensation. But they were the only ones who were screaming. The most sensational feeling they could supply any guy was their hole followed by a paper bag and a muzzle. But in any ugly patch there was always one girl that stood out and she wasn't anything too special at that. Sylvia had dark brown hair and blue eyes, but it really was her heavenly tits that made all the boys sink their eyes down to that nice bouncy flesh.

During spares she'd be out there in the smokers' circle with her girlfriends. She'd sit across from me, blowing her smoke rings and laugh each time she caught me staring at her. She liked playing her little games. At one moment she'd be all friendly and then, a teasing bitch.

But ever since the helpful Nadine, I wondered about the contours of that fat fucking hole of hers. I observed her mouth working hard to puff out two circles in my direction; maybe she would blow me.

Her blue eyes watched me watching her. I gave her a wink and she laughed high and crackling.

"Hey, sleepy-eye, is that one still dreaming about me?" She'd make her blue eyes pout followed by her swelling bottom lip.

"You would like that, wouldn't you?"

"I don't think my thirty year old boy-friend would like that."

"You mean the posters hanging up on your wall or was it that Willy you pack away?"

"Fuck off and leave me the fuck alone." She came up with her friends and stood there for a minute. "And Chris." She poked her fingernail into my chest. "If you don't leave me alone, I will tell him. He used to be in the army."

"Bring it on, baby. If that what it takes to get into your pussy—"

She slapped me.

"Fuck off."

She stormed off with her pack.

"You're really falling for her." Kel smacked me on the back.

"All she needs is a man to fuck her right and she wouldn't be all up there. I think she's had too many pussy cats."

And with that last statement the bell rang.

After my last class, I was heading back to Kel's car and both of them were there waiting. I was about to head over when I was blocked by a thrusting chest and bad breath streaming straight into my nostrils.

"What the fuck?" I backed away and the sweet one came into the picture.

"Hey, Chris." She gave me one of her tricky smiles.

It clicked together, this piece of old meat belonged to Sylvia. "Chris, tell me are you still dreaming because Sylvia says you are?" He poked his fat finger into the centre of my chest.

I looked up at this toppled blond hair boy with big stupid blue eyes and dwarf white eyebrows.

"She's been telling me that you've been bothering her?" He folded his arms against his chest with his hands rolled into two thick fists.

I looked at my friends who pulled out and Drew commanding me with his arm to run. I observed Sylvia's hunk of meat and gave one last glance at Drew's arm rushing me in.

I made a decision; I took the cheap shot and kneed him. He fell and fuck did he howl. Sylvia dropped her bag. I was about to join my friends when Sylvia grabbed my bag and then me.

"Rob, Rob!" she was yelling out. I could feel her gigantic titanics rubbing into my back.

I pulled her in. Gave her a quick kiss which was a smash of teeth and I smacked her off. She went tumbling over Rob and I could see the big guy getting up so I gave him a kick in the ass. Drew was already in the car with the back door swung open.

"You're dead, Chris!" she was yelling. "Dead!"

I got in the car and watched as she helped Rob back to his giant feet.

"Wow, I think she's really coming around there."

"I think she likes it a bit rough."

"You really fucking gave it to her, man."

"It was a gentle love tap."

At Drew's house, we headed to our usual corner of drunkenness, the little red entertaining bar where Drew prepared our traditional mixed drinks.

"Kel, did you hear from Packer, yet?"

"Yeah and I'm in. That means me and Chris will be roommates. And you're still going to stay in rez?"

"I have no choice. Otherwise, my parents told me I had to get a job to support myself and they know that's not going to happen."

"My dad got me a job." I told them all about it. "And that's because he loves me and knows what's best for me."

"Way to go, Chrissy Boy." Kel slapped me on the back.

Drew handed us drinks. "To Chris and Sylvia. Cheers."

It was 9:02, 9:02 was blinking through my wincing eyes as I felt the headache set in place for the night. I glanced over at Drew and Kel—they were still sleeping. Kel's bottom lip kept mumbling something and Drew rested peacefully. I got up feeling the thick film of liquor coating my mouth and throat. I gave them each a kick in the leg.

"Let's go."

Kel drove over the St. Maurice Bridge, which was the only way out of Bury. Wolston's lights flickered through the sea's fog. Kel drove up Bow Street into the atmosphere of the huge Victorian homes of Wolston which led straight to the city centre. Instead of going to the city centre we went down on Union Street. Union Street was deserted, but around eleven, the street would be packed with people scattering in and out of places. Line-ups outside waiting to get inside as the clusters of girls tried to entice the bulky bouncers.

We parked by the newly constructed Mertle Park which used to be the factory district at the beginning of Wolston's industrial history according to the stone plaque. The park was nicely done like most of Wolston's parks. It had lots of flowers and hedges growing past the black steel fences which kept the surrounding streets out.

We walked around the neighbourhood which was populated by men with minuscule dogs. We ended up near the flat gravel properties that were protected by huge metal fences. We leaned against the fence and Drew pulled out his surprise. Gently placing the pill in our hands, we all downed it. Me and Kel, the virgins to this new drug, waiting and walking for the new sensation to kick in.

"Nothing's happening." Kel looked over at Drew.

"Just wait, man."

With all of our senses still intact, we searched for the red brick factory with two smoke stacks that resembled every other building. Fortunately, we spotted two zealous silver wig ravers entering the factory. We climbed over the old fence. You could see the damage of the missing, 'No Trespassing' sign.

Inside everything was booming immaculately, it felt like the bricks that kept it together were also booming. Lights were flashing all over the place, exposing different groups of people dancing and a lot of passing hands and swallowing mouths turning into happy looming faces. Everyone seemed to be smiling and my own lips and mouth were stretched.

I felt so light walking on the cement floor and feeling the beating music filter through my body. The other bodies pushed against me; it felt completely fantastic. I pulled Drew over. "Thank you, man. This is fantastic!" I shouted out the words, hearing them form and bellow through my throat and tongue.

My attention turned over to the sweet reality: girls in multitudes. Nice and plentiful. Drugged silly out of their minds and smiling wide and glaring with love all around them. I looked about trying to find a girl through the multitudes that was close to me. I could see thighs thumping to the beat behind Drew. I followed her thighs up past the frisky red pleated skirt to her bouncing ponytail. She turned around. She was wearing a red Main Line tightie. The blue lights smacked each white letter, exploding on her chest. Her skirt went round and round, never high enough.

I glared at her rosy lips opening wide into laughter. She read my shirt and mouthed it out, "Doctor." Her big red lips ended in laughter.

She turned back to her girls. I grabbed Drew by the shirt and switched him over to my side. I felt her body beside me moving up and down, feeling her laughter jerk her body. I rested my head on her and she rested her head on mine. Her ponytail was pricking the back of my head.

She turned around and held my waist as she danced from the back, rubbing against me. It felt like I was fucking dreaming. My hands found their own way to rest on her thighs. I turned around dancing with her, wanting to hold her close and feel her up. I held on to her wrists, feeling her strong pulse through my thumb.

She broke away and wrapped her arms around my neck. I kissed her and it felt incredible. Kissing became a whole new territory. Our tongues fought to feel each other's mouths out. I pulled her away as she continued on bopping madly. She jumped on me and I held her.

"Are you tired, Doctor?" she shouted into my ear.

"No," I said. But my body said yes and I carried her out of the mass of moving bodies.

I dropped my arms and she landed on her feet and wobbled there, giggling. We walked around in the back. Each room was filled with hot, touchy lovers who were whispering into each other's ears, creating a humming sound. She ran ahead into the dark hallway and stood against the wall. I sat down and she sat down on top of me.

She bent down and caught my tongue between her teeth. She held it there, giggling. I pushed her head forward and we sat there with our devouring lips.

The instinct of a man kicked inside my pants and I slid her cautiously onto the floor. I felt under the Main Line shirt, feeling one tit coming out through the M and the other through the N. My hand went up her thigh and I propped her skirt up to reveal her red panties.

The pressure of my tenting pants was building and I responded by taking off her panties. I unzipped my pants and I hoped to God she was on the pill. That thought lost its momentum as I shoved it into her moist pussy and I pushed her up with her head bopping away.

And it happened; I rested on top of her listening to her heartbeat with my dick still hard with no pressing out and her body jerking away to my finger flicking.

I rolled off eventually with my attention stuck on the lights hitting the ceiling above me. I saw bobs of her hair and her red tits being covered up but it didn't stay there too long. I lay there looking up. I couldn't take my eyes off the lights. I was in total stupefied suspense of the next colour. And I knew there was a formulated pattern but it was passing too quickly for me to count or categorize.

I don't know how long I sat there. I remember getting up and seeing the zealous silver wig ravers. I headed down looking through the rooms which were still filled with people. I squished through the bumping bodies hoping to find Drew or Kel. Instead, I found the doorway and I went out feeling the fresh air smack my face and wake me up. I sat outside against the building and the bouncer came up. He was carrying a black bag.

"Water?"

"Yeah."

"Five."

I gave him a five and he gave me water. I became focused,

feeling that cool spring hydrate my body and the ocean breeze mixed with the stale smell of gravel. I couldn't take my eyes off the black sky with little specks of stars trying to come through the black clouds. I went over to the bouncer; he wasn't doing too much but lighting a cool smoke for himself.

The first thing that came out of my mouth was, "It's a beautiful night."

He looked at me a bit stray-like. "Want to go in?" He took control of the door handle.

"No." And like a fucking pussy I asked, "Can I hang out here?"

"Fuck, whatever."

The door opened and two other ravers jumped out long lost in love with each other. I held the door and entered the booming with sweating bodies all over the place. I searched for any sign of Kel and Drew.

I found myself back to where the rooms were. Three girls surrounded Drew. They were relaxing and laughing softly to one another. I stepped into the room and Drew's eyes sparkled, "Chris, where were you?"

Kel stepped in and took a seat by his blonde of the night; she was wearing tight plastic clothes. He squeezed her tightly, making the sounds of a Crispy bar. Drew laughed with his arms around two girls. One wore a sparkling silver wig and resembled a man. The other girl had sparkles in her brown hair and she wore a silver dress that revealed her green panties.

"Come and have a puff," Kel said lifting his arm from his true blonde sweetheart and taking up the pipe.

"It's magical," his blonde responded, giving me a wink of assurance as she took her puff.

I took the pipe and sat down on the cement floor, taking a big puff with that slow calculating blow. I fell back with an ah.

"This is your friend, Chris?" I could hear her asking Kel as her hand played through my hair.

The silver wig girl came up to me with a quick wave. She sat down beside me.

"Hi, I'm Tasha. Over there, that's Sasha, we're twins."

I looked at both of them. She was right, they were twins but I got the ugly one.

"Right."

Tasha grinned and shook her metallic pieces of hair. I wanted to rip it off with her red-lipstick that strayed from her lips to her teeth and all over the pipe like she was giving it a blow job. I really didn't care for her.

She placed her arms around me, mistaking me for the strong silent type. Or else I was making up for the lack of Drew. I glanced over at Drew who was nipping at Sasha's neck until the magical pipe got passed over to him. I relaxed as Tasha went on about herself, and the blonde above played with my hair. That was nice.

I stared at the metal ceiling. I looked back to her. She smiled that girlie way as her metallic strands of hair dragged bits of lipstick across her face. She was getting all messed up by herself.

Her twangy voice settled down after her long talk. She sat back with her body touching mine. She looked at me and said, "What do you think?"

"No one listens to you. No one gives a fuck what you're saying, right!"

She sat there like a good ugly dummy smiling all eagerly taking the blow. I sat back again, feeling the grin on my face, thinking of the Main Line girl. Now, she was a nice piece: her lying back, breasts pressed tight up against her shirt as I ripped off her weary red panties and her deep eyes relaxed as I played with her growing clit. Getting all wet and myself plunging right into it with those tits ready to explode and pop my eye out.

...

Me and my friends were at our first school dance. We were watching the older students go for it on the dance floor, the girls doing those sexy moves as the guys followed them up on it. The girls with their twirling skirts going a bit high and some revealing those special fancy panties not just the cotton white ones you see in the porno-mag where the little school girl takes them off carefully wetting herself in the process. No, these girls were into lacy panties. They already had the night planned out, but there was this one girl, she was wearing a tight purple dress. She was a big girl, mind you, and that dress only covered half her tits.

She twisted with her boyfriend who planted his hands heavily on her waist causing the top to rotate down. And she would stop and pull it back up.

The inevitable happened—her tits came flying out, the left tit poked him in the eye. He went back grabbing his eye and the strobe light gave everything that accurate slowness. She snatched her fisted tits and was screaming out: "Rob! Rob!"

Finally, the strobe light shut off and the coloured lights twittered around as she pulled up her dress and went flying down after him. The gymnasium filled with sounds of music and laughter. She and Rob left with him still holding his eye. She was waving goodbye, smiling and trying hard to laugh at herself. The next day, Rob showed up with a black eye.

...

I heard myself laughing.

"What are you laughing at?" I heard her asking.

Then out of the blue, her massive red lips came towards me in full effect. With her tongue lashing out to lick her lips and then the fucking pucker. "What are you doing?" I pushed her away from me. Kel and Drew glared at me as if they were telling me to keep the peace.

"What's the matter?" Kel asked, and Sasha turned towards her twin sister with her eyes breaking through the glitter.

"Nothing, I just want a bit more of this." I took the pipe from Tasha and I gave them a cheery smirk, hoping I didn't ruin any of their chances. I turned back to the teary-eyed Tasha because I rejected her fucking mess of red lips. I stared at her not feeling a bit sorry.

"I'm sorry, I'm just seeing someone and I'm the sensitive type." I shrugged my shoulders and took a puff.

"The nice guy, right? That's really sweet." Everything must be sweet to this red-faced cunt. "Because most guys I get with don't give a fuck." Here we go again. Instead of enjoying the memories I had to focus on her to make sure she wouldn't try to kiss me again. "I have a boyfriend but we go out with others. I met him at one of these raves. Is your girlfriend here tonight?"

"No, she's off on a school trip. One of those school trips that takes you around Europe showing you all those historical sites."

"That so nice, Chris. Are you two in love?"

"Yeah, I miss her, that's why they took me out. They told me that I was moping too much."

"That's what friends are for."

"Are you in love?"

"Yeah, we just had our one year anniversary."

"Is he here tonight?"

"Yeah. He's also wearing a silver wig. We always dress the same. It's funny how we met because one night I was wearing a red wig and he was wearing a red wig. It was practically the same one except that he had a silver bow. Anyways, that night we just hit it off."

That's when Drew got up with Sasha and headed for a darker room. And from there I got up.

"Where are you going?" she asked picking up the pipe. "Don't you want anymore?"

I pretended that I didn't hear her and walked out. I thought I'd entertained her enough until Drew made his exit. I headed back to the bodies of fast-moving people and joined in getting pushed from group to group, finding new bodies to admire as they flickered around. But the Main Line girl was out of my site. Feeling the music again and feeling fucking free with multitudes of bodies all pushing up against me, I found another girl.

The time continued to waver and the crowd was sagging a bit

too much. I headed back to the rooms to find Drew and Kel.

They got up and headed towards me, looking completely pissed as they went on about something but at this point nothing was making much sense.

Outside, the dark sky was now becoming day with a thick morning blue advancing as the sun calmly edged out and the birds were twittering about. The bouncer was still there.

"Do you want water?"

We all bought water and sat down with our backs against the building. We sat staring out at the sky as if it was doing something.

Late late afternoon—early evening I woke up with a headache. I could hear the game from the hallway, the announcer shouting, "He scores!" Followed by my father's response, "Fuck."

I heard the sound of a can being flicked open. There he was sitting in his navy blue tracksuit mesmerized by the game holding the can tightly in his hand. If mum were here he'd have it in a glass. And if mum were here, I probably would've had a rude awakening from one of them to join them for lunch.

"Good morning, Dad."

"Right, Chris." He raised his eyebrow and one eye as it quickly returned to the game.

"Did mum call?"

"No, but I'm sure everything's alright," He said taking a sip of his beer. "She's a big girl and can take care of herself."

"What's with the can?"

"Mum's away. Did you have fun last night? Come on you little bastards, get it out of there."

"Yeah."

"What did you do?"

"Usual. What's the score?"

"God, they're playing like shit. Four to absolutely nothing."

The phone gave its high pitched ring, it was even louder than the television. The phone was lying by his side and he picked it up. "Hello? ... Good and how's everything? ... That's great.... How much longer? ... Right.... Yeah.... Alright.... Bye." He handed me the phone taking a gulp of his beer.

"Hi, Mum."

"How are you?"

"Good. How about you?"

"I'm great, it's beautiful out here. I wish both of you were out here. But I was telling your father that I'm going to be a bit longer. I'll be back in a week's time. So you and your dad can have some good quality time. And don't you give him a hard time, now."

"You know I won't. It's usually the other way around."

"Right, Chris, and I mean it. Chris, I have to go."

"To the beach?"

"It's a business trip."

"Working on a Saturday?"

"That's what I say," my dad whispered, finishing the can of beer.

"That's right. I love you."

"I love you too, Mum."

"Bye."

"Bye. Mum sounds good."

"It must be one hell of a trip for her to be out there for another week."

"I'm going back to bed."

"Still feeling under?" he said trying to sound all concerned with both eyes on me.

"Yeah."

"Holy fuck, they just missed. Oh fuck."

I went back to bed to nurse a headache with a Tylenol that wasn't kicking in soon enough.

Hub

The stale air of Saber filled Ashley's car.

It was grey out and Saber seemed more grey and disjointed. There were kids all around playing with invisible bouncing balls and shouting about some new game or some other kid breaking the rules. The older crowd talked with one or two friends as they walked around watching the chasing kids. My house came up with the empty front garden and cement path as the only ornament and the screened front door, rusted up with years of banging and rain.

The lights were on, more than likely the TV's blue flashing lights. Ashley parked behind my father's prized car. We got out. Ashley came up behind me couple-like, and kissed my head as if to say it would be over soon. I pulled away and took his hand, smiling at what was to come next.

"Ashley, let me be the first to introduce you to Saber." I gave him a kiss to make him feel normal.

I opened the screen door to the loudness of my father's voice.

"Eliza, hon-nay!" My mother came up laughing and smashed,

not resembling at all the voice I heard over the phone. "How's my baby?" She hugged me tightly.

"Good," I said pulling away.

"Your father won big again. It's amazing. I really didn't think he was capable of winning twice. You should've seen it, Eliza!"

"Mum," I said grabbing her to hold her down. "This is Ashley."

"Ashley, you can call me Maril." She held out her hand. "I've already put your stuff in bags. It's in your room."

"Thank you, Mum." I forced myself into a normal grin. I looked at Ashley, he was grinning at it all. I dragged him close by me, past my father and his gang of friends which my mother joined.

"This is crazy!"

"Yeah, I'm sure it is." My kid stuff still loomed around. Mostly painted pictures and the poster. I took the big black garbage bag. "This is it."

"Is it always like this?"

"Is what?"

"Your parents' house."

"No, just when he wins so now that's been twice. Usually my parents are never around. Both of them work."

"Ah." He hugged me from the back and kissed my neck. "Remind me to tell you the story of my uncle and his Jade."

"Is that supposed to even things out, my little rich boy?"

"Which one was your dad?"

"The one sitting in the centre of the sofa, the big one."

He took the bag and we headed out. Paul was dancing with my mum. My father got up to take his place because he was the winner this time.

"Bye Eliza!" they all shouted.

I gave them a wave.

The screen door slammed on my way out.

. . .

She was tanned and all smiles, giving my father an amiable hug and me a huge hug.

"Were you boys good while I was gone?"

"Yeah," I said.

"Really." She gave me a kiss on my cheek. "I'll be right back." She patted my cheek.

She followed my dad with the luggage to the bedroom and I sat down to watch the game. After five minutes their bedroom door was slammed shut, and she came out crying with her purse.

"What's the matter?" I asked about to get up.

"Not now!" She opened the front door, slamming it and I watched her drive away.

I walked to the bedroom and knocked on the door.

"What?" my dad yelled.

I came in. He was watching the game loudly on the television. He looked towards me a bit surprised. "Do you mind shutting the door," he said calmly.

I shut the door. What the fuck was he onto? I stood outside the door wondering if I should ask. Instead, I turned around and left home to finish watching the game at Kel's house.

My last day of exams, I came home to find both my parents in my father's den working over papers.

"I'm done." They looked at me both grinning.

"That's great, Chris," my mum replied giving her honourable smile. "Come sit here." She touched the seat beside her.

I came and she gave me a hug. My father gave me a handshake.

"I'll do it," my mother told my father.

"Do what?"

"Your father and I have something to tell you. Now, you're not going to be happy about it, but it is for the best, the best for us. All of us. Chris, me and your father have just signed divorce papers. Now, it may come as a surprise, but really it's for the best."

I couldn't believe it. She kept rubbing my shoulder with her hand. "You're joking?" I observed both of them hoping for a yes.

My mum shook her head and her pink lips formed and whispered, "No." Tears filled her eyes.

"No. Chris, it's for the best as your Mother says. We have different interests and we're tired of pretending."

"What the fuck do you mean?" They tilted their heads and nodded at me.

"Is there anything you want to say?"

"All this while you were pretending for the sake of me. Is that the truth?"

My mother was trying to protect me as she squeezed me harder. "Not like that. We have our differences and tried—"

"What, was he cheating on you?"

"Fucking hell no," my father replied.

"Then what?" I didn't get it.

"Differences, that's all. It sometimes happens in a relationship."

"Me and your mother have totally different interests and staying together isn't in the picture any longer."

I sat there with my mum's squeezing arms around me, both of them waiting for a response and all I did was sit there. My mother tried hard to make my father's words more sweet as she wiped tears away from her eyes.

"Do you want to say anything?" My mother raised her tearful caring eyes on me.

"No, I don't, thanks."

"How are you feeling?"

"Great."

"Chris, come on, we're here for you." My dad was trying to reach out from his desk.

"I told you, I don't have anything to say." I wasn't going to cry. What the fuck, since they were pretending all along. "What's going to happen with the house?"

"Nothing. Your mother is moving out and everything will go on as normal."

"But I'm still moving out?"

"If that's what you want."

"Yeah I do. Where are you moving to?"

"I have a place in Wolston near Devins Park. It's right by the ocean."

"When did you find this place?"

My mum glared at my dad and he nodded his head saying it was okay. "A while ago."

"When are you going?"

"Today."

It was all fucking great, I had actors for parents, maybe that's why I never wanted a girlfriend. I didn't feel like giving goodbye and hello kisses and listening to their sad stories. It was just too much drama on top of the anniversaries.

"Can I go now?"

"If you want."

I got up and left them to finish signing. I looked in my parents room and my mum's stuff was already gone. Nothing of her remained. Even her stuff around the house was gone and our family photos were missing. Fucking parents. Everything was already gone and I had never noticed because I was living in the never never world that they so happily created for me.

Post

I was living with my dad who walked around for three days with bandages on his head because he finally got his plugs. Before he kept his hair buzzed because he was balding at the front of his head. He and Mum argued many times over him getting plugs. She always said that he didn't need it and that would end it. Until the next time he brought it up, pointing out new facts or friends of his who were wearing bandages, or their hair was growing back and it looked absolutely natural. But his head remained unplugged.

After a week of separation he came home with bandages on top of his head and for three days he rested at home carrying around his painkillers with the television on full blast.

The first time I saw his plugs was when I came home for supper; he was sitting there all casual with his crown of bandages, eating his macaroni and cheese.

"What happened to you?"

"A little operation, it should be off in no time."

"Is it plugs?"

"Transplant."

"Does it hurt?"

Instead of answering me, he shook a white bottle of painkillers.

It was amazing how each new grain of hair changed his personality. He was a new man. I sat with him in front of the television with my own glass of wine because there was no beer left. The old man had drunk it all and it was showing with that tummy of his. He slurped down the wine and sat there with his eyes on the new newscaster. She had permed hair and was wearing a serious shade of red-lipstick.

"She's a piece," he said as he gulped, while flashing his one eye back at me, waiting for a manly response.

"Right." I rolled my eyes. Taking my dad as a real man in the world was hard to do and place. My father was salivating over the ladies.

My mum's place had huge windows overlooking the ocean and she had scented candles coupled with seashells everywhere. The furniture was ivory coloured mixed with deep maple and the walls were cream.

"If you ever want to sleepover, this is for you." She flicked on the light in the second bedroom with one blue sheeted bed. The walls were papered in blue and white stripes.

She had her private den with an exercise contraption looking outside onto the windy ocean.

"What do you think?" She placed her arms around me.

"It's nice."

"That's what I thought, too. When do you move out?"

"A week from now. Me and Kel, and Drew's staying up in residence."

"Can't wait?" She poured me juice as she eyed me up for an answer.

"Yeah."

"Are you looking forward to school?"

"Yeah."

Question after question before supper was ready. I thought about telling her about dad's new plugs but I decided, since she never asked about his well being, or what it was like living with him, that she didn't want to know.

At the end of the grand tour was the new family wall. It was photographs of me or me and her. She pointed out each photograph recapturing the memory and giving me a grin and a hug.

Crash

Weeks later, Miss Clarbet approached me and Matthew. I thought from her glare that she was going to complain about my weight. I was a little over the scale as usual. I loved ballet but I hated that damn scale and watching everything I ate and drank. I was ready to tell her off because I went hungry most of the day. I was trying hard to be good. I could just see those words forming, "That's not good enough."

"I wanted to tell you two. There's an audition, six weeks from now. It's with the Metro Ballet Company. A very rare opportunity. And the reason why I ask you two is because I think you are perfect for each other." Matthew and I grinned at each other. "And this company needs a pair. So, do you want to?"

"Yeah." We both said.

I couldn't believe this old thin-stick bitch that's been tapping her fucking magic wand at my feet everyday or yelling at me to stretch out my arms to reach for the inevitable. Now, it was going to pay off. She gave us our papers with her name signed on it and we filled out the rest. After class she came up again still with that hard, narrow look.

"Now, if you two want to make it, you'll have to practice, practice till each step becomes your breath. That's what my teacher told me. And to practice you must stay after class and do the routine. Remember, each step must become you. Become both of you."

"Stay tonight?"

"Yes, I will help you."

She did. We stayed and practised. I actually enjoyed the pain because I knew I was trying out for something. I had to have it. That's what kept me going. Having to have it. Having to have something. Something I wanted. It was all I needed. It became an obsession where all I thought about was the moves of my painful body. I felt I was living in one of those films about dancers trying like the little steam engine to make it.

Matthew and I studied the mirror. As I allowed my body to fall and gain strength so I could reach the sky and Miss Clarbet below telling me to, "reach, reach." She even stretched out her arms. I reached out, feeling everything grow into a new body. The first practice ended.

I was completely tired. After class, Matthew met up with me like he always did, like the good doggy he was. Smiling, always. But this time he hugged my tired body.

"What?" I asked pulling away.

He held me in his arms as we walked out into the cool air.

"After all her bitching it's paying off."

"I know. I thought I was going to be doing it forever an when I was forty an too old they would've sent me away."

I reached my corner and we parted. I was going over the steps in my head. The steps changed into the idea of the Metro Ballet Company and travelling the world and maybe becoming The One.

I walked towards Ashley who was coming out of his little

hidden scene in the living room. "Hey, Eliza." Ashley hugged and kissed me. He walked with me to the front of the room where someone else sat. A boy sniffing cocaine. "Eliza, this is Jonathan. A very dear friend of mine."

"Hello."

"Me and Jon were doing a little treat. Do you want some?"

"Ashley, I think—"

"Come on, you'll feel better. Come on, I want you to."

I was going to say I was too tired, but I decided under the advice of Ashley that I would. The whole night passed with over-excitement. I sat in the centre of the two with the blue lights on. All of us waiting for our turn to pass up the torturous dry moments to talk. To get dissolved in our own voices. That's what I discovered best. I loved my voice. I could just dissolve in it. Hearing and feeling it echo through my throat, my voice sounded so beautiful. The words I spoke were all shit, but it felt so real and touchable at the moment.

"That's fucking great E. I always knew."

It broke with Ashley getting all excited over my practised success. He began talking about how we met; it was a beautiful picture. I kept saying, "Yeah," nice and low nodding my head.

And it started—we came down like an airplane crash. Sick of each other and sniffing up more to get more out of each other. Jon sniffed, Ashley and I hugged and kissed in short snippets. Jon raised his head and Ashley and I sank into the couch. Jon rested his head against my shoulder and he was talking about something. Ashley kept laughing and then tensing up.

"I'm tired," I said as I stretched myself.

"I'll be right back," Ashley told John. Ashley got up and walked with me. "I just want to tuck you in."

I walked into the dark bedroom pulling him to the bed. We fucked through the intensity of it all. Once he kissed me good night and closed the door, I stared outside. It was hard sleeping that night with my heart racing and wanting to be left alone.

The next morning I got up, feeling my broken head, sore eyes and throat. I dressed in my uniform and went into the living room to get Ashley to drive me. He was there with Jon, both of them lying under the covers. I thought about waking him up and telling him to get ready for school. Instead, I just kissed him and his eyes stayed still, stiller than ever. But he moved his head slightly to make himself more comfortable on Jon's chest.

I suppose out of forgetfulness, I was a bit stunned by Ashley and Jon. Part of me, probably the bigger part, expected anything. I wasn't too shocked because I knew that he wanted me to live with him. So why get involved in questioning? Where was that going to take me?

I took the train to school, a bit pissed because I wanted to be driven. I guess at the moment, I was greedy, maybe spoiled, but I hardly knew him.

The Cutters

It was Ashley's thing, which was nice because at the beginning I was already formulating the idea that his life concerned three things: drugs, boys and me. Out of nowhere came the discovery that he had a band, The Cutters. He was the lead singer.

The first time I saw him on stage was at the Union Club. All the lights were turned off. People screamed already excited by the bleak darkness. A black light came on Ashley; he glared at the audience giving that cryptic smile of his and faintly the music tickled in the background. Suddenly, the loudness followed by the lights came on with the band.

Ashley's voice crept through the crashing music. Everything was absolutely cryptic about it.

Ashley captured everyone there, their eyes and ears intensely on Ashley who stood there tall and gleaming in the light. His eyes never left the crowd until the moment of ecstasy, high ecstasy when he shut his eyes and his voice was the only thing heard. The band played and his eyes opened. It was amazing to watch

Ashley; thinking of the absolute attention he had from everyone. He had it all. He had all the control and he used it. After a while, I couldn't wait till it became me with everyone's individual eyes on me. Wanting me. I wanted to feel the gravitational pull of it all. Instead, I held my breath on a smoke and blew it out.

And Me

Me and Kel wanted to make the place feel a bit more lived in, and we badly needed to try our new state of the art stereo system which was supplied compliments of Kel's parents. My mother gave me a massive television of my choice. It was big enough to watch the hockey games and make the viewer feel like they were part of the game. The rest of the furnishings were also supplied by our parents so that we would only have to worry about our studies.

I rang up Drew at his new place. Drew's girlfriend, Sweet, answered. She turned out to be his and our drug dealer.

"Who is it, Sweetie?" Drew shouted.

"Chris."

I could hear the phone being passed into Drew's hand.

"We're having the party of the century."

"Finally, man."

The essentials were arranged.

Kel rang up Amanda telling her to bring herself and friends. Kel saw them as some new fuck lassies for me, excluding Nadine.

She was a bit upset and supposedly enthralled with a new toy which occupied all her precious time.

Me and Kel got the beer and hard liquor for the sweet ladies. I really needed more ladies. I made sure I supplied them with the right fundamentals so everything would be easily accessible.

If me and Kel ran into any sweeties or guys that knew pretty girls we told them about it, this being the kind of neighbourhood where parties were openly welcomed since most of the young crowd were single and eager to find a mate.

In nice and tight summer patterns the girls showed up, some of them carrying their sweet candied liquor. Me and Kel, until Amanda showed up, were introducing ourselves and giving a very warm welcome to the girls.

The whole night, girls slipped by in conversation until I met this one. First, she came up to ask for another drink and from there we started talking.

Amanda staggered over to me and placed her arm around me, "You like him, sister?" she asked mumbling over the word sister and falling onto the girl's knees.

"Fuck off," I told her, watching her body wobble under those words for clarification. "She's had a bit too many. She's going out with Kel, over there."

"He's mine, sister." Amanda thumbed herself in the chest.

"Why don't you go tell him that?" She tapped Amanda's chin with her sparkled fingernail. Amanda stood there drunk, and lost her grip on my shoulder. Carefully, she headed back to Kel holding her head up.

"I don't want to scare you." She placed her arm around my neck. "You see that little boy that's nodding off near the window?"

I looked over and he kept nodding off only to get pushed up by the person he was sitting beside.

"Yeah."

She placed her other arm around me and brought me closer. All I could think of was, I'm in there. "He's my boyfriend, but don't worry he won't know. He's too high right now. He really does sleep like a baby." She sighed.

"What do you mean?" I stood there feeling paranoia coming on strong under her arms.

"I told you not to worry." She bit her lip. "He never knows what's going on." She was going to add more words.

I gave her a kiss, hoping that her boyfriend would be out of it.

"Come on," I whispered, taking her hand. I showed her to my room and locked the door behind us. And from there Chris lived on.

After, I looked at her with the white sheet pulled up, her red hair surrounding her shoulders. I was really trying hard to remember her name.

"What?"

"What's your name?"

"Julia, and you?"

"Chris."

"Mmmm." She gave me a kiss on the cheek. "Chris, let me give you my number and if you ever need a little of Julia give me a call." She got up, dressing. Her little ass squeezed into those tight jeans. I watched her place on her bra and lean forward with everything coming forward to pick up her tight-tee. Her blue eyes caught mine. "Pervert." She grinned and bit her lip. She wrote her number down. "And you don't have to worry about Joel."

"Joel?"

"My boyfriend. I'm giving you my cell." She showed me that she left the paper with her number on the desk.

We went back out and I observed her shoving Joel awake. He grunted and flinched but he noticed her and she pulled him up. She walked up to me with her boyfriend as he wiped his eyes. She gave me a wink. "Great party."

"Yeah, right," her boyfriend said and they left.

The party was still going strong with the passing of various spliffs. Unfortunately, Amanda materialized beside me but fortunately, she held a spliff and she was anxiously shoving it at me. I eyed up some other girls in the far corner, giggling with their colourful bottled beverage.

"How's it going, babe?" She laughed under her words and placed her arm around me. Unfortunately, she took me out of the sea of pretty faces to land on hers which was a bright-intoxicated crimson.

"Great," I replied flatly.

"I'm feeling really good. Did you find any takers?"

"What?"

"Any girls, sweetie?" she said giving me a kiss on the cheek.

I stared back at the girls. They were involved with someone else. A thick sweet marijuana cloud mixed with smokes glowed in the centre of the room.

"Why don't you find Kel?"

"He's playing with the stereo." We passed the joint around.

"What about that redhead. Did you give her a little Chris?"

I laughed and she laughed and pulled me closer. I shoved her away and stole the spliff from her.

"You're so sweet, Chrissy boy."

Laughter broke out and I sat on one of the barstools in the kitchen and she sat beside me. She looked at me with her heavy eyes.

"What happened with that redhead?"

"I gave her the big Chris."

"I bet you did. Nadine sure talked about it."

"What?"

She covered up her mouth as if she just bombed a secret. "She talked about how you gave her the big Chris. Why do you think I tried helping her out?"

"Fuck off." I sucked back thinking of my encounter with Nadine.

"I'm serious there, big boy."

"Well." I gave her a bright eyed smile.

"And that little redhead seemed pretty pleased with you. Some men just have it and others don't know what to do. I'm lucky, though, because Kel is pretty good. At least he—"

"Wait!" I held my ears not wanting to get enticed into what Kel was like in her hole.

"Shut up Chris. Now, I know two great guys, Chris." She touched her heart and a burp followed with her waving hand to excuse herself.

"Who's the other?"

"You, for fuck sakes."

"And what are you supposed to do with that hefty knowledge?"

"I don't know." She rolled her eyes. "Give me that." She took the spliff and took a huge suck. Right there she looked like a red balloon. I knocked myself off the stool and onto the floor exploding into laughter. Her balloon face bumbled down at me, mouthing the words, "Are you okay?"

I got off the floor, still laughing at Amanda as she handed me the spliff. I took it and sat there staring at the scene: the beats of the cool Snoop passing through the air, everyone chilling out in the smouldering atmosphere and Amanda's laughter high up there. I shrugged her big head off as I inhaled the itty bitty back.

There was a crowd around the coffee-table playing some sort of game. One guy, red and thick, kept getting yelled at because it was his turn.

"It's your fucking turn, cunt!" the girl told him.

He responded, thrilled out of his fucking mind. The girl, being a good sport resorted to physical abuse and he treated it as if she was tickling him.

Drew was on the couch, laughing at the redhead and Kel was still mystified by the stereo. I got up and I heard Amanda ask me, "Where are you going?"

"Bed." The word just trembled on my lips, reinforcing the

letter B. "Bed." All I could think about were my pillows and the cloud which happened to be my mattress.

I got up in the middle of the morning, although it felt like night because it was dreary out with a pale sun severing through the blinds. I threw on a shirt and pants.

The windows were wide open to let out the smoke. Some people were lounging around. I went to the fridge and took out a bottle of water. I heard Kel's door open and the paddle of feet. I turned around half expecting Kel but it was Amanda wearing one of Kel's white t-shirts that was barely covering her. She stood there watching me drink.

"You want some?"

"No." Her eyes went down like she was ashamed of something. "What're you doing?"

I wiped my mouth. "Going to bed." I walked past her.

"Can I come with you?"

I turned around and she was stretching and yawning with her big brown tits forcing themselves against Kel's t-shirt. She tried hard to give me the sweetest smile her ugly face could manage.

"Can I come to bed with you?" Her blue eyes stared hard at me.

"No."

"Kel doesn't have to know." She placed her hand on my shoulder.

"Fuck off."

"Pussy."

I locked the door as I went back to bed.

I heard her creep up and tap slightly. "Chris, come on. I'm not asking you for your number." A long pause with a lot of breathing. "I didn't mean to call you pussy. Chris?" Tap tap. "Chris?"

I was waiting for the summer to end and school to start. I was getting really tired of hearing Amanda getting banged with her screams for Kel. The fuck machine was his name. Her screaming and his fists banging the wall, "Fuck me, fuck me fuck machine!"

I found Julia's number and called her up.

"Hello," she said loudly longing on l's.

"Julia, it's Chris."

"Chris, my boy. How's it going, hun?"

"Good and you?"

"Fabulous."

"You want to go out?"

"Yeah, that would be great."

"Where should I get you?"

"I'm working at Sticky Hair on Rover Street, close to Connor Road. You know where that is, right?"

"Yeah."

"Can you get me now?"

"In fifteen."

"Okay, babe, see you."

Click. I took my jacket and two helmets and left. I scootered myself up to Rover Street, passing all the little funky boutiques of ravers' gear and left over punk ideas and there was Sticky Hair Boutique.

Julia was waiting outside. She was wearing a green dress which fluttered up with the afternoon wind.

"Julia."

"Chris, baby," She gave me a hug and kissed my helmet.

"Get on." I passed her a helmet and she crawled on. Her legs squeezed mine and her arms wrapped tightly around my waist.

I scootered to St. Maurice Park because it was a beautiful day. Kel and Amanda were home.

"You're a hairdresser?"

"Mmmm, and what about you?"

"A student."

"In what?" she asked getting on top of me, undoing my

buttons.

"Business."

I started to undo her top. "Oh, does that mean you're going to open up your own business?" She took off her top that showed off her black lace bra.

"No, my dad has his own factory and I'll take that over when the old man croaks."

"What does the factory make?" she asked toying with my hair.

"Boxes. Cardboard boxes."

"Oh, exciting."

To shut up this conversation that wasn't going anywhere. I pulled her down and we fucked. I banged her ass right into the grass.

After, we both got up and removed grass and leaves from each other. Most of it was knotted in her hair.

"Chris, I don't mean to rush and go, but I'm having supper with my fiancé's parents tonight and I have to get home before he's there."

"Is that Joel?"

I cuddled her in my arms as she fixed my hair. "Yeah. We have to do this again, though. I really like being with you. And you're absolutely great. Has anyone ever told you that before? You're fabulous, baby."

"No. Tell me, Julia, how long have you been dating?" I thought I should act a little bit jealous and hurt.

"About three years. He asked me a year ago to marry him, but I've been waiting to save up enough money to pay for the wedding and all that. Tonight with his parents we're going to talk about it. My friends at the salon can't believe I said yes to this yuppie, especially my old boyfriend—we're best friends. Sometimes I can't believe it either. But he loves me and that's what counts right, babe?" She gave me a kiss.

We walked back to the scooter and she went on about the

wedding and Joel.

Julia was a great release, even though she talked endlessly about the wedding plans and then laughed about her fiancé. She was a fantastic fuck.

Hiding

One night I brought Matthew home to my place after ballet class. It was just going to start out with unwinding the night with a couple of drinks and that was all.

We both sat down on the couch. I got the drinks and Matthew lit the cigarettes. And what was missing or at least what was missing for the burning smokes was the ashtray. As I searched, the brain Matthew found something in the coffee-table. I came back from the kitchen and there was Ashley's cocaine shining in the little plastic coloured bags of blue, green and yellow.

Both of us laughed. I shrugged my shoulders like any good drug addict. Shrugging them like, "Oh gosh, you found it, well you know, an really it is alright."

We broke it on the little glass mirror Ashley always used. We wrapped up a bill and started sniffing. All the way it went up there like a fucking roller coaster in my nose. Each turn of the coaster banging me hard and then the sudden interest to wait, to wait for the drip and at the same time finding out whether this was Matthew's first time. I believe it was because, like the course of the drug, you listen with complete enlightenment to the person's voice.

Time banged on and the conversation swayed onto the Company. He talked on about his girlfriend or girl problems—they swayed into each other. I talked about Ashley.

We sat there, his arms around me and my head resting on his chest, both of us taking turns to listen and talk. It was a perfect set-up.

Time stopped and we looked at each other with that sense of a kind eye. He licked his lips to moisten them.

We both bent into a kiss and the door opened and slammed. Time began again as I rushed to put Ashley's co-ordinated baggies back in the door and then, we held the drinks like we were drinking the whole time.

The whole year I lived with Ashley was a blur.

I came out of it on the last day thinking that I hadn't done anything. In a sense, nothing really happened with Ashley. And I didn't try hard enough to sort it out.

On a nice rainy evening in late July, right after ballet class I came home. Everything was dark. I searched for Ashley to see if he was hiding out. He wasn't around. I went into the bedroom and relaxed on the bed. This is what I usually did. I went over all the steps in my head and slowly those steps fell into being. I got up, flicked on the lights, looked in the closet and watched my clothes hanging there.

The future events played in my head. I'd be gone soon. And I wanted to leave now. Quick and easy. I didn't want a party of departure.

I threw my clothes on the bed. I found one of Ashley's suitcases. I knew he wouldn't mind. I stuffed my clothes and other stuff of mine in it. I closed the closet, grabbed my jacket, placed the hood over my head, carried the suitcase and headed out.

With Ashley's place in the distance, I thought I should've left a note. But nothing I could write would be what I wanted.

The train served as a shelter for a moment. Once I got off at Shepherd Lane, I walked to Matthew's apartment in St. Maurice Bay. I walked up the steps to the door and knocked.

He opened the door and smiled at me and he noticed the suitcase. That served as some sort of uninvited hint. I came in as he moved out of the way. I put my suitcase down as he closed and locked the door. I took off the hood.

"Before you ask—"

As he was getting a beer for a guest, I sat there for the first time admiring his cosy home with all the essentials of his life on display. His life really didn't consist of much: a stereo, small television and plants spewing about from the two windows. He came over carrying the beers and sat beside me.

"Cheers."

I noticed the various doilies neatly placed under each plant giving that fatal delicacy. I couldn't really imagine him sitting there after dance class in front of the tube knitting those doilies. Or going out to the nearest church to buy doilies. And it all summed up into the beer tickling my throat as I started giggling trying to hold it in.

"Did your mum knit those doilies for you, or you got some sort of secret hobby?"

"My mum brings them over with the plants. It adds a nice female touch."

"That's one way to put it."

"At Christmas time she's over at the church knitting Christmas coloured doilies."

"Up in Bury?" Gulp the question goes down.

"Yeah, at Saint Teresa. She started doing this after my dad died. She joined—What are you laughing at?"

"Because you are going on an on an on. What else can you tell me about those doilies?"

"What did your mum ever knit for you?"

"Nothing at all, I can proudly say."

"Maybe a portrait of the family out of glued beer caps."

"That's right." He was laughing it all up. "Ah, that's fucking raw of you now."

"Come on and admit it."

"No, you're not getting a thing out of me."

After the exaggerated slurs, he studied my slouching appearance on the sofa. I was sipping the beer and smiling openly at him. He sat back touching and curling my damp hair. "Eliza, you are skipping out on goodbyes hiding up here. Admit it!"

"Yeah, so?" I touched his face in response almost speaking in silent ballet terms: I did it all for you. The idea of saying, "my love," seemed too patently old but baby was new.

"So, baby." I leaned back on the sofa and he followed with a slight boyish jump. "Yes, I left, but it was only a matter of time. I wasn't going to marry Ashley. An you know that. Before I left an I told you how he used to leave messages to me saying how he wouldn't be home tonight an you didn't see me crying. So skipping out goodbyes doesn't even come into mind. I mean it's Ashley."

"Did you leave any note?"

"No."

"You left him crying?"

I glared at him, why was I being accused for leaving Ashley in a tear choker moment. Now that would've been a laugh, Ashley crying. It wouldn't be me.

"If he does cry, it would be good for him. What about all the ones you left? Did you give them the I love you too, Matthew?"

"Exactly. But you should already know that saying goodbyes is the best invention that was ever thought of. See and that's what you've missed."

"So."

We both drank and the words sputtered out on more sane

topics and silly past-time jokes. Sipping more to wash it all down and swallow that sore laughter, at the sudden end of the drunkenness coming back into search of reality's feelings. "I really don't think he misses me that much." The words repeated themselves and tried hard to hit that sense of human emotion, but I missed them every time in the eyes of Matthew. Lost in his smile and it all felt good. Really good. I took a quick sip and brought my legs up and over Matthew. He contemplated me in that wicked delicate way which made me think of the doilies.

He came in like a big fish underwater and we kissed, smacking each other roughly over our splitting lips trying to catch up with our chasing over-salivated dull tongues. Both of us tearing each other's shirts off. Both of us in drunken ah. And, it was all released as he lay on top of me.

We got up, put on our shirts and he dragged me to my new bed. We sank in bed together and slept arm in arm.

Too drunk to comment or make a slander, and too tired to worry about all the rest that we forgot.

First Job

I parked my scooter among the staff automobiles that were all wrecked with rust, dents or half-painted jobs. My dad's new black sport Jaguar was the only car that had nothing wrong with it.

Inside the waiting area, I could hear the rumbling sounds of the heavy machinery humming through the two steel doors which announced Staff Only in red.

The receptionist had her old white blond hair hiked up in a bun and her lips covered in thick pink-lipstick; her glasses dangled from her nose as her eyes narrowed down to read a pink sheer slip. Her blue tinted eyes looked up at me as she cautiously removed her glasses.

"Chris, Charles's son right?" she asked with the excited nod of her head.

"Yeah."

"Hi, I'm Debbie, I'm the receptionist." She pointed to the rectangular sign on the desk and held out her hand which I shook, making her blue bangles jingle.

"Nice to meet you," I told her.

"You're going to be helping your old dad out. He's not that old right?" She paused and we both grinned. "I love that new car he got. A convertible, too." I followed her to my dad's office. "He's been expecting you." She nodded her head to reinforce the period after that statement.

"Charles, your son's here." She moved aside presenting me to my father whose plugged hair had already become a nice puff. When he looked up from his papers, the hair dangled in his eyes and he pushed it away only to have it rebound.

"Chris." I went in. The smell of fresh cardboard was in the air.

"Hey, Dad."

"Sit down."

"How's everything going? The hair looks great. Did anyone notice yet?"

He grinned feeling his hefty shiny locks. "It's going great, and so far no complaints."

"What's does Debbie think of it?"

"She can't take her hands off it. I'm afraid that she's going to wear it down. You like the Jag?"

"Yeah, it's nice."

"Very sporty. And how's that scooter?"

"Not as nice as yours," I told him flatly.

"Eventually you'll get your own."

"How's the housework coming?"

"Great. Close to being done. You'll have to come down for dinner. How was your first week of classes?"

"Good."

"Went to them all?" he asked.

"Yeah," I told him grinning like a good prospective student. He looked down at his papers. Unfortunately, the old man didn't believe me.

"Alright." He gathered his hairy-paper-buried eyes on me. "Today." A big pause and swallow from the man. "We are going to get you started with delivering boxes. Now, these are small deliveries. For the bigger deliveries I contract outside businesses." He leaned forward. "You'll be driving with Cody Baxter. He is the one I assigned for you to work with. Everyone calls him Cod. He's one of my longest workers and he's a good boy."

He pressed a button on his phone.

"Deb, send Cod up please." He turned back to me. "So, how does driving sound to you?"

"Fine."

There was a knock.

"Come in," my father shouted as he stepped out from his desk.

Cod came in. He was wearing jeans and a dark blue shirt with Imperial Boxing embroidered in yellow. The company's shirt was flying open to show his white t-shirt which greatly emphasized a perfect ball of a beer belly. The one side of the shirt that wasn't escaping to rest on his back was holding a box of smokes in the pocket.

"Hello." He gave a song-shout to it.

"Cod, this is Chris my son."

"Yeah, I know, I heard all about it from Debbie."

"Hi."

We shook hands.

"How are you?"

"Good. I can't complain." He examined my father steadily with his red-veined blue eyes. "I see that's coming along good." He tapped the top of his buzzed head towards my dad.

"Thanks for noticing."

"Hey, I got to keep you on your toes." He gave my dad a point. "An how's that sweet Debbie? She's still patting you like a dog?" He laughed heavily.

"You know how that goes."

"That's how it started balding in the first place. All I know is, she pats my belly an tells me I got to take it slow on the bevy." He turned towards me. "Chris, just wait till she starts on you."

"Alright, Cod and Chris, I think it's getting past time to make those deliveries."

"Right-o chief."

"Cod, do up your shirt. You know the rules."

"Right-o." He buttoned up his shirt.

"See you boys later."

"Alright, follow me."

We left.

"Are you excited about your first day at work?"

"I don't know."

"That's what I said when I started, but it pays. An don't worry, I'll show you the ropes to this place inside an out. That's why your dad gave you to me because this place is like my second home an I treat it as that."

We walked down the hallway to the stairs that led to the basement.

"Now, this is the basement where the lockers are."

"C. Jamison, here's the key."

"You got yourself a bike?"

"A scooter."

"Not bad, gets you around."

I opened it up and there was the shirt hanging there. I placed my helmet in and buttoned my new work shirt over my white t-shirt and I rested my smokes in my shirt.

"That's my boy."

We went outside, walking up the cement stairs where the white trucks with Imperial Boxing written in blue were parked.

"Okay, I'll do the first one an you watch. Watch everything I do."

He got in the driver's side and I got in the passenger's side. The interior smelled of cardboard and mouldy car seats. He started it up and put the radio on to the oldies station.

"First step is to relax. An you do that by taking a smoke." He took out a smoke and lit it and I did the same.

"Here we go."

He started backing up and the truck grunted at being forced into reverse.

"Pick up that clipboard."

I picked it up.

"What's the first one?"

"300 Piper Street. Mello Boutique."

"Now, this is how the system works, you start with the deliveries furthest away an you work your way down. Mello Boutique deals with all that fancy glass shit." He switched into drive and the car grumbled to get out of the parking lot. "Are you going to school?"

"Packer School of Business, I go at night."

"Doris my wife, we have three kids, is always talking about sending them to university. That's the way to go she always says. Personally, I feel it is more educational to learn from the streets an from living, instead of reading it in some book."

"My dad pays for it. He wanted to send me."

"Ah, that's good. He's a good man, your father is. Although, to tell you the truth, I don't know what he was thinking about those plugs. Some of the boys in the factory got those wigs an they wear their hats to keep them on. But once they snap them off, the rug goes. That's another thing I learned, if the hair goes just let it go. But I'll bet you anything, a year from now, with Debbie's patting ways, all his hair is going to be worn down. I've warned him to stop that hand of hers. Tell me, why do you think your dad got those plugs?"

"Girls."

"Exactly, an don't we all. A nice little young pussy is sweet. An there's nothing wrong with it."

I laughed at Cod's sophisticated lecture on pussies because I knew he was coming from some sort of experience.

"But getting these young chicks, hair doesn't do it. Sometimes they fancy a shaved head an they don't mind if you've been balding a bit. You can always say to them that you're a fabulous lover. You know how the ladies like to grab. I swear that's what happened to mine. But I like keeping mine short an simple. When I had hair I never knew what to do with it. This way, I shaved it off an I have nothing to worry about. But your dad doesn't listen. The car was a brilliant move. That definitely guarantees fresh pussies."

Piper Street was coming up and since there were no back streets, we backed in front of the boutique with displays of glass sculptures filling the windows.

"Okay, I want you to go in there an get Richie Rich to sign. Once you get that, come back, open up the trunk an pull out the boxes. How many did they order?"

"One."

"Right."

I took the clipboard and pen and headed inside with the automated bells echoing my entrance. A long legged creature wearing a tight black dress and a necklace with a colourful glass object dangling between her breasts, looked up tentatively with a friendly smile.

"Hi. A delivery?" she asked cheerfully.

I grinned back. "Yeah."

"Let me get Richard for you." She tilted her head and turned around. She'd be a perfect fuck.

Richard came out dressed in black with a shaved head and a small goatee, a total of three mature hairs curving underneath his witchy chin.

"Hi, you must be new."

I handed him the clipboard.

"Yes, that's great. What's your name?"

"Chris. And I'll just bring in the box?"

"Yes, that would be great."

I took the clipboard and pen back and I threw it into the truck.

"Everything's alright?" Cod yelled as he picked up the clipboard.

"Yeah." I went to the back of the truck and pulled up the lever and took the box that was labelled: Mello Boutique. Rich was waiting at the entrance and held the door open.

"Just follow Mel to the back."

I followed the perfect fuck to the back. Her heels made her skinny ass jiggle. She opened a cupboard. "Just place it in there." She bent over and pointed so I'd know where to put it. I grinned nicely at her as I placed the box in slow and steady. "Thank you," she replied stretching her body.

"No problem."

She walked me out again and joined up with Rich.

"Thanks, Chris."

"No problem."

"See you next time."

I returned to the truck.

"Not bad, eh? Too bad." He lit a cigarette and watched me from the corner of his eye. "Too bad that Mel is tied up with that fag Richie Rich there. I'll bet you, if either of us gave her a proper bang, she wouldn't know what hit her. That's the problem, some of these beautiful women are stuck with these rich fuckers, who may know their wines, but when it comes to women all they know is that they have a little prick an they got a hole. Poor, poor Mel, to be ravaged like that is a real crime. Do you have a girlfriend?"

"No."

"I remember my days like that. Free an going. Ladies all about waiting for fast Cod to pull in. When I met Doris, I didn't think nothing of it. She was a real sweet bone, to be honest. Alright, here we are. How many boxes do they get? Two?"

It was another glass store but the art this time was more functional. At least it looked that way with a jug on a pedestal and a purple green vase beside it. This place was located on Shandy Avenue. I walked in again as Cod got the two boxes ready. I asked the young boy, who was wearing a black turtleneck and black pants with a brown leather belt, "Is Carole Jackson in?"

"Let me get her."

Carole, old and frail, rushed in with her flowery silk dress that exaggerated each move she made. She resembled a piece of glass herself.

"Hello there."

"Hi." I took the pen from my ear. "Sign here." I pointed.

She picked up the pen. "This seems right. Two boxes. Yes." She signed away.

Her male assistant opened the door for Cod.

"Mrs. Jackson!" He bellowed it out into the empty gallery.

"Hello, Cody, just put it in the usual place."

"You're going to drive now," he told me.

I started the rumbling truck, the radio blared on and I lit a smoke as Cod did the same, smiling, seeing that I was quick learner.

"What was I talking about?"

"About Doris."

"Doris, it was that one sweet bang that got me stuck with her. She got pregnant an that, my friend, ended my life of freedom." He picked up the clipboard. "We only have two more to do. You see what takes long with these deliveries is the traffic."

The next stop was a gift store on Mount Road and the last stop was on Dudley Avenue another gift store.

After I drove into Saber with Cod's instructions to go to the pub that was on Docker's Row. It was still mid-afternoon, a couple of drunks staggered but not too many yet.

We sat down at the table and the waitress whose numerous wrinkles reflected her life came up.

"Hey, Cod, dear." She placed her arm lovingly around him.

"Bren, I'd like to introduce you to my new friend an co-worker, Chris."

"The pleasure is mine." She gave me a wink. "Boys, what will it be?"

I pointed to him to decide. Since he decided on everything else why stop him from ordering the beer.

"The usual please." He gave her a grin.

"Always."

She walked away. "That Bren is a real sweetheart. Her husband sits in that corner."

"Which one?"

"The one that's sleeping in the corner there."

"Ah."

"He was laid off awhile ago an never got back on his feet. He used to be a good guy. In fact, at one time I'd call him one of my best. An Bren, she never had to work but she's on her feet non-stop now. She's a real sweetheart married to that pussy of a man. In my time, I used to date her. Now, she was a real good one always ready to go when I came a knocking. An in the end she married that filth. At the time, he was probably better than any of us. So, in one way she made the better decision."

She came back with the beer.

"Thank you, Bren."

"Cheers," we said in unison clinking the mugs together.

"Now, this place is usually crowded with men from the factories after closing time. But I personally like to come here after a hectic day of driving an all that delivering. But mind you, we're going to be working together, an you don't mind keeping this a secret now, do you?" He observed me with his red veins redder as he held the beer.

"You don't have to worry, Cod. I think it's a great idea and you never have to worry. How's that?"

He laughed at my little commentary. "Great."

"And lookie what I got here." I took out my safety mints. "Don't be a scared little pussy now."

"Great. Fucking great. You see, I wasn't too sure. Since I've been doing all the talking trying to show you, today at least, one part of the factory. The killer of the job is for a whole day you're working inside. When your father wants me to deliver, I look forward to doing it, it's a chance to get away. So trust me, after a while you'll be enjoying days like these. An what's really nice about delivering is, it usually takes a whole day." He took a sip. "An tomorrow you'll be working inside with me. Come for seven-thirty in the morning an I'll show you everything an we don't have to wear these shirts. It's only for representing the company." He took a long hard gulp. "When do your courses start?"

"At six."

"Ah, you're enjoying it?"

"It's school, nothing too exciting. I take about two classes at night and at ten I'm out. It's really nothing."

And with that we drank it down. I paid for the beer.

"This is basically where I live, down here on Bensley Street. I used to live up near Mertle Park but the price went up when the fags moved in. It was fairly nice, but since they have all the time in the world they fixed it up. Most of this area is where the factory families live. It's a fairly kept dump. One day, I'll introduce you to Doris, she's a real gem."

We left Saber and entered the dusty area of the factories. Less than thirty minutes before it was time to clock out. He parked the truck and we headed inside.

Debbie was on the phone. She mouthed hello to us and returned to the conversation. "Oh God, I know.... Yeah, I tried but.... Right, but."

We headed up to see my father.

"Come in."

We both stepped in and he looked up all excited still trying to get control over the natural motion of his hair.

"How did Chris do Cod?"

"He was great. He's a natural."

"Great. Cod, you can clock out and Chris stay here."

"See you tomorrow," Cod said to the both of us.

I took the chair across from my dad.

"What'd you think so far?"

"It's work."

"What time is your course tonight?"

"In about thirty minutes."

"I was thinking about going out for dinner, but since you have classes, we'll have to do it another time." He grinned and ran his hand through his hair. "You can clock out."

EXIT

The bags were packed, waiting with me near the front door. Matthew finished talking with his trusted house-sitter, the neighbour, a woman with twins. Their father left them thinking that she was a freak for having twins. Or it could've been maybe she was the devil but he was gone. And she didn't care if you were to ask her. It was for the better.

She was nice and seemed normal, though. The twin girls seemed fine, maybe too cute to be normal. To some that would've been godsent.

They both came out and she was smiling. She gave Matthew a hug like he was her own child. I thought of my mother as she came by all knowing and gave me a hug. "Take care," she whispered as she smiled on her way out.

It was still cold and damp out but the sun was making a graceful appearance for the morning.

The taxi pulled up and we stuffed our bags in the trunk and got in. We drove into the busy heart of Wolston, passing all those fortunate and unfortunate memories as he held my hand and kissed it reassuringly. Our eyes met, and it occurred to me that I'd never been this much in love before.

Not really. Instead, we got in the taxi and zoomed off trying to miss the morning traffic. But it was already there. Business people buzzing on the cement, not really watching the traffic and going out in bunches of crossing suits.

"What was her name again?"

"Jane Hermock."

We arrived at the ferry docks. On the ferry we stayed outside with our coffees. The morning air fell into the day's habit of mist mixed with the scent of active dead seaweed as the seagulls circulated for the hiding clams, finding them and knocking them against the echoing rocks.

As the boat got on its chilly ride, Wolston disappeared behind the thick, massive fog, hiding everything deep away. Me and Matthew hugged each other. I was thinking of my new bed. I needed sleep.

"From here we embark on new territory," said Matthew.

New territory high up in the cold mist. All the other little islands which surrounded this new territory were hidden from site. It was exciting to be standing in the freezing cold and waking up to something new. I was so excited the coffee was just provoking me and later Matthew into hysterics followed by dangerous moves of imitating other ballerinas. We stood there arm in arm pretending to swim for a second and next resting, feeling the damp coolness sink in.

As I was in Matthew's arms, I rummaged through his pockets as he slept. I found the disposable camera he bought. I took a picture of us. Memories to remember and the song rings on.

The boat started to dock and we met up with a bus filled with everything foreign because it really was foreign.

Me and Matthew took the bus and train into Paris. My French consisted of not many words at all, bonjour, je ne sais pas and la pomme—that one I remembered because it was the one French word that made me hungry for apples. The word apple just never did it for me, it made my saliva gather up in the back of my throat.

Paris, a romantic documentary, was a new beginning for me. A new beginning because I didn't understand a word of French. Matthew shamefully knew as much as me.

We got to our hotel which would be our home for a while. Getting off the bus and into the hotel room was a relief for a bit. It felt fantastic lying on the bed and feeling this new foreign comfort. I lay there staring at the old stylized ceiling. I imagined my feet putting on a tiny little ballet on the ceiling. My feet matching the invisible score to the dramatic lighting of the hotel's reading lights.

It didn't last too long because they both fell effortlessly down, bouncing on the bed out of frustrated impulse because they couldn't withstand the gravity.

I wondered endlessly at the shadowed blankness of the ceiling and I couldn't believe I was here. I mean, how many other times would I experience this same sensation, being amazed each new time and each time lasting for two minutes at the most. Each feeling broken up into little fragments equalling two minutes. Two minutes floated around in me like sensational spurts.

In the corner, a flash of light struck the wall followed by a steamy entrance of Matthew in a hand towel.

La Compagnie

Meeting the company. The company stared blankly at us as the director introduced the new dancers. They stood there in their tights, arms folded against each other, waiting to hear the new names as they pointed their toes, which were edging to be warmed. We all grinned. Once the intros were over, we all formed a line in front of the mirror and did our warm-ups. Although it was just warm-ups, it seemed to define the moment of respect within the company. But like any good performer they soon lost their own snooping, interrogating eyes and fell in love with their own bodies. That's what I loved about being a performer, you were allowed to publicly absorb yourself.

It felt good to perform for the first time to a paying audience. Each individual light standing out to show each practised expression of the body, the face, the hands, the legs and the feet were perfected. Everybody stretched out towards the centre of each light and backed away as the lead dancers took their place and the corps de ballet became their shadows. We stood there with the lights passing us to aim on Anna and Mikal doing their long awaited duet.

Mikal held her high as she stretched out to grab her lost emotion of love. She collapsed through his arms down to his legs where she held onto her dying wish. My part came into play as we gathered around her, giving her the strength of her spiritual soul to recline to her feet again. We echoed each move she performed while she soaked all of the light and the audience's moving eyes to catch each twirl and foot movement. It ended in a sounding collision of hands.

After this particular performance, Anna walked up in her kimono to Mikal who was standing outside his dressing room. The rest of the ballerinas and me watched the dramatic scene unfold.

"Mikal, you bastard! You almost dropped me! You know what that would've meant?"

"Anna, Anna my dear, my love."

"Listen, I won't take this! I don't need to wonder during every single performance, if tonight is going to be the night when you drop me!"

"I didn't, you fat cow!"

"Fuck off!"

She walked past the rest of us and slammed her door. Mikal slammed his and that's when the rest of us laughed, hoping sooner or later one of us would get chosen.

I headed out leaving the gossipy crowd to discuss who would be the next leads. I met Matthew and we headed home. All I could think about was a long warm shower. I could almost feel it as Matthew placed his arm around me. The heavy warm drops soothed each painful muscle.

After reclining into the warm bed with eyes already heavy and sleepy, I dreamt about threatening lights peering through the dry icy fog and that would start a new dream, something inconsistent and not too memorable.

The company, to show that it appreciated our hard work, gave us a costume party. Me and Matthew picked out the same daisy patterned dress but his was blue and yellow, and mine was red and yellow. Next came the long blond wigs. We were going as twins. Marcy and Darcy. He was Marcy and I was Darcy. The twin idea really mocked the idea of being clowns because our faces were painted unnatural: white, white skin with big blue peacock eyes and scarlet lips.

The stars of the company came as stars. Mikal came as Anna as Giselle, which was an excellent portrayal, and Anna came as Mikal as Prince Albrecht. They came hand in hand. Anna tried lifting Mikal only to make him fall. It was amazing because they hated each other and yet they were laughing and working together. Maybe it was true, the rumour that both of them were seeing a head doctor.

Mikal came over to us. "So, what do you think of my costume?" He did a little twirl.

"Very nice."

"Both of you look good, too," he said sizing Matthew up. "What about a dance?"

Matthew took his hand and led him onto the floor.

Rich, one of the male dancers, came up to me. He was dressed like a witch except taking the French notion of a bad, very bad witch.

"That Mikal is something. He has the worst attitude but he

really is something to look at. Don't you think so?"

"He's not really—"

"You mean personality."

"No, I mean everything. He does nothing for me."

"I'm glad you think so because you're too sweet to get burned, baby. Eliza baby, you should warn Matthew about him."

"Me warn Matthew?" I giggled. Rich was always a little protective of everyone, warning them of invisible tragedies. He liked to be the mother of all situations.

"Yes, I'd warn him. Mikal, word has it and trust me, I know that Mikal is a real heartbreaker."

"I really don't think I have to worry about—"

"Mikal, ah, works magic when he has too."

"I'm sure he does."

"But he's no good, really no good. And I'm not just saying that he really is no good. Tell him please." He placed an assuring arm around me. I wished right there and then, that he called me baby and I'd go: "yes mummy," with my crimped eyelashes fluttering for my little mummy.

"I will."

Rich left.

I watched Matthew work the scene. Matthew kept winking at me as he danced all dainty getting into the character of the dress, feeling it out. After the dance ended, he came back grabbing my arm excitedly.

"To be quite truthful with you, I think that's the most laughable dancing I've ever seen."

"I did it for you."

"I'm sure you did."

"What did that Rich want?"

"He wanted me to warn you of Mikal."

"Yeah, you better because that Mikal is something, something sublime."

"I know, I was standing in awe, the way he danced an, an—"

I touched his arm.

"And I was the lucky one."

"Why are you laughing?"

"I think I need another drink."

Both of us sat down with new drinks trying to look like twins as we sipped our drinks and sucked our cigarettes.

"My face is burning."

"So is mine. I don't think you're supposed to drink an wear this stuff."

I pulled Matthew onto the dance floor and we had one last go at hanging onto each other in the darkening party with carefully placed lanterns.

"E-liz-a, I don't feel too well."

"I'm burning."

Burning and not feeling well. We left the few remaining people who still had the energy to stand up with great co-ordination to say goodbye with two kisses. Each hug came with a pelting stomach. Each kiss glued our lips together.

We resembled two scratched up putty cats, going home together arm in arm, realizing that the man we fought over was nothing. Matthew's hair was starting to look lopsided. The dampness on the sidewalk did not make the old brick road easy to stand on with high heels. The sound of each heel diverging into a motorized headache as little cars zoomed by hitting each sunken puddle.

Finding our hotel room became a living nightmare. We tried each keyhole and each one debating with hardened ease that it wasn't the right key. We landed on the stairs and carefully climbed to the fourth floor. I fell down and he came tumbling even harder, hitting my side causing me to throw up over the railing. You really had to feel sorry for the maids. They were the ones who had to clean it up. After wiping away the liquored saliva from my chin and lips, I hugged Matthew.

"Just think, they're the ones that are going to clean it up."

"I'm not."

Not, not heading down and into my stomach.

Matthew went on about not doing this or that. I fell back on the stairs and I could feel myself falling to the third floor. Slipping down and finding my head dragging on each new carpeted step. I fell asleep with the step edging into my neck, making a new comfortable dent in my neck.

The messenger came in, flying down below with a vacuum which sucked in the last dirt and stopped at my foot. I gazed up at the uniformed messenger. Her foreign words dug into my head for some sort of translated response. Instead, I scratched my face and yawned, tasting the left-overs.

She scooted me up, pressing at my feet with the vacuum, and then, she blabbed at Matthew who was leaning against the wall drooling over his dress. I poked at him and he came up. We walked up to the fifth floor turned our keys and we were in.

I yawned big and wide, scratching at my face. "I feel like my father." The words just came out after the big yawn. I could feel him in me wanting to come out.

"What?" Matthew asked pulling off his dress.

"I need to throw up." I slammed the door of the washroom.

"Whatever!"

I pulled-tore off my dress, bumping into everything because I forgot about the zipper in the back. Finally, I just knelt and let it all out in the toilet, where it swallowed the bastard of my father.

"Bye, bye, Daddy."

After that, I took a shower and I tried to make something in me feel right, searching for my usual reality. I knew then it wouldn't work out. Nothing seemed good.

I stepped out and Matthew was lying on the bed. He turned around to avoid the noise of me getting dressed.

"How are you?" he asked.

"Fine." A sharp and edged word that would wake him up and give him that sore head which just pounded. I watched his hand touch and squeeze his brow.

"How are you? Are you alright?" I asked with a fake concern.

"Alright." He opened his eyes; they were red and sore. "Where are you going?"

I grabbed my coat. It was raining outside again. "For a walk." I wanted to be alone in the city. Or at least try to be.

A Great Teacher

Cod was a great teacher. He showed me all the ropes to the job and always showed the proper time for awarding oneself breaks so that one didn't have to suffer from exhaustion. Cod justified that the breaks were a time to conserve and build up energy.

One day we got onto familiar ground besides the beer, smokes and pussies. It was gambling. Cod took his chances on the races.

"I haven't gambled much since the last time."

"Why don't I take you after work today? Once we get our paycheques, we'll go an cash them. I know a little place for that an I'll introduce you to the races. I know a little place for that too an it's not too far away. Do you have school on Friday?" he asked scratching his chin.

"I'll make a sacrifice."

"Meet me in the parking lot an just follow me."

"Alright."

We headed back in to finish our shift. Today, I worked inside the factory at one of the pressing machines. Pressing the machine down to flatten out the cardboard. After a while, you got used to the smell. Even though I had to wear a mask, I could still feel the fumes taking up residence in my head.

I got on my scooter and followed his four-door wreck which was burning oil down into Saber. We went to the one and only 'Cash n Go' and I followed his steaming oil through Saber and up near the factories on Caper Drive. We stopped outside of Crooke's Pub.

"This is what you call a family generation pub. Passed down to the next Crooke."

We went inside and it was loud and busy with other factory workers. Television monitors were set up all over the place showing the races and sports. Cod went up to the pub.

"Hello Neil."

"Hey Cod. What will it be?"

"Two of mine for my new-found friend Chris, Chris Jamison." Cod placed his arm around me. "This is Neil Crooke."

We both nodded our heads in respect. He kept his hands underneath his armpits as he sized me up, recognizing the name over the face.

"You're Jamison's boy, right?" he asked giving me a hard squint.

"Yeah."

He set the two beers down. We picked them up. "Where's John tonight?"

"In the back."

I followed Cod and there was John with his table which served as his desk.

"John."

"Cod," the old man said.

"How's it going? How much money did these losers lose?"

"Ah, my big one just came in."

"Chris, this is the man that I pay for his spot. But tonight I feel like you'll be paying me back."

"Is that right, Cod?"

"John, this is Chris."

We shook hands.

"Now, give us the score?"

He handed us a sheet with the horses names filled up with the odds.

"Alright, Chris, I think we should go with Bella here, what do you say?" He looked up from his sheet.

"No." I pointed to Rush. "Rush."

"Alright, Rush."

We lay down our money and John took it. John looked up. "Rush?"

Cod nodded his head. We took back our forms and found a seat in front of one of the monitors.

"That John is a Saint. There's another place you can go up in Saber but that one is always hopeless. I mean once or a couple of times I've won but never big. That's why I come to this one. Who did you deal with?"

"It was usually done through my friend Kel who knew someone. I made a small fortune. That you know still brings a smile upon your face but I haven't done it since."

"I did probably a little bit before I met Doris an slowly when you start seeing some of that free money come into your hand. It feels fucking fantastic. After Doris moved in an we had our first kid, I thought what the hell, I've got nothing to lose. So I started playing again to see what I could win for my family as I explained many times to Doris, but she doesn't get it. Because she forgets the times I won big an that's when she loves me the most. They always do when you win. No arguments, nothing, just completely happy to have known you. Just you wait till you get yourself a girl an you'll see. If you win, they'll be flat on their back. An the way I met Doris was at a pub an I won an she was coming on strong an it kind of happened that way. Now watch it." He pointed to the monitor.

The races were off and there was Benny struggling to keep up with Rush and another one was trying to throw Rush off but he kept on him, gaining more speed. "Fucking, yes."

"Yes!"

We drank our beers and Cod indicated another one. He took out a cigarette. The waitress came back and placed the beers down.

"Thanks, Love."

We picked up our glasses and cheered them down.

"Usually, if I win, sometimes, depending how much I won back, I'll bet again but lately I've been trying to keep winnings instead of losing them. Because that Saint over there is how he makes his money. Fuck, I must be his favourite customer. He always gives me bullshit advice."

We both finished our beers and went up to John.

"Pay us, John boy."

He took out his canister of money and paid us out.

"Thanks."

He waved his hand in response. We headed out with a thick wad of cash in our pockets. It felt fucking great and I decided to stop by Julia's for a quick celebration fuck.

Doris

After work, we both lost our paycheques to John the Saint. Cod was pissed out of his mind. I wasn't much better off. I drove his car back home not listening much to his directions because when he said make a turn we had already passed the street.

"Thank God, you don't have to go back to a bitch of a wife. That's all I got ." He said as he hacked up another hurling cough.

I pulled over and the door quickly opened like it was going to fall off. He vomited again this time wiping his face with his shirt because he ran out of towels from the pub.

"Good."

With two more stops, I was at Cod's house. I didn't really want to help him stand up because he had gathered quite a pile of bile on his white shirt. Before leaving the car, he grabbed his plaid shirt from the backseat and put it on. He wanted to look good for Doris.

"You need help?"

"Na."

He walked up the broken stairs and opened the squeaky door.

"Doris!" he screamed.

"Fucking shut up, the kids are sleeping." I could see her though the screen door in a flowered nightie. "You're a fucking mess."

"Be nice, love. I want to introduce you to my friend."

I gave her a small grin. She glared over at us and crossed her fat arms.

"Fine, introduce me." She kept her arms tight and walked outside followed by Cod who held on the door for balance. "Hello, there."

"Doris, my dear, this is Chris."

"Hi."

"So, you're the one who brings him home like this. You know he has kids. Three that he's got to feed."

"Shut up, you bitch."

"Three bloody kids!"

I quickly walked away from Cod's angry wife who was advancing towards me. In the distance I could hear Cod trying to shut her up but her big squeaky voice trailed off, "three bloody kids!"

Mum

"Hello, Eliza?"

"Hi, Mum. How's everything going?"

"Alright. How's the dancing? Is it still paying?"

"Yeah, are you working?"

"Yeah, I started again. I had to. I have—" Her voice broke off. "No choice."

"Are you alright?"

"Eliza, I want to tell you that your father, he's dead."

Her words hung in the air, dead-father-dead. "What?" That's all I could think of at the moment.

"He's dead. He died two days ago. I've been trying to call but you're never there. He died, at least what they tell me, the doctors, of a heart attack. He was at the pub like usual, you know. Paul called me an told me he was rushed to the hospital. Supposedly, he went to the washroom an just fell down—dead. I was in total shock. I never would've thought. I always assumed I'd be the first to go."

"Don't say that."

"Yeah."

"Are you okay?"

"I've just been in shock, I'm fine, really. I'm just really amazed, Eliza. Your father is dead."

"Do you want me to come home?"

"No, no don't worry. Your father is in a better place an he doesn't owe anybody anything. He really is better off. He'll make less trouble in the grave than he did being alive. Sad to say—"

"But you'll be okay?"

"I'll survive an that you should know. Paul an Lisa are both helping out. I don't know where to begin with his things. Part of me wants to sell them. I'm sure I'd make a small profit. I just don't know. I guess I'm still in shock. How about you?"

"I don't know."

"That's how I felt. But you'll be okay. Maybe I should just sell his things. It isn't like they have any value. It's amazing how he just went out like that!"

"Yeah, I can't believe he went out like that in a washroom. One moment he's there at his usual game an the next he's dead. When's the funeral?"

"Eliza, don't even think about flying out now. Anyways, the funeral will be in two days. I just want to get this over with."

That's where everything stopped. My mother went on as I listened, both of us not really finding any sort of loss but trying hard to see some sort of light for him. Instead, shock took the feeling of any sensational loss. Shock that he was actually gone. My mother remained calm and asked me once in awhile, "Are you okay?"

Fine is how I felt that day. My father was dead. The only expense she was worried about was the funeral. So he'd be cremated. My mother didn't need me to come flying into her arms. She didn't need anything. Her voice remained calm during the whole conversation. I could almost hear her breath saying never better.

Once she hung up, I sat there feeling the loss but nothing came except I thought about the comedies and that made me laugh. I could hear him saying, "Never better," like some sort of battery commercial that kept going and going. Never better was my father.

All that remained of him were his words for bad decisions in life. I laughed to myself reluctantly trying to find a long distance comfort into the day's disappearing afternoon light.

Flash

When it came to performing, all the expression that I didn't practice came up in the lights with the audience watching. It all came out. The emotions flowed right through. At the end of each dance I was amazed at how I did it. How I carried it off. I really couldn't stand it anymore being in the back. Never being seen.

The lights and the audience clapping is what kept me going. When I saw those blinding lights all shining on me, I couldn't help but feel that intoxicating pull.

The audience was outlined in haloes. The light would switch their attention onto the stars of the show. Everything went dark and unnoticeable as I caught my breath.

Five years seemed too long for me to live in the back. I couldn't take it living in the back. Back. Back. Back. It was a fucking nightmare. Smiling there in the back. Thinking of the moments—moments floating up like a special documentary of my life. Laughing at me as I stood grinning, framing the stars of the show. Laughing at me because I wasn't good enough to last.

The Moments—me lying in bed gazing at the ceiling thinking of the same performance, playing like a broken record. The MOMENT that tops it, is thinking of Anna's moves and actually taking the time out to practice them and she takes all the parts. And that white ceiling glaring back at me as I see those yellow fleshy lights all around.

I've been staring at the lights; it gives me something to do when I'm in the back. Squinting at the lights gives me a familiar blind feeling but I don't want to think about feeling. The feeling hitting me in my stomach. Feeling bare—naked—gone in front of the lights.

My last performance for the company I was in complete pain. I gave a performance that I've done numerous times before. But this time the gelatin grin felt like it was cracking under the heat of the lights. My feet were sliced up by the cloth that tried to protect them. Everything was killing me.

Hot, pasty and melting—melting all that gently placed makeup into mush on my face.

The lights were blinking madly at me. It felt as if the audience had cameras and it all stopped to begin into the hollow clapping of smashing hands. After, I changed quickly and bandaged up my blistering feet and washed my eyes out because every face was flashing at me.

I headed into the street still seeing the blinking lights. I had my hood over my head trying to protect myself from the drizzling rain.

Out of the damp blue air, a guy stepped into my path carrying red roses. I moved to the side to let him pass. Somebody wanted to get lucky tonight with a dozen red roses.

"Hey, hey Elizabeth Fellows, hello."

I turned around. For the first time I heard my full name being used on friendly terms. I didn't know what to expect as I turned around to face him as he held the red roses, shivering under his jacket. His red lips perked into a smile.

"Do I know you?" I asked defensively.

He stepped forward. "No, but I've been watching you."

"What?" I questioned, backing away from him. Psycho is what flashed into my head.

"I've seen you on the stage and I came to give you this since it's your last performance." He handed me the roses. I stood there dumbfounded. I noticed him nodding at me to take the roses.

I took them. "Thank you."

"I didn't mean to frighten you back there. I thought you were beautiful on the stage."

"Thank you." I stood there with the roses holding them tightly.

I didn't like the silence of standing there holding his roses. "Have a good night."

"Elizabeth, why don't we go out for a drink?"

A drink. I sized up the situation. A harmless drink as my father's words loomed in my head. It wasn't really a knowledgeable comfort but something familiar stood in my way.

"That would be nice."

We went to a local pub.

"Richard Parks."

"Call me Eliza, everyone does. When you first said Elizabeth, I thought maybe you were my instructor. How long have you been watching me?" The question stood in the air, hanging there, waiting for a response.

"I've been watching the show. I'm an usher. The first time you just captivated me."

"I'm in the back."

"I know. All the others did nothing, you had it all."

"Now that's a big statement."

"You think I'm crazy?"

"No. Why, are you?" This is when I really wanted to know the answer.

"No, I don't think so." He chuckled.

"I'm just amazed that you got a glimpse of me."

"I got more than a glimpse. I mean, you had it all. When you came out on the stage—"

"No need for a step by step."

"I'm writing a book."

"What about?"

"I can't say just yet."

"Oh."

"Do you write?"

"No."

"I would have thought you wrote."

"No, I just dance."

"I could tell, you have a real passion."

"Ah." When was I gonna get out of here? This passionate man bored the hell out of me. And what bothered me more about it was that he had everything already planned out. He had me planned out like I was a piece of property for sale. Where was this sign he saw?

He ordered another set of drinks. Wanting to get me drunk and easy. He had it all planned out.

"The reason why I approached you is because I want to make you part of my book. I want you to be who my male character Jeffery Stokes loves to the end. I want you to be the one."

The way he said "you" stood out. You, you, you. All of a sudden, I became a form of words which he wanted to take and snip to his liking. He wanted to make me the love of his book. The book I thought never existed in the first place, because if it did, why would he be waiting for someone to come and form his direction.

He took my hand and stroked it. "Maybe if it got published, you could be on the front cover, because you would be the love, the main point to the whole novel."

I took my hand away. The drinks had put me in a sour mood because I was already bored out of my mind. "Fuck off, psycho!"

I got up, watching from the corner of my eye his quick desperate movements to grab my hand. I ran out not really wanting to make a scene because I didn't want to end up seeing it on the number one best-sellers list.

I walked home with too many secret thoughts trying to peek through. When I stepped through the door Matthew was already there. His smiling face took away everything. Matthew tucked away those unavoidable thoughts and my dead father with his wise words under the covers.

Exit 2

I got up feeling absolutely smashed. Matthew was lying beside me. I remembered the night before, "fuck me sweet an simple." It ended that night. The night of preconceived decisions ended sweet and simply.

That's when it happened. We packed up as we drank bottles of beer and smoked cigarettes. We got it all done. Matthew was nice, warm and was snoring, it sounded like he was catching a cold because he had a ripple sound forming underneath his breathing.

We left London quicker than we planned. Travelling became faster the more and more we did it. I had no need to sneak pictures of the new forsaken land. It was finding my bed that was more important.

We took the ferry back home, heading out on the choppy seas, the wind tangling my hair, breaking my lips and giving me too much air to breathe.

The other islands disappeared into the winter's fog, Matthew sat inside recovering from a massive headache. Maybe he was thinking it was a wrong choice, but I loved it out there, freezing under my jeans holding myself against the wind. After a while it got too cold and I took up the seat beside him.

"How are you feeling?"

"It's passing."

I couldn't wait to step off the ferry and find a new home with a new life. Drop by to see my mum. I couldn't wait to see her because I was excited by her new life.

Matthew wasn't doing too well but he wasn't turning green yet. His body flowed with the weight of the boat's movements. Each deep sway of the waves pushed the boat and Matthew's eyes would jerk open and shut to rest in his new position.

"Are you happy leaving?"

"I don't feel any regrets at all." He tried hard to give me a grin. I smiled back hoping to God he wasn't going to be sick.

"I feel that way too. I really believed that we weren't getting anyplace." All I could think of was the word back, back. Being there in the back, I couldn't take it and those lights. The whole company experience summed up into nothing as I sat there staring out, waiting for Wolston's night lights to appear through the light fog. It was hard sitting in the plastic curved seats and searching through the fog to find Wolston.

The fluorescent lights beamed down, gently buzzing me to sleep but keeping me awake and aware of the other passengers on the boat staring at me.

I opened my eyes and there was Wolston glistening under the light rain and no fog.

I actually smiled because I didn't know what to expect at the moment. All I saw was the glistening lights and I was home.

On

On foot. On land. I was waiting for a taxi with Matthew as the rain pelted down on us.

Both of us walked in the rain, carrying our luggage and trying hard to get a taxi to notice us. Both of us stood there dripping, waving our arms around as each occupied taxi drove by, hoping the occupants' heads in the back-seats were an illusion.

Finally, a taxi zoomed in as we rushed right in, throwing the luggage in first and then us.

"Careful, there."

"Sorry."

"Where to?"

"513 Shepherd Lane, St. Maurice," I told the man as Matthew slammed the door and the taxi took off.

I watched the new shiny city pass me and stop. Few people were on the street; they were either running against the wind or walking cautiously and tugging their umbrellas with the wind pushing against them.

Everything stopped in Wolston. Every place and everyone seemed more foreign here than in the foreign cities.

The taxi stopped at Shepherd Lane. I paid the bill as Matthew got out taking the luggage and running to the landing. I entered Matthew's dark home. I removed my hood and walked into the living area where Matthew was standing. I took off my wet jacket and felt a chill.

Matthew read the note his mother left as I went to the bedroom. It was a small bedroom with a small bed where I only spent a few nights last time. Now, it seemed tiny because my sleepover was going to be more than one night. I unpacked my bags and filled up the empty spaces in the closet. I lay on the bed and noticed his little plants. The plants now stood or grew squared around the window and underneath the growing masses his Mum had knit new coloured doilies. Red, orange and blue.

I walked towards the perfectly squared growing leaves and I saw the secret nails edging the leaves so they wouldn't block the view.

I heard Matthew turn on the stereo as I went to the washroom. I wanted to be alone and the closest I got to was flossing, brushing my teeth and washing my face. The stereo played a radio tune. Popular in Wolston. I liked it here. The warm water spit at my face with each hand smacking it.

On――TO

Matthew called up Julie Moore, an old friend of his. Moore lived up on Harold Street.

"She used to blow bubbles with her saliva when she was pissed," he told me.

"I'm guessing she was a party freak?"

"Yeah, she really was a freak show. I used to call her fishy girl. She looked like a fish when she did it, that was what was even freakier about it."

"Did you have romantic—"

"All elegant tonight, are you?"

"Presentable is the word."

"I didn't know you were for that."

"Didn't you?"

"No, you've got to be kidding."

Once we arrived, Julie opened the huge wooden door and greeted Matthew with a hug and hugged me after. She dragged us into the room where her husband sat. He smiled at his guests. Old friends, how nice!

"Matthew and Eliza, meet my husband Sean."

He greeted both of us with a firm handshake revealing his white teeth, which shockingly were as brilliant as Julie's teeth. The idea that he was a dentist was illuminating in his bleached teeth.

We sat down as the jolly husband delivered the drinks and the conversation began. Matthew placed his arm around me trying to create a couple-like atmosphere. I cuddled into him to feel less awkward in front of the cheery couple.

Sean was a professor which explained his small wooden pipe and how he sat with his legs tightly closed, holding that small package in. Those were my father's words and thoughts. My father hated pansy-assed-educated-pisser-wankers as he called them. Always liquoring you up to tell their long stories concerning their over-paid studies that was of no interest to anyone.

We were all jolly as me and Matthew traded with them hidden secrets of our intense relationship. All those knotty details made both of their faces red. The liquor made our stories sound really interesting and valid with each giggle of the couple. The laughter gave me a comfortable position in the house of dead leather and proper liquor glasses.

We teased each other with a lasting relationship of honesty and it clicked like the truth was placed right before us in their light reflecting teeth, which kept me awake.

Me and Matthew had been together for some time. Our relationship had always been based on friendship. Did me and Matthew actually fit the definition for that? Fuck it, now the fairy couple was playing with my mind and the cool liquor was turning sour. I wanted to fight but my little arms and fists were only good for pulling out hair. So being a brute was out of the question.

Being good hosts, they ordered us a taxi.

"Matthew, are we together?" I asked holding in the hurtful laughter because my liquored throat was burning.

"Are you starting to believe it too?" His eyes glanced over.

"We're friends, right?" I asked pronging the intensity of our relationship.

"Too much of a married life, love." He slurred his words.

I was out there searching for my own place and a job. The job, out of no surprise, was a checkout girl again. I was working at a grocer in St. Maurice. After two days of working there I found a little apartment. The tenants before left a bed and a kitchen table with two chairs and a slightly awkward coffee-table. One of the feet was shorter so the tenants doing a little home improvement glued a new foot on. Except it was a lighter colour of wood.

The whole place was painted white covering up all the grease marks and crayon drawings that were there before because when the sunlight hit it, it would reveal the wall behind the paint. If you ran your fingers along the walls in the kitchen you could feel the grease coming through the thin layer of white paint.

Matthew helped me move my stuff and he gave me a plant to keep me company. He placed his heart warming plant in the living area.

"So Matthew, sweetie, you're not going to be too lonely are you?" I put my arm around him as his head sank into my shoulders.

"I'll manage."

Checkout Girl

"I know I failed." Kel was just sore because he gave me a copy of his excellent penmanship notes.

"Well, you went to half the classes." I told him.

"And you went to them all, is that what you're telling me?"

We stepped inside the grocer. I looked from Kel onto the checkout girl bending over in her green uniform. Her cute ass made the dress rise up to reveal white thighs covered in black nylon. She stood up and pulled the dress down. Her ponytail followed her searching face as she bit her bottom puckering lip. She grabbed a bunch of cigarettes from the counter above and bent over confiscating the cigarettes in her bag. I couldn't take my eyes off her. I wanted badly to step up behind her and just give it to her, the way she moved under the tight polyester dress seemed to be screaming for Chris to come and help.

We walked over to the liquor section and picked out our starters for tonight and I headed towards checkout girl number 8. I carried the beer and placed it on the conveyor belt. I stared her down as she helped the older customer. Her green eyes glared down at the groceries and then to the money in the till. Her red lips gave a hearty thank you with a smile that ended as quick as it went up. Her long fingers reached out for the beer and she dinged it through. Her eyes flashed up at me and I observed her very attentively seeing her lips form into a pretty little smile.

"You think you have enough there?" she asked gazing right at me as Kel flipped through a magazine while slamming my foot to make a move.

I took her on as she edged her body forward putting the beer nice and careful into the bag. I grabbed her hand and she followed the concerned gesture with her eyes peering lovingly into mine. "What time do you get off?"

And right there a fat popper sneaked up behind her. She glimpsed over and back at me, licking her moist lips. She was one fucking sweet package. I released her hand.

"It's against rules for me to say. Thirty-five, fifteen is the total."

I took out the money and crushed it into her hand. Her hand folded over my hand. "Tonight, I'll be at the Union Club." I released her hand and gave her a wink. I looked back as she watched me leave. I was awestruck, completely fucking gone for number 8.

Eliza

We finished off our beers and took the train up to the Union Club. There was a line up, and Drew was already starting to rack up who he was going to bone for the night. Some girls peered over while others not so elegant told Drew to fuck off.

We were in. The place was crowded and booming. I squeezed through the crowded bar and ordered three pints. I glanced up to pay the bartender and on the other side I saw her. She was absolutely gorgeous. A fucking gem in a crowd that was around her. I gave her a smile of recognition and she returned it. I quickly passed the pints to Drew and Kel.

"Cheers." I gave a fast one and started walking as they tagged behind.

"Where are you going?"

"She's over there."

"Well, my boy." Drew walked up to my speed and placed his arm around me. "Let's get Chris screwed tonight. Cheers."

I popped a cigarette into my mouth, lighting it and walked over to where I thought she should be. There she was sipping at her beer. She was wearing a short black dress that snuggled her just right. Her eyes spotted me and Kel moved in the way going up to her.

"Hello, there. My old pal Chris here wants to meet you." He winked at me. "But he's a little shy, as you can see. Now, I can vouch that he's a gentleman. He won't take advantage like the other ones and he always means well. He's a good mother's boy, too. Although, truthfully, he doesn't live with his mother. But—"

"Alright, get out. Yeah, yeah Kelly." He hated when you called him that.

"Like I say, he's a gentleman and he won't dare lay a finger on you."

"Thank you, Kel." I shoved him away.

They disappeared into the crowd and I walked up to her, nice and close. That's what I liked about going to the club—you had no choice but to invade their space to pass any form of communication and of course, to be an attentive listener.

"Chris!" I wanted to kiss her neck as she bent forward. She smelled good too.

"Eliza!"

"Eliza, don't listen to him!"

"So, you do take advantage is that what you're saying?"

"No, no."

She was gorgeous as she moved her body to the music. "Do you dance, or are you just going to watch?" She raised her eyebrow smiling with her mouth open so I could see that juicy tongue of hers.

"Both."

"Drink up then, Chrissy. I want to dance with you."

We drank up our beers and I took her glass and mine and left them on a table. She pulled me onto the dance floor, squeezing past everybody else and we danced. I held onto her pretty little body as she jumped up and down.

I pulled her closer and shouted into her ear, "You don't come here often?"

She crawled up to me. "Why do you say that?" I took advantage of pure instinct and held her there.

"I've never seen you here before."

She burst out laughing, throwing her head back, so I could admire and peep down into that heaving chest of laughter.

"I thought you said that you never did me before."

I held onto her tighter. "But I will! You don't have to worry!"

"You're not much of a mother's boy, are you?"

"It's only up to you, baby."

The way she threw her head back and showed off her long neck was truly a path of ecstasy and I couldn't take it anymore. I bent in and kissed her hot flesh, and she tightly held me, agreeing to it all. She came up all divine with her eyes half-closed and I would have kissed her, except Kel shoved between us with new pints.

"This is for a lucky night!" He hit his elbow against my side. Like he was an old man sharing a dirty joke.

I placed my arm around Eliza. "Cheers!" I couldn't believe it as I watched her beer disappear. She gazed at me, her eyes big and hazy. She was a real good girl and she was my girl.

Kel placed his arm around us. "Now, fuck! I have to find Amanda! Chris, did you see her man?"

"You didn't bring her."

"Fucking right! Come on, let's get fucked! Come on, Drew's holding seats back there. Come on!"

We headed to the back where Drew was sitting with some

new-found girl. They were necking and she was giggling during the whole process.

"Stop biting me!" she shouted and noticed us looking on with drunken grins.

"Ah! What, baby?" He noticed us and nodded. "Hey all, this is Cherry with a C!"

"Just like those ripe Cherries."

"Isn't that right, baby?"

"Hey Freaks! Is this a gang bang?"

"You wish baby!" Drew forced her face to look straight into his.

"I thought it was!" Kel said coming in closer.

"Fucking Freaks! I'm out of here!" There went Cherry, out of the booth.

Drew unsuccessfully tried to grab her. "Come on, baby, we'll be quick about it! You're not being much of a teammate, love!" he bellowed out, and all he got out of her was her middle finger. He winked at Eliza. "Chris, is this a new one to the team?"

"I don't think so!"

"She's mine, man!" Her body sank into mine as I squeezed her closer.

"Ah, I see, I'm Drew!"

"Eliza!"

"Welcome to our little gang!"

"Shut the fuck up!"

"I didn't like that Cherry one, you know what I mean? She wasn't too much into the biting game."

We all sat down. Sitting with the boys is not what I had in mind for Eliza. I quickly drank my beer and of course, my new lovely did the same with no reserve. The question came up to her after passing various drunken insults.

"What do we do next, Eliza?"

"Dance!"

We all danced. After awhile, me and Eliza were holding each

other up for the night. All I could think about was holding her close, feeling the edge of her skirt close to her thigh and kissing her neck.

"Now Chris, love, do you want to go to my place?"

Her words moved me so much that I wrapped my arm around her and we headed out.

"Wooooo!" I screamed on the empty street as a car sloshed by trying to stop at the red light with its backside skidding.

I tried getting a taxi but she directed me to the train because there weren't any taxis. Finally, we made our way onto the train and up to her place.

Her door seemed many steps away. We carried each other up the stairs to have one of us trip on the other's shoes causing us to fall down on the wet stairs. We didn't feel any pain in the slightest as we fell against the concrete steps. She was about to get up and I held her sweet ass which was already wet from falling all over the place. She sat on top of me, taking the cigarette out of my mouth and smoking it.

"I'm so fucked."

"Right, yeah, I want to be fucked," I told her as I took my smoke back.

"Is that right?" She watched me carefully for a response.

I was about to kiss her but she pulled away running up the stairs. She unlocked the door and I came in. She shut the door and rested herself against it. She looked absolutely stunning while the rest of room spun.

I curved my hands around her back and brought her close to me and we kissed. Our tongues pulled each other in for closer action. It never felt this good. Everything tingled as I held her body closer, feeling it out and then I pulled away. My eyes half-closed and the drunken feeling of the hot liquor swirled up, and she was doing no better because gravity was beginning to take possession. She pushed me against the wall where we fumbled till the lights were flicked on.

Light-headed and feeling fantastic but sick with the walls and her tumbling on me, we ended up falling through a doorway. We stayed there for a moment. I was trying to hold down my stomach, and my head felt like it was twisted all around.

"Can I have your number?" I coughed it out.

"Yeah." She pulled herself up and I lay there as I heard the distinct sound of a pen jotting down the number. I got up and walked over to her to write down mine. I took the paper and placed it in my pocket.

She walked me to the door and we kissed each other good night.

I was feeling fucking great but sick at the same time. I kept checking my pocket to make sure that I hadn't dropped her number. Finally after two torturous blocks to home, I dragged myself up the stairs and spit out the residue of the dark liquor. Unfortunately, I took my keys out on the third staircase and I dropped them over the railing as I spewed over the flying keys. I walked back down holding my stomach because it was all out of place, almost collapsing down the stairs.

I found my keys. They were a bit wet from the digested liquor but I wiped them on my rain drenched jeans. I walked up very carefully, this time holding onto the rail with my hand and the other hand holding tightly onto the keys. The sixth floor, number six, was in reach and my door was right there.

Checkout

My mum quit her job at Hives and was now living with Paul. Every time she quit her job I was there to replace her in the work community. She was out, and I checked in.

I was ringing the groceries through for a customer, and I usually kept my eyes down because the groceries were more interesting than the customers watching you ring in the correct prices.

This particular customer had a lot of beer. Not like I haven't seen it before but it stood out. I glanced up to see who it was and met these blue, blue eyes staring at me with little lips edging into an excitable smile. I smiled back with my eyes flashing into his.

"You think you have enough there?" I asked keeping my mouth open with a smile.

He grabbed my hand. "What time do you get off?" His eyes stared into mine and sparkled.

My boss sneaked up behind me, waiting for the appropriate answer to this stranger as I packed the beers.

"It's against rules for me to say. It comes to thirty fifty-five."

He paid, holding and crushing my hand with the cool bills and coins. "Tonight, I'll be at the Union Club." He winked, picking up the groceries.

I watched him disappear. I felt spasms of smiles coming over on my lips. My boss didn't want customers coming onto the checkout girls. He said it was bad for business. He believed that we would start giving discounts and eventually freebies just to get a date because I supposed, we must've looked that desperate to him. He was a bit sore, according to the gossip from the older checkout girls, about his wife leaving him for a customer that would only checkout at her till.

I stood there charging in other goods as my mind floated to those blue eyes and how much I wanted him. My lips loosely kept whispering it. I had to get control, otherwise I'm sure one of the older customers would notice because they liked to stare at the youth to find something wrong just so they could give advice. Instead, I grinned at them. Maybe that was the first time I had.

Once I got home I was planning to go to the Union Club, but Matthew called me up and wanted me to go out with him and his new friend Charlie. I was already forming an excuse in my mind.

He said, "Let's go to the Union."

I was silent.

"Eliza?"

"Yeah."

The Union Club's door had a slight line situation. My stomach tickled me with each new male face passing, casually thinking of possibilities in the back of the head that it could be him and once they turned around it wasn't.

Matthew and Charlie both agreed on whatever with a little laughter.

Inside another manic panic struck my bitty eyes searching for those blue eyes. My mind debated the embarrassment of being obsessed with someone.

Matthew pulled both of us on the dance floor, ripping me away from my short lived obsession.

I turned around to find someone else sneaking up close who wanted to dance. It was so dark I couldn't make out much of a face except when the coloured lights tittered through each bleached spike. It made me think of Ashley but it wasn't because his eyes were too dark. This one was trying too hard to impress me by mocking each move I did. He wanted to communicate through the movement of his body—the relationship dancer. I got sick of watching my male-self because he was a boring-repetitive dancer.

I walked over to the crowded bar and slipped through the drunken line up. I ordered a beer. I needed something right there and then.

With the head and all, I took a sip and looked up. That's when I found him. His blue eyes spotted me with his lips hanging open in that enlightened little boy, ah. I smiled to him, already knowing the ahs of his expression. The crowd pushed both of our stares away into strangers' eyes.

I waited at the end of the drunken crowd and he came in the centre of his friends, they were all holding pints.

"Hello there. My old pal Chris here wants to meet you, but he's a little shy. As you can see. Now, I can vouch that he's a gentleman. He won't take advantage like the other ones and he always means well. He's a good mother's boy, too. Although, truthfully he doesn't live with his mother. But—"

"Alright, get out. Yeah, yeah Kelly."

"Like I say, he's a gentleman and he wouldn't dare lay a finger on you."

"Thank you, Kel."

They left and Chris came forward holding his pint of beer and smiling with a cigarette hanging out of his mouth.

"I'm Chris!"

"Eliza!" both of us shouted with anticipation.

"Eliza, don't listen to them."
"You do take advantage, is that what you're saying?"
"No, no."
"Do you want to dance, or are you just going to watch?"
"Both."
"Drink up then, Chrissy. I want to dance with you."

We both guzzled it down, feeling light headed from it all. It gave me the urges to drag him on the dance floor and he held onto my waist as we chugged and slightly pushed the other dancers away. He felt so strong even though he had that boyish thinness about him. I held onto his neck as his hands jumped around my waist and tickled the dip in my back. The ebbing beats came crashing in so we could catch our breath as we swayed together.

"You don't come here often?" asked Chris. His lips touched my earlobe.

"Why do you say that?" I crawled up to him and he held me tightly.

"I come here after my night classes and I've never seen you here before."

I laughed because I thought he said he never did me before and I thought there was some sort of list. "I thought you said that you never did me before."

"That's true enough, but I will! You don't have to worry!"
"You're a sure one for being a mother's boy, aren't you?"
"It's only up to you, baby."

The beats went fast and I bent my neck backwards as he kissed, taking full advantage. His lips felt so good. I squeezed him tenaciously, wanting to hold him in and he came up. The moment was placed with our eyes staring into the other's and Kelly interrupted us with two pints of beer.

"This is for a lucky night!"

"Cheers!" Chris had his arm around my shoulders already. We clinked our pints and drank them down. I downed it pretty fast as Chris observed with animated amazement at one of my secret talents.

"Now, fuck! I have to find Amanda! Chris, did you see her, man?"

"You didn't bring her."

"Fucking right! Come on, let's get fucked! Come here you two, Drew's holding seats back there. Come on!"

We left the dance floor to go back to where the red booths were. Drew was sitting there necking with some girl.

"Stop biting me!" she shouted, throwing her head back and catching three boys and me leering at her.

"Hey all, this is Cherry with a C."

"Yeah, with a C just like those ripe red cherries."

"Isn't that right, baby?"

"Hey freaks! Is this some sort of gang bang?" She glanced around her and stopped at me questioning my part.

"You wish, baby!" Drew grabbed her chin forcing her face to him.

"I thought it was!" shouted Kelly.

"Fucking freaks! I'm out of here!" Cherry climbed over the booth.

"Come on, baby, we'll be quick about it!" He tried grabbing her hand. "You're not being much of a teammate, love!" He ended in a loud wicked laugh and took a gulp of his beer. "So, this is a new one to the team?" He noticed me as if I was the next one.

"I don't think so!" I told him.

"She's mine man!" Chris held me closer.

"Ah, I see, I'm Drew!"

"Eliza!"

"Welcome to our little gang!"

"Shut the fuck up, Drew!"

"I didn't like that Cherry one, you know what I mean? She wasn't too much into the biting game!"

We all sat down.

"Tonight is pretty lame for chicks, I mean, except for you

Chris, you're getting lucky I see!"

"An he's all mine! I think tonight we're just going single. Isn't that right, Chris?"

"What about you?"

"She's mine. I don't think I need an explanation."

"What a lovely couple!"

"That's right!"

"I found some good ones, but I thought that Amanda was here so I was being a gentleman."

"Amanda, she's not here, man!"

"I know!"

"What kind of shit are you on?"

"He's just fucking pissed and in love with his forever Amanda!"

"I wish Chris, I just don't fucking know!"

"Enough with all that love, brother!"

"So, Eliza, how did you get stuck with that loser?"

"An not you? Is that what you're asking Drew?"

"Yeah, baby you got it right!"

"Because I like a man, boy!"

"See man, I'm a man and you're just a boy. A fucking little boy!"

"Yeah, yeah, I hear you!"

"What's the score tonight?"

"Pissed and maybe, just maybe, I can get that ripe Cherry. I like how she fled. She won't find anyone else in this place."

"Except me?"

"That's right. Kel, I thought the amazing Amanda was here?"

"You know it!"

"Drink up you fucking pussies!"

"Chris, I like her!"

"Cheers!"

They all drank up.

"What do we do next, Eliza?"

"Dance!"

The whole time was spent dancing as the music filtered onto the sleepy tunes which gave everyone a chance to gather their stuff and go. Both of us swayed together as the other ones talked. I kept admiring Chris's strawberry lips in amazement.

"Now Chris, love, do you want to go to my place?" The loveliness of words was flowing through. Everything was lovely. I was a happy drunk.

"Wooooo!" Both of us screamed as we held onto each other outside.

"What are we doing?"

"Trying to get a taxi."

"There's no taxis around! Train Chris, the train!"

We carried each other into the station almost falling on the stairs as the station's bright lights snapped our eyes open. The train came to a metal grating stop, we piled in. We sat together with our heads resting on each other. The train came to the third stop and we got off feeling the cool morning air.

Once we got to my place, we walked inside and I locked the door. I waited, and I smiled as he sluggishly slipped his arms around me and our lips came together as our beer tipped tongues twisted. We fell to the floor. My eyes fell on him in a lovely daze. I had never felt my eyes so heavy before. They closed as my lips stayed warm against his.

God, all I could think about was how bad, really bad I wanted him. I wanted to stay in his arms always. I was turning into mush that night. The night me and Chris met.

Nice One

We got together after two days.

After work I went home to change into something casual but attractive. Jeans and a tight shirt were the answer to that. I let my hair which was long with a slight, slight wave flow on its own. I was set. I waited to hear Chris's knock on the door. I sat on the sofa dreamy-eyed with my ears perked like some sort of sick manic. My palms were sweating with each passing second. I felt his pressure on my heart but it was just my heart pumping blood and throbbing louder and faster because the silence was so thick.

A loud and anxious knock broke the silence in the air. I opened the door and there was Chris grinning widely at me and I smiled back.

We sank into the pub's seats with a pitcher of beer and Chris kept his arm around me as his fingers played with my hair. He liked to lean in and smell my hair.

"I work for my father and I do all the shit that workers do. He wants to make me well informed and he wants me to know everything about the company. I get so many lectures, I'm even talking like him. I'm not complaining about it. But I mean, I've been working there for years now. Doing the same shit, and going to night school for business. He pays for it, otherwise he knows that I'd be up there in Greece on the beaches with my mum and her lady friends. That's what he fucking thinks."

"At least your daddy is still alive."

"Why, is yours dead?"

"Yeah."

"Oh Eliza, I'm sorry. I mean, I might be acting like an ass because—" He glommed up at the ceiling for a quick answer.

"Because you love me." I gave him that you astonish me grin and he caught onto the game and kissed me with his boyish strawberry lips, teasing me with his deliciousness. He knew that I was enjoying this. His wide blue eye followed by his little lazy blue eye ogling over at me in that familiar cocky loving way. I sat there staring back as he lit my cigarette and his. The moment of smashed silence kicked as we blew the smoke to the side.

"Eliza, I love you." He said it with that smile of his.

"When you say it like that, I don't know what you mean." Both of us flirted with the idea of some sort of love.

"I love you and I'm sorry."

"About what?"

"About your father."

"It really is nothing to be sorry about because it's really funny. My mother called me up an I was in London at the time performing up there. She called me an says, 'Eliza dear, your father, he's dead. He died in the washroom at one of the pubs.' He had a heart attack after one of his gambling games, probably bet his life on the table. The funeral went on an my mum took the ashes an spread them over Dockers Row where Caper Cove is. Now, when I moved back to Wolston, I call her up an she tells me she's living with Paul, who was one of my dad's friends. He used to be married but his wife recently died."

"Convenient, two widows fall in love."

"Yeah, that's what I say an she tells me, I'm like my father. Which is a bad thing. After that, I ask is there going to be any future wedding bells an she says, 'No' an explains how living together is practically the same thing."

"At least she's honest."

"Ah, yeah, now she is. She can be. The comical aspect is that Paul is another gambler but he always breaks even. My father basically lost more than he won. My mother tells me, 'that Paul is a good one Eliza.' She wants to reassure me that he'd never hurt her or lose all her money. She put so much money into my father's gambling."

"Your father never won?"

"Well, he won big twice but I'm sure after all the glory parties he lost it all. One time, he actually lost me in a bet. That was completely gone." I laughed paralyzed because the words were spreading too easy.

"What do you mean he lost you? Did he actually use you as a bet?"

"My father actually thought he had a winning hand after he lost everything. I was just sitting there colouring an he bet me."

"You're not kidding?"

"No, I'm serious my father actually bet me. The next day, I went to the stranger's house an helped him out. I thought the whole time he was my new babysitter. Nothing happened though. Nothing sexual, an I was way too young. Now, that is what you call a real loser at gambling, right? Right to the end. Fucking unreal my father was."

"My poor Eliza."

He hugged and kissed me.

"Another?" I asked holding the pitcher.

"Another."

I poured the beer into the glasses.

"Where was your mother during all this?"

"She was pissed but she couldn't do anything."

"That's fucked!"

"I'm so glad you think so, because if you didn't think it was, there would be something wrong with you. An all of this—"

"I want you to know that I would never gamble you off."

"Ah, now that is sweet isn't it?" I kissed him. He believed it because he was too sweet. "Now Chris, tell me about your parents."

"My parents are divorced. My father still lives up in Bury in the same house. He owns Imperial Boxing, it's a small boxing company. He wants his little boy, Chrissy here, to take up his load when he dies. He trusts me."

"Poor little Chris." I gave him a pat on his back.

"I know, I know. Now, my mother, she's over on Greece's beaches living it up with her friends. She sends me little postcards, always signing off with 'love Mum' or better yet 'thinking of you.' She used to be one of those bastard attorneys, that's why she literally lives on Greece's beaches. The reason they probably got divorced was because my father was having some sort of seedy affair. At least, I like to think that. It gives a good reason for them breaking up and explains why he loves controlling my life. Both of them don't even speak to each other. I'm the channeler as my father puts it. I hate it though. I remember when they told me. My last day at high school. I just sat through it and they explained I could express myself. I don't know what they wanted me to say. I just sat there. I had nothing to say to them. But my parents, I guess, are happy now. They both think openly that the other one is crazy. Both of them are. But I'm pretty sane despite them."

"Postcards love mum." I laughed at this bit.

"Neither of our parents loved us Eliza. We are in a world that doesn't want us."

I crawled on top of him and we kissed. "You're saying that we are two lonely people?"

"Destined and desperately in love."

"I like that bit." Both of us felt the wanting of the other. The heat, warmth of our breath felt so good against the barley taste in our mouths. We finished our drinks as I sat on him. Our lips played, until the playing turned too sensuous under our wet lips.

We left with great urgency back to his place. His roommate Kelly was out. He pulled me along into his room. It was dark, with clothes piled on a single chair. He sat down on the bed and pulled me close to him. He lifted up my shirt to kiss my belly. I pushed him down onto the bed.

The bed pushed back and forth against the wall with the springs madly creaking. I lay there pulling my hair at the raising tension and him responding by ducking to bite and suck at my nipples long and hard. My legs crushed him with the long releases of Ahhhhhhhh.

And it ended with plain excitement as he lied down beside me.

"Nice one."

"I was expecting a bit more than that."

"Great, fucking great, Chris."

"There you go. Come here."

His forearms were so strong. I kissed them, letting him know in my own way that I approved of them.

This was more than any good that I knew before. His head rested on mine while I listened to his heartbeat. Beating into my ear and keeping me awake.

I noticed he was awake, staring into my eyes. All I could think about was food. Together, we bathed our used bodies and dressed into our old clothes.

"So, what do you have to eat?"

He took me into the small kitchen and searched the refrigerator. Kelly and Amanda stepped through the door.

"Chris!"

Chris propped up. "Kel." Chris pulled me in. "I want to introduce you."

"She's the one from the Union."

"Eliza, Kel and Amanda."

"What are you two doing now?"

"I think we're going to get something to eat."

"We have an exam this Friday in stats."

"Alright, you got all the notes?"

"Yeah."

"I'll be right back."

Chris went off to his room.

"Hey there Chrissy-boy, you shouldn't be missing as much as you are!"

"Amanda, shut up!" Kel went to Chris's room and I was left with Amanda.

"So, you two met at the Union, eh?"

"Relatively." She came closer, looking like she had some sort of dirty secret she was about to spill.

"Chris is pretty good, but I have to tell you something. It's girl talk. I've never seen Chris with a girl."

"You mean he's a fairy?"

She giggled. "No, no, I just mean, that I've never seen him bring anyone home. He's usually a one nighter. I just thought you should know. Like any girl getting involved they should know the score."

"That's nice." I didn't know what to think because I didn't

trust her little protruding blue eyes and dark rooted blond hair. "Can I ask you something?" I was pursuing her eager need for girl talk.

"Yeah."

"Did you an Chris ever get it on?" I asked lifting up my eyebrows to her. She liked the thought because she grinned.

"No, I've been with Kel forever now. I mean Eliza don't get me wrong Chris is a—"

"Amanda, are you pissing around with Eliza?" Chris put his arm around me.

"No, I was just giving her some girl advice."

"Ah, some of that stuff. That's always reasonable but Christ, how would you know anything about that?"

"I'm a girl."

"Yeah, let's go."

"Fuck you, Chris! See you later, Eliza!"

Chris and I left.

"What was she saying to you? Giving you some of my history?"

"Somewhat. She summed up your personality in two words, one nighter."

"A one nighter."

"Mm. An I'm guessing from that point she was warning me that I'm going to be dumped. Kicked to the curb!"

"Eliza—"

"No, Chris, don't speak." I held his lips with my finger. "Sh. I'm just going to call this great day quits before you kick me out. You sly dog! I would've never seen it coming from you!"

"No, Eliza—"

"Hush, don't ruin it." I giggled under this serious moment. We kissed. Kissed kissed kissed kissed kissed.

Mine

I picked her up and gave her a big hug and a kiss. And I asked, "You remember me?"

"I think so, Chris. Although, I tried hard to forget you." She raised her eyebrow and gave me a kiss to know that she was kidding.

"I couldn't forget a creature like you."

"Right, nice an drunk."

"You want to go for a beer?" I embraced her.

"That would be very nice."

"Great."

"Did you work?"

"Yeah, it was the same."

"Did you take any more smokes this time?"

"Of course. How did you know?"

"When I first saw you, I saw you hide the stash."

"What, an that is why you're going out with me?" She flashed her eyes and I lit her a smoke.

"No, it was when you were bending over."

"So that's why, the cigs were just a bonus then?" Her eyes were exuberant and her voice ended in a high spirited giggle as her body knocked mine.

"Because you have a nice fucking fat ass that just begs to be slapped." I gave her a kiss and squeezed her tight ass. She took it in beautifully.

We walked into Hector's Gate. I got a pitcher of beer. I sat close with my arm around her, twirling her long hair as I told her about my job and night classes which I skipped quite frequently. I found myself listening with great attention to her life, growing up in Saber and coming from a family of gamblers and how she herself got gambled off. The way she told it, not feeling anything at all, that's what I loved most about her. It was how I felt about my parents. Nothing. They were simply figureheads in the past which happened to be looming around with general concerns and their dispensable money.

"What were you performing in London? Were you an actress?"

"Ballet. I lived in Paris for awhile an then I went to London. I was with a ballet company."

Ballet, the word ballet strung off a whole bunch of stereotypes, very flexible and durable individuals.

"And why are you working at the grocer?"

"I quit the company." She rested on my chest and lit both of us a smoke. "I needed a change."

"And the grocer was the answer."

"Yeah, Bury boy, I'm going back to my roots." She edged her head up and I kissed her.

Eliza got on top of me and ran her fingers through my hair and I rested my hands on her happy ass.

"Come on."

We left and I took her back to my place and gave her a short tour and the last spot was my room to the bed. I pulled off her tight shirt that made her breasts bounce under her black lace bra.

I took off my shirt and I pushed her down on her back and kissed her little belly and I took off her jeans. I got on top of her, feeling those breasts and pinching at her sweet nipples as I took off the bra that was attached at the front, nice and easy. I took off my jeans and boxers as she took off her tiny black panties. She crawled up to me and I moved my dick into her, and I slid right in with her long ballet legs wrapped closely around me.

I felt her tremble underneath the quick pulse of my pussy finger. Her liquid pulled me heavenly inside her. I fucking jammed right into her. It felt fucking great as I rested a moment on her.

"Nice one."

"I was expecting more than that."

"Great, fucking great, Chris."

After our little nap, I walked her home. Everything seemed normal with her and I didn't know how that happened. I couldn't stop admiring her.

Outside her place before saying goodbye, I playfully squeezed her tightly.

"Come on, try and break free!"

She tried pulling out but she was stuck.

"Poor thing, can't get out!"

She stopped struggling and just stayed there. She placed her head back. "Let me go, please." She tried wiggling herself free.

I let her go, and I took possession of her again and kissed the back of her neck. I whispered into her ear, "You like that, don't you?"

Instead of answering, she gave me a kiss on the cheek and took the smoke from my smiling lips.

"Do you want to come to my place for a drink?"

"Yeah."

I was starting a new life with three aspects: Eliza at the top, gambling, friends, school and work smashed in between.

Mum and Paul

Chris and I were on the train to Saber. He was going to meet my mum and Paul. This was my first time back to my mum's in a long while.

As we walked together arm in arm, I noticed that Saber hadn't changed much except for a new group of children playing soccer with a blue ball. They were yelling and screaming and swearing to mother of God that they had made a goal. And off to the side, two girls skipped rope as the ball passed in front of them.

"Get it, John!" they both screamed.

"Is that what you were like?"

"No, I was shy."

"Ah, so you lived in a bubble?"

"No, I went out there sometimes but I wasn't out there all the time chasing rats or a shit covered ball. I was taking ballet lessons."

"Snob to the whole Saber experience as you say."

"Shut up, Bury boy. Here's the house."

The house seemed new with a fresh coat of white paint and

an added blue trim edging out the house as the neighbours' paint was peeling off. Even the cement path had been fixed. It was now a smooth base of cement leading right up to the front door. I knocked on the screen door which for the first time stood in its place. The door tentatively opened and there was my mum looking the same as always. She rushed right into my arms and gave me a hug almost knocking Chris down who moved aside for the whole mum experience.

It felt good to hug her after a long time and feel that same warmth.

"Oh my God, I can't believe you're here!"

We stood there hugging each other for a while. Paul entered my view. He didn't know what to do. He kept scratching his head and turning back to the television or just stood there waiting for my mother to make a move. We both let go of the hugging position to end in holding hands.

"Mum, you look great." I was speechless so I thought the inevitable.

"But you look better, you look fabulous!"

"Mum an Paul." Awkward as it sounded, I wanted them to know Chris. "This is Chris."

"Hi." He did a slight clumsy wave.

"Hi," they said back.

"I made tea. Eliza, come help me."

Chris and Paul sat down in front of the tube. I went with my mum to the kitchen.

"Chris is very cute. He's good to you?" Her green eyes looked up under her light green eyeshadow.

"Yeah, he is." I said it all dreamy. "An Paul makes you happy?"

"Yeah, he really is good to me. Did you see all the work he did for me? The house looks great now, it's not a dump anymore. Paul did it all."

"It really does look great."

"But how is my little girl doing?"

"I'm really happy right now. I'm still working at the grocer, but soon, hopefully, I'll be doing something with ballet. An Chris, he's really nice."

"You two look really great."

"Do you still work?"

"No, finally. I think that whole aspect of my life is over now. Dead an gone. Paul an I go to church. It must seem to you that I have this new life. Going to church, no longer working, an feeling fabulous. Paul works at one of the factories, but he usually is good about his gambling. He doesn't take chances. Now Eliza, don't go telling him I just said that. Watch, I'll be stuck with your father again if you do." She ended in laughter. "Paul always breaks even. An I'm so happy about everything. So are you an Chris living together?"

"No, not yet, we really just met each other. He works at Imperial Boxing. His father owns it, so he works there boxing things up an he's going to night school."

"That's really good. A factory owner. Who would of thought? Paul used to work at one of the fisheries. Your father did a little bit of that. He really stunk an he quit because he couldn't take that dead smell. Help me bring the tea into the other room."

I brought the teapot followed by her bringing the cups and saucers, sugar and cream on a silver tray. We entered the room where both of them were discussing each other's work in the factories. They moved over so mother and daughter could take the couch together. I poured the tea in the cups and my mother asked if either of them wanted sugar or cream.

"This you may not know Eliza an Chris, but me an Paul for a little while were once boyfriend an girlfriend. It was really innocent at the time. It was before I met your father, Eliza. Me an Paul were about thirteen. I was mixed with the wrong bunch, an Paul joined us. I showed him the ropes of hitting cars with eggs. We'd steal the eggs from the market because if we took them from home we would've been beaten. It was out on Bury Road where all the newer cars would pass. So me an Paul ducked under the bushes an waited for a car to pass an he smacked the front window. Paul's first hit. An from there he continued on throwing excellent shots an we became the best of friends."

"It was more like you let me become your friend."

"Well, I didn't want no wimp for a friend."

"An I introduced your mother to your father, Eliza."

"It wasn't like it was a blind date. An when you introduced me to him we were just friends at the time."

"I was always too shy around your mother. An like mother an daughter, they're absolutely beautiful."

Me and my mother laughed as Chris and Paul agreed with glaring grins.

That night I watched Paul talk about his work, I kept wondering was this my new dad? Was I supposed to call him dad? He grinned when Chris made a joke out of his job comparing it with his. They both laughed over the same work lingo. Paul would stare and squint at my mother and me in deep fascination. It seemed his eyes were trying to find that younger version of my mother, especially when me and her joined together in laughter.

Paul was all opposites of my father. My father seemed huge like a big boat. Paul was tall and thin with tight curly short red hair and blue eyes. He liked to hold my mother's hand. He really did love her and I knew my mother loved him. The way they talked of their first shared ice cream, both of them lit up with a smile and their eyes were all over each other. Their timeline went from innocent childhood beginnings to now. The rest, the centre of it, my father, never happened.

I glanced over at Chris and he was enjoying himself, fitting right in. As they carried on with lovely stories, I was curious to know if they had been in love when my parents were together. I kept the question to myself because I already knew the answer.

The memories of my father in this house had already been

sold, packed up and gone to the highest bidder.

Now the home was dressed with Paul's furniture, except for the golden tv-trays. Those were my mum's, folded in the corner by the television because Paul's coffee table replaced them.

"Eliza, your room is still the same. I didn't sell or give anything away."

"So, when do you expect me to come home?"

"Tonight."

"And what about me?" Chris's blue eyes popped open to the question.

"You can have the couch."

"An don't worry, Chris, there's always breakfast. We can eat an go to work together. Hit the pub an come home to our two lovely misses."

"So proper there, Paul. Come with me, Eliza."

"Thank you, my love!"

I followed my mum to my old room where the ballet poster still was posted.

"It's still the same."

"The only place here that is."

"Where did you get all that new furniture?"

"Most of it was brought over from Paul's home after your father died. I decided to sell it all since Paul was moving in an I needed the extra money. Your father would've wanted it that way. But the house looks pretty, doesn't it? God, it was such a rat hole before. I truly believed that it would've stayed that way. But it is really nice, isn't it?"

"Yeah."

"What do you think of Paul?"

"I knew him before."

"Yeah I know, but what do you think of him now?"

"I think he's nice. I'm not supposed to be calling him dad, am I?"

"No, I just wanted to know what you thought of him."

"I think he's nice."

"Yes, I think so too. He takes care of me an I don't have to fight anymore over the loss of money. Chris is very charming."

"He's cute."

"Are you in love with him?"

"Mum, please no lectures." She kissed my brow.

I helped my mum with the dishes as we shared a smoke in between.

"Paul thought about papering or painting the kitchen instead of this yellow. I haven't decided myself yet. What do you think, paper flowers or colours?"

"I don't know."

"You see the dilemmas I face now. I feel like a lady of leisure. I don't dare tell Paul that, otherwise I might have to work again."

"I don't think so."

After we finished, we returned to the living room. Me and Chris decided it was time to go and I hugged my mum goodbye. She didn't want to let go and neither did I. She smelled too good and Paul came over for our first family hug. I was so used to squeezing that I thought I would break him. He seemed so small in my arms, although he was tall. Tall and delicate.

Wicklow Street filtered out under the tall lights which lit up the vacant street. In the distance a couple of shouts played over the sounds of fucked-up vehicles.

We got up to the train's entrance.

"Next is to meet your parents."

"They won't be like this. You'll be falling asleep."

"What was Paul like?"

"He's good, works hard and loves your mother with all his heart." Chris grabbed his heart as he pelted me with his big sad eyes.

"I'm not taking pity on you."

"But I love you."

"You do now?"

"Ah, come here." He gave me a big squeeze. "I'm taking you home with me." I told him. "That was my plan."

Family

"Chris Jamison, report to the main office." Debbie's voice rang over the speakers. You could hear the slapping of her tongue against her afternoon chewing gum. Cod and I were both at the vending machines; we were on one of our many breaks so that our constitution would not be too damaged. I went up the spiral stairs and knocked on my dad's door.

"Come in."

"Hi, Dad."

"Kel told me that you're hardly around and gave me Eliza's phone number?" He regarded me with a question mark. Did I say that right, E-L-I-Z-A?

"Eliza, she's my girlfriend and I've been staying at her place lately."

"How come you never told me?"

"Never really thought about it. Not like it was that poster piece you got." I was referring to his girlfriend Cheryl Brown who owned Brown Real Estate.

"Are you going to move in with her?" His questioning eyebrow rose to an accurate point.

"I thought about it."

"I would like to meet her. Maybe we can have dinner together with Cheryl and Eliza."

"Yeah, we should."

"Did you meet her at school?"

"No, I picked her up at the local grocer."

"Ah."

"She's a ballerina. She's from Saber."

"Does she still live there?"

"No, she lives close to where my place is, two blocks up. Tonight, I'm going down to Saber to meet her mum. Her father died a while back."

"I would like to meet Eliza. We'll have to go out for supper sometime."

"Yeah, that's great."

"I'm glad you think so." He said, his voice defensive. "Can you take out that trash as you're heading down?" He pointed to his small bin filled with lunch bags.

"Right-o."

The phone rang.

"Yeah, put her on... Hello, Cheryl... Yes, I got the tickets."

I took the trash out and headed back to finish up. To finish with Cod who was browsing through the horseracing newspaper.

"How did it go? Did he break your balls?"

"No, I've been seeing this girl Eliza Fellows."

"Right."

"Did you know her father?"

"Ah."

"She's from Saber. Anyways, he wants to meet her with that cardboard piece Cheryl."

"He's dating her?"

"Yeah, personally I feel that he's being used. He's a man with a company and for his age a fair set of hair, now. And her seeing and feeling that makes her feel that he can get her anything. If she rubs him in his right place. You know?"

"She's some good fucking pussy for your dad. Now, if he buys her a ring fight it all you want. Otherwise, leave it alone. Let that old guy just do his thing." Cod was older and more out of shape than my dad but he talked like he had it going on with every young pussy that came his way.

Me and Eliza waited outside her childhood house. Eliza's mum abruptly rushed out and gave Eliza the hug of a lifetime. Behind the hugging couple must have been Paul, tall and red, and awkward as could be. He kept scratching his head and I gave him a slight wave as mother and daughter continued hugging. He gave a sophisticated nod as he watched the girls hug. As soon as they broke, my eyes were on the mother. She was still attractive and moved very much like Eliza did. Eliza introduced me and that's when Paul stepped forward and we shook hands. I watched Eliza at this. She basically kept a fair distance so that all that could be attempted was a handshake. Their place was a relative dump; it was Saber; not much expected. Except outside it was painted up. Eliza gave me a quick tour which didn't last too long.

"You're sure that's it?" I asked placing my arm around her.

Eliza's mum came up behind her. "Where did you grow up?" she asked glowing at Eliza and then at me.

"In Bury. Now I live in St. Maurice Bay."

"This must seem quite small. Paul's mother lives in Bury, too. I've been there a couple of times an it is really gorgeous. The gardens, especially. Eliza was saying that—"

"Did you put the tea on?"

"Not yet. Why don't you, darling?"

Eliza left and her mother continued on. "You're working at Imperial Boxing an your family owns it?"

"Yeah, pretty much my father started it and he wants to pass it on."

"Paul works up there too."

"Mum."

Eliza's mum went into the kitchen. There was a small table for two in the centre of the room. There was an old white stove with a small counter and a big old fridge that hummed loudly beside a smaller counter where one metal sink with separate taps for cold and hot. Eliza poured tea into their Christmas decorated teapot. I went into the living room where the television was on one of the comedies.

"I hear you work at that local boxing company, right?" Paul asked.

"Yeah, and what about you?"

"Reinforced Plastics. I take care of moulding the pipes an valves an all that. Maril was saying that your father owns it?"

"Yeah."

"Do you have your own office?"

"No, I do the work that everyone else does."

"At Reinforced, he has his nephew working there an he has his own office, but the scandal was that he was taking a bit more than he should have, so we have someone else now. I guess he must be doing his job. So, your old man has you working?" he asked.

"Yeah. Do you go to that pub on Dockers Row?"

"Sometimes."

"Cod—"

"Old Cod boy." He nodded gleefully in recognition.

"He's been showing me around."

"He's a good boy that Cod. We went to school together an I'm guessing that he's gambling pretty high because sometimes his wife is in there with her friends an she's always complaining about him. Before me an Maril started going out, I used to go there quite a lot an I'd see one of them in there. But I don't go there as much as I used to. To me, the place has gone a bit downhill, not like it was one of those top notch places to begin with, but it's gotten pretty filthy. The beer itself tastes like water. I usually don't see Cod in there anymore. Anyways, I heard he goes to a place closer to where he works."

"Crooke's."

"Right. I remember some nights Cod's wife would come there looking for him. She's a fighter."

Eliza and her mum returned with a tray stacked with tea and biscuits. She put the tray down on the golden flower TV trays which Eliza propped up. Paul, a rather softy type of guy, helped Eliza's mum.

"What are you boys talking about?" Eliza's mum asked as she passed us each a blue paper napkin.

"Work."

Eliza poured the tea in the cups and supplied the milk and sugar for anyone who asked for it. I sat back into the seat as Softy Paul, with a giant red smile on his face, talked about meeting and obviously falling in love with Eliza's mum. He liked to call her Marilyn when he was talking about the past. Otherwise, he called her Maril.

I searched around for their family photo area and all I found were a couple of photos in simple metal frames on the television. There was a small hospital photo when Eliza was a baby, and a picture when Eliza was a child at a funeral with her mum. There was a photo of Maril and Paul in front of the house with two giant pots of red flowers on each side. Both of them were grinning with their arms around each other.

Paul caught me looking at the photo. "That's me an Marilyn in that one. After we painted the house. She planted those herself."

"Are you looking at pictures?" Maril asked as she took the last sip of her tea.

"Yeah," Paul answered placing his teacup gently down.

"I have a lot more, but I never really got into buying a picture frame an putting them up. I just thought it was a nice idea to do it. That's Eliza an her grandmother there at Aunt Doris's funeral. Eliza was quite young there. I don't know even if Eliza remembers her grandmother." Maril placed her arm around Eliza and gave her a hearty kiss on the brow. "She was hospitalized. Her health was never that good an sadly she was a bit nutty. That was a real long time ago."

Maril sat there staring off and Paul noticed and picked up his teacup moving it like it was a service bell.

"More tea, please."

Maril poured his tea. "Anyone else?"

"No thanks."

"No Mum, but me an Chris should get going."

Eliza got up and I followed her. I turned around to Paul.

"So, maybe I'll see you up there sometime or at Dockers."

"Yeah."

"Chris, I hope to see you again."

"Likewise."

She turned to Eliza, taking her in her arms and whispered in her ear and Paul came around and gave Eliza a hug. Eliza rolled her eyes to her new family addition. From there we left onto the dark streets of Saber.

Mucker

Chris and I, we, us, became part of our speech. We became a set. Going out meant we went out together. After work, school on his part, we headed out. Chris's things were casually staying over. The toothbrush played a big part, dirty boxers mixed with mine. A couple of his shirts he forgot and left for the next sleep-over were hanging in my closet.

The day of the big move came on a Sunday after he had spent the night at my place. He got up with his boxers on and made coffee as I stayed in bed waiting for the aroma to wake me up. He came in carrying two cups.

"Here you go."

We sat there for sometime sipping the coffee in silence.

"You know, love, we should get a tube in here."

"Why do you say that?"

"Besides spending so much time in here, it would be nice in the morning to watch the news or something. I should buy one."

"Maybe I like the peace an quiet of the day."

"Why am I here, then?" He pouted.

"Fine, buy one," I told him giving an amused look. "Is that better?"

"You know, I think today, I'm just going to move in."

"That was my plan."

"And it worked."

We kissed, holding in each other's morning breath so it seemed more like a peck. A bird's kiss.

After waking up, we headed down to Chris's old place. His room didn't have much in there. We piled his clothes and books into boxes.

Amanda came in and observed with excitement the vacancy. "Moving out?"

"One reason to move in with you, Eliza. I'm moving out."

"Are you going to be moving in, Amanda? Chris told me, you were all excited about it."

"Maybe, I would like to."

Kel sneaked up behind her holding beers. "You want any before you go?"

I took one and threw one to Chris and before I could open it, Amanda pulled me out and onto the couch.

"You two are in love?"

I shrugged my shoulders. "Maybe." Girl talk was on the way.

"Ah, I've been trying to convince Kel to let me move in. I'm practically here all the time." She took a long sip. "I mean, I never would've thought Chris would've settled down so quickly. Don't get me wrong." She touched my knee. "It would just seem that me and Kel would've moved in first."

"Really?"

"Yeah. Me and Kel have been going out for ages, and you and Chris have just started that long journey. It just doesn't make any fucking sense that you're moving in first." Amanda was searching her pockets and brought out a spliff and I supplied the lighter for her. "I don't know what Kel's problem is with me moving in." She passed me the spliff. "You know, then he could fuck me all the time." I exploded into laughter and right about then, the boys ended our little girl talk.

Chris brought the little TV and placed it in our room. I hung up the rest of his logo t-shirts and plaid shirts. He blasted the stereo playing "Funky Cold Medina," and I came into the room watering the plants. He closed the curtains.
"What are you doing?"
He changed a white bulb to a black light. He left and came back carrying a small strobe light.
"This is for the hit." He put it on and we were in a club atmosphere.
"Come on, baby!"
He came up from behind and shook me. Chris held a water can and the fragmented water came pouring down on me.
"Dick!" I screamed at him.
"Yeah, my love!"

Moving In

The day I moved in with Eliza. Of course, most of my daily objects had already ended up there. I made sure of that. In the end, I didn't have much to move out. Eliza helped me with the rest of the packing which was two boxes plus the hefty television.

Amanda and Kel returned from their weekender date and Amanda anxiously wanted to see me out so that she could negotiate with Kel the question of her desperate occupancy.

She stepped into the room and took surveillance. "I see you're moving out."

"Yeah."

"Are you moving in here? Chris was saying that," Eliza asked as she got up and sat down on the bed.

"I'm thinking about it."

Kel came up behind with four bottles of beer and grinned casually across her big tits. "You want any before you go?"

"Yeah." Eliza got up and took one and threw me the other.

"Come with me." Amanda decisively took Eliza's hand and dragged her away.

Kel sluggishly came in and carefully shut the door. "I don't know what I'm going to do."

"About what?"

"You're moving out and Amanda wants to move in. I told her, I don't know. Anyways, I could ask Drew to move in." Kel sighed with despair. "Chris, this just amazes me, you moving in with a girl and you don't know how much Amanda is pleading to move in. And speaking of Eliza. Did you tell her yet?"

"No, I think it's better not to. It was a bad round and that's it. She doesn't have to know. You know there's no point to that. Kel, next week I'll get my paycheque and I'll give it to them. They already know that. But there's no way I'm going to tell Eliza. I'm not going to purposely upset her with that. It doesn't even concern her."

"You don't know a fucking thing about races."

"Yes, mum." Kel was a bit panicky about my situation. He was worried that they knew where I lived. "And look, Cod dealt with them before. So don't worry, they're not going to come and terrorize you. They didn't come for his kids about it and tear little bits off of them." I watched him as he steadily sipped his beer. "Look, I'm going to pay it off."

"Alright."

"And there's no reason why I should tell Eliza. I don't feel like fighting about it with her. It's not worth it. Anyways, everything is under control."

"Alright, alright. Are you done?"

"Yeah."

We both got up and headed into the living room where the girls were talking and passing a hefty spliff.

"Boys, you want any?" asked Eliza as she held it.

I snatched it from her and nodded over to Kel who was already having his second beer. "Do you think it would be a good idea?" I asked edging my eyebrows at him.

"Why?" he asked all confused as if something was wrong

with him. He grabbed the spliff and slouched back in pure leisure onto the chair.

"No reason."

Amanda burst out laughing, holding her breasts. "Oh fuck, Kel stop being a pussy." She screamed at him and took the spliff.

"Forget you all. Except you Eliza, you never gave me any problems." He tapped her knee as his charming smile crept upon his face.

We sat around like a big family passing around the diminishing spliff. I had Eliza under my arm. I loved her so much. When she would laugh her whole body moved and crashed into mine.

I wasn't listening much to Amanda but watching the blank television screen reflecting me, Eliza, Amanda and a slice of Kel's perturbed twitching foot.

The deal. It got way out of hand. So did all my luck that night. Me and Cod had just won and we decided to bet it all on the next round because we were feeling great. Only, that lasted for a second when the wrong horse came in first place and ours came disturbingly last.

We were finishing our drinks pathetically. Both of us surveyed the crowded pub and ignored the races above. Cod motioned to two losers wearing black leather bombers.

"Hey Brian, how's it going?"

"Good. This here is Carl an Cod an?" He glowered at me as he stuck out his ear and flicked his lobe with his pointy finger towards me for a response.

"Chris," Cod told him.

"How are you, Cod?"

"Alright."

"You don't sound alright."

"Lost."

"Ah, Cod boy, I'm sure Doris is going to be on your ass. You want to name your game? Is your friend here game for it?"

Cod and Brian observed me. At this point, I realized Brian was going to get us out of hell and I saw Cod's desperation in his puppy eyes. He wasn't going home unless he had something. I nodded towards Cod.

"Yeah, he's good."

"Alright."

From there Brian set us up. Everything looked great. Royale was in the lead and it was beautiful. Brian and Carl whispered amongst themselves. Royale was up there. Far away from the other ranging horses and somehow out of nowhere Destiny poked herself through, followed by the pack and Royale stayed behind the asses not even making an eager attempt as Destiny fucking gracefully crossed the winning line.

Me and Cod sat back, lighting our last smoke of the night. I could hear Brian and Carl's squeaky leather bomber jackets approaching us to deliver our chosen destinies.

"Sorry to see that lady of luck." There was a long pause as they lit their smokes. "An poor, poor Cod going home to that bitch of a lady." They laughed that up for a good long second. "Cod, you know the rules an I know next week you're good for it. An what about Chris here. Are you good for it?"

"I'm good for it," I told him ending it with a gulp of my pint.

He came around and glared hard into my eyes releasing his tight lips into a pleasurable grin.

"That's good. That's real good. Now, if you want to go again—"

"No thanks, Brian," Cod interrupted.

"Alright, next time boys."

They left. And we left, going home with empty pockets. We said nothing much about the event. I was too drunk and I thought next week I'd worry about it. Payday was coming up and it would go over to them and I'd be done with it. The paranoia finally filled me as I thought of Eliza. I saw the outcome of it being all bad if Eliza found out. I could handle her screaming but I didn't want her to leave. I couldn't risk it.

She was lying on me, finishing up her beer and I was getting all sweaty over the situation.

"Chris and me." I looked over to Kel who was sitting up really erect and grinning uncontrollably now. "And Drew, too, we'd go to the hockey games and do a little bit of gambling. It was a fun way to make easy cash. Of course, at times, we would lose. But that last time was heaven sent."

"I never knew you gambled," she said shocked, glancing up at me.

"I did," I said trying to control the fear in my voice. She trusted and believed in good old Chris and that was essential in our relationship. I bent down and gave her a kiss on her brow.

Dad and Poster Girl

After making deliveries, Debbie announced my name over the speakers, this time in her early morning professional voice. "Chris Jamison, report to the office, please."

I walked up from the locker room and knocked on my dad's door.

"Come in."

I entered and there was the woman from the posters in a blue suit standing behind my father smiling at me. It was my dad's girlfriend, Cheryl.

"Chris, I would like you to meet Cheryl Brown."

In response, she rushed out from behind the desk and held out her board-stiff hand for me to shake.

"I recognize you from the posters." I shook her hand and her grin grew into her, 'you're sold' smile.

"Very nice to meet you, Chris." She gave me a let's-make-a-deal nod.

"Likewise." I took my hand back.

"Cheryl, we'll be meeting Miss Elizabeth Fellows tonight."

I told my dad before that I only wanted him to meet her. I

didn't want poster girl tagging along with her nods and stardom red smiles. "Eliza, Dad."

He looked at me. "Eliza, right."

"Charlie tells me that you're going to business school and that eventually this will be your own. That must be so exciting for you." She clasped her hands together and released them to dangle straight by her side.

"Somewhat," I replied flatly. It was the Imperial Empire of cardboard boxes, how else was I supposed to reply.

"Well, Chris, you should be getting back to work." My dad gave me a friendly grin to show that he was saving me in some way.

"Chris, it was nice meeting you and I'll see you tonight with Eliza."

I was already feeling the buzz of the cocktails by the time my dad and Cheryl arrived at our table.

I whispered into Eliza's ear telling her my dad had plugs. She smiled but kept her laughter down to a minimum. There was Cheryl looking gleeful in her crimson suit. Her and my dad held hands as they lovingly walked past the other tables with monstrous smiles.

Me and Eliza stood up to meet the new-found couple. I tried hard to give them a big grin without a heartfelt laugh.

"Hi, Dad."

"Chris, how are you?" His curious eyebrow sharpened upwards.

"Good, and you?"

"Fantastic."

"Hi, Chris," Cheryl squeaked.

"Cheryl, how are you?"

"Great." She replied very excitingly as my dad did an exquisite gesture of pulling out the chair for her.

I placed my arm around Eliza. "Dad and Cheryl, this is

Eliza."

The evening was set. My dad interrogated me about school and work. Cheryl sat there happily holding my dad's arm and tossing her head to show her grin and incredible white teeth.

I loosened my tie as my dad started asking questions about Cod. Since the wine was circulating in my veins, I took it personally.

The question came underneath that nice sweet tone of his. "He still has two children and his wife is still Doris?"

I took a sip of wine and said, "We have reached the drunken hour! And your dear old son is unfortunately pissed out of his fucking mind!" I took my wine glass and gently tipped it to my dear old dad. I gave Cheryl a smile and she didn't know what the fuck to do except look towards my dad for an answer.

"Is this fucking normal, Charlie?" she whispered under her grin.

"It fucking is, honey." I looked to Eliza who was controlling her laughter.

"Beautiful, eh!" I gave Eliza a wink.

"What about Cod?" His voice snapped as he ground up his food and breathed oppressively over what he was eating.

I stared my father down as I answered him. "Cod, he has one more child and his wife is still Doris. She's a lovely bitch, too! And she loves to holler!"

"Chris!"

"But she does, just ask Cod. He talks about her all the time!"

"Tell me Eliza, how can you live with that?" He used his eyes to point at me.

I gazed towards my lovely love and she was about to burst out laughing. I watched her take a hard swallow. "Usually, he's more agreeable!"

"Hear that dad, I'm usually more agreeable. So proper and with such elegance my dear Eliza delivers the truth."

"I think that's enough out of you, Chris!"

"Too bad, it wasn't that easy, right?" I glared at him. I thought I should apologize for my dad. Cod's wise words rang in my head, you don't want to ruin it for your dad. "Sorry, Cheryl, that you had to see this! Dad doesn't mean what he does. He is a genuine man," I told her flatly as she grinned and accepted my peace treaty.

"That he is." She did a genuine pause giving her enough time to pick up her wine glass and turn her attention to my father. "Let us make a toast to Chris's father, Charles Jamison for being a genuine man."

We all raised our glasses.

"Cheers!" she said.

"Cheers!" I watched my dad finish off his wine and turn to Cheryl, giving an assuring grin.

I followed up with my manners. "That was beautiful, Cheryl."

"Yes, it was." My dad took the opportunity to pick up her shiny golden hand and kiss it.

"Cheryl?"

"Yes?"

"Did you do anymore posters lately or do you use the same ones from before?"

"Actually, we just use the same ones. I find that easy because it is not like I'm modelling."

I noticed my dad watching me as I snorted little bits of laughter and I responded to Cheryl's answer. "That's what I thought Cheryl, because when I see the new ones posted they look so similar to the old ones. The same red dress looks like the blue dress, right?"

"They're the same ones but the blue suits are the new posters."

"Did you ever give my dad a poster so he can hang it up? You could be his pin-up girl?"

"I've never thought of it."

"I just gave you an idea now."

I grinned and took a big gulp of wine. I observed my father

and Cheryl sitting there with grins and holding hands. I sat there thinking about my mum and him. I never saw them do that. Cheryl, that fucking fat cow sitting there all cheery-like. I looked at Eliza who was finishing up her mashed potatoes. I picked up her hand.

"So, Chris and Eliza, what do you two have planned for tonight?"

"We're going up to Kel's tonight for a party."

I got up, followed by Eliza. I placed my arm around her for a little balance. I gave my dad a gentle smile. "Thanks, Dad."

He eyed me carefully and then patted his fluffed out rug. I could see a joke building up in him and I knew it was at my expense when he looked over at Eliza after she thanked him for a pleasant dining experience.

"You're welcome, Eliza." He paused and winked at me. "And I want to thank you in advance for taking my son." He nodded at me. "I really don't see how you did it."

"Ha, ha, real funny, Dad." The old man wanted to impress his lady.

Payback

Me and Cod left together to go to Crooke's. Our paycheques were cashed and rested in our pockets. It felt good and sad to enter Crooke's. The races highlighted above and good old John sat in the corner.

"What time did they say they'd be here?"

"Thirty minutes."

"A whole fucking paycheque gone to them. What are you going to tell Doris?"

"I've got a plan. I've dealt with them before. They'll probably be trying to get us to bet. Now, I know from experience that I'm not going to bet my whole paycheque this time. I'm just going to do a little bit because I have to. I really have no choice." He ended with a shrug and drank his beer. "So, how is that Eliza?"

"Good."

"Have you told her yet?"

"What?"

"That you're gambling?"

"No, I told you her father used to gamble and she's a bit sensitive about it. I don't want to upset her because I honestly love her. I like to keep her away from harm."

"That's my boy. You're a smart one, Jamison."

"Hello, boys."

"You have the cash?"

"That's what I want to talk to you about."

"Ah, good old Cod boy, very dependable to make a living. Now tell me, Cod."

"That I'm good for the money."

"Before you go into any sob story, how much? An what about little Chrissy here. Is he going to try an play with the big boys?"

I ignored the two cunts who were right up in my face. "I'm up."

"Great. Before you gentlemen place your bets, give me the cash from last week."

We handed him the cash and he quickly made it disappear into his big bomber jacket. I mindfully examined the sheet and picked out Coal.

"Coal."

"I'll go with that," Cod replied.

"An what are you placing at?"

I looked him straight in the eyes. "Double."

"Very good. Cod?"

"Same."

"Alright."

They disappeared and we sat there waiting for the races to begin. We didn't even discuss the choice or the money placed. We just sat there staring at the screen. I glanced over at Cod and he wasn't doing the greatest as it got closer to the races. He kept wiping his brow every couple of seconds. I felt guilty about it. He had a family and I didn't. I felt that I shouldn't have talked and I should have let Cod do all of the talking. But I couldn't stand the cunt's face right across from mine, breathing down on me like he was better, the fuck-face.

All worries disappeared as the horses lined up and they were off. Coal was doing real good, fighting to get his say among the other horses and then, there he was crossing the finishing line.

"Wooooo. Yes. Yes." We shouted. The few people in the bar looked around. Brian and Carl came up, giving a cold hard glare as they dished out the money.

"Very good. Anything more I can do for you boys?"

"No thanks." I gave them a smile.

"Alright, then. I'll catch up with you later." They left.

I waited for them to leave. Then I got up. "Everyone, this round is on me."

They all roared with excitement followed by running up to the bar. As they returned to their seats they nodded their head with a gigantic grin of approval. It was fantastic. The cash separated into two pockets.

"That was fucking unbelievable. I was thinking the whole time this isn't good an now look. We're riding fucking high."

"Cod, it's fucking fantastic. Pockets filled to the brim. Those gangsters gone to find some other bastards and I hope that they'll fucking win, too."

We drank pint after pint and then Neil gave us some shots. We were both drunk., I was completely smashed. When Neil wasn't looking I took a little bit more of that special liquor. I couldn't help myself. I sat on a chair, holding the bottle.

"Does anyone have a smoke for me?" I shouted across the bar.

An old lady gave me a smile as her tight blue spandex body sat beside me. She brought up her dirty white banana bag. I watched her open it. It seemed like her hand was forever in the bag digging for the cigarettes. She brought out her pack and knocked it open for me.

My hand, sweaty with anticipation, dug into the pack struggling for a little control of that white stick. I popped it between my lips. Her lighter came into view and I sucked hard to light up. Menthol, like sick medicine on my tongue.

"How are you feeling?" She swept away the fire to light her own cigarette which absorbed her hot pink-lipstick.

"Fantastic."

"Shelley."

She was all blurry. "What?" I shouted, sucking hard on that smoke. I felt a heavy hand rest on my shoulder.

"Ah, he's had enough." Cod swirled me around.

"He doesn't look too hot."

"Come on." I stood on my feet. "Can you walk?"

"Yeah."

I followed Cod as the pub around me swirled and people moved out of the way. Outside, the air smacked me right in the stomach. All that dark liquor I took came right out on the gravel road. I sat down for a bit hacking up the dark liquor. Then Cod came from nowhere and pulled me up. He dragged me to the car and put me in the backseat where I collapsed. I felt my pockets for the money and it was still there. The old car jerked and slid all over the gravel parking lot. I fumbled with the window to get it down so I could vomit. From there I passed out on the backseat, feeling each massive movement of Cod's wreck.

"What?" I asked as Cod shook me.

"Come on, you're home."

I felt my pockets again. "Holy fuck Cod." I tried to slap him on the back but there was nothing there. "We won. We've fucking won!"

"That's right. Now come on, you've got to look nice for Eliza." Cod was always a gentleman. He took my shirt and wiped off my chin and mouth.

"Is that better?" I gave him a grin. He was fucking great. I thought about Doris and I convulsed into laughter. "Doris is gonna love you, man. She really is."

"Tell me something I don't know."

We walked up each stair and it made my stomach feel worse. "You've got your keys?"

I went into my pockets, fighting with the numerous bills to get out my keys and Cod grabbed them out of my hand.

"The first door."

He placed the keys in and unlocked the door. I saw Eliza looking at me and then Cod. She didn't seem too happy with her arms crossed. I couldn't help myself to stop laughing. Cod dragged me further into the bedroom and placed me on the bed. I heard the front door shut and lock and Eliza came in the room and flicked on the lights. I rubbed my eyes as she stood in the doorway looking on.

"Eliza, Eli-za I couldn't believe it."

"Believe what?" She came closer and I tried to sit up and give her a hug. Instead, I grabbed her legs and hugged them. They felt so good right now. I stared at her ass as my lips kissed her thighs. I loved her so much.

"Believe what?"

I squinted at her. "I came this close." I wanted to show her, so I used my fingers so she would understand. I told her again so she'd understand the example my fingers were giving her.

"This close for what?"

I felt the dampness on my shirt and the liquor-vomit resting at the back of my throat. "God, I'm fucking sick and where's Cod?"

"He left. He went home."

"Oh." I stopped staring at her because it was hurting my eyes too much. "Oh, Eliza, baby I just need to sleep." I pulled at her jeans to bring her down. I wanted to kiss her. "Eliza, let me kiss you?" I fell back down on the bed and the lights went off and I rested there as she undressed me. The bed felt so fucking great. I moved my head on the pillow trying to find the most comfortable point. I would tell her everything in the morning. It would be great.

Back On

I was sick of it.

Nailing people's goods through and packing them. The job gave me that kick that I needed to find myself and get hold of that dying aspiration to dance again.

I was ringing through crackers and pâté. I looked up to take the cash being handed to me and I saw Mrs. Lynn.

"Mrs. Lynn?" I asked.

"Yes, do I know you?" She spotted my name tag and her lips formed a smile of recognition.

"Eliza, oh my God. How have you been?"

"Good an you?"

"Good. I heard that you were in a dance company?"

"I was but I came back an I've been doing this since. I had to take a break from it."

"Are you through with dancing?"

"No, no I'm getting sick of this. I just needed something to make money. Are you still teaching?"

"No, I gave that up recently so now the theatre is looking for a teacher."

And it clicked like it was given on some sort of silver platter that this was an opportunity. Opportunity spelling each letter in the air above her dyed hair.

"Do you mind if I ask you something?"

"What?"

"Do you think that I could take your place? That's if the position hasn't been filled."

"I think that would be absolutely fine. I mean you were in a company and it's a community theatre. I'll tell them. When can you bring a resumé by?"

"Tomorrow?"

"Good, what about at noon?"

"Fine!"

"I'll talk to you then because I have to go, but the job has no applicants so far and I think you would be the best for them. For a second, I thought you had given up on ballet. It rather scared me, Eliza."

"No, don't ever worry about that. It's in the blood, you know."

"Yes, I do. I'll see you at noon!"

It all unfolded there for me then. The whole landscape of life just opened up and took me back in. I was worthy of another chance, but a different chance in life. Teacher. I loved the idea of it all as my brain answered all the trivial questions of an interview. I answered them even though I had to stop to inform the total to the paying customers. I sounded pretty smart in my mind's eye.

At the end of the day I left my job.

Matthew

I went down to the St. Maurice theatre taking the keys that they gave me. I entered the studio where the barre and the wall of mirrors surrounded me. I dumped my duffel bag on the floor, turned on the small little stereo and stretched.

I hadn't watched myself in a full set of mirrors in a long time. I could tell where my body's pain stopped fighting and became relaxed till I started to stretch it out to the right painful position.

Matthew came in with his eyes dancing around the mirrors. "This is great. You own your own studio."

"Fabulous."

We stretched together.

"God, I look horrible."

"I know." I told him smiling as he glared at me.

"Well, you're not as firm as you used to be." He stuck out his tongue.

"You're telling me that!" I stretched my leg and extended my body upon it. "Oh, that feels good."

"Where's Chris?"

I raised my head and answered Matthew through the mirror. "He's with Kel an both of them are getting a party ready. Do you want to come?"

"I've met the duo."

"What, are you jealous?"

"No, I'll bring Charlie. She's really—"

"Are you in love with her, is that what you are getting at?"

"I don't know—"

"Ah, that's love!"

"You know we live together and we're going to London. What amazes me more over my little relationship is that you don't want to come. Instead, you want to perform in front of these mirrors and for children. Where's the fame, Eliza?"

"I wanted something else, that's all. An if I want to return to the stage, I will. I'm not afraid of closing off my options right now."

"You think you're a princess always going to have that red carpet out for you."

"Yeah, I do. Come on. Do you remember our ballet?"

"Yes."

We tried doing our little duet which got us into the company. Except this time we needed to work. Our bodies were too soft and our feet were sloppy. Instead of finishing our ballet I spun circles around Matthew.

"Princess!"

I stopped in the centre of spinning which wasn't good because it left me wobbly. All the mirrors reflected about ten Elizas and Matthews.

I gently fell to the floor and I watched Matthew who was still dancing.

"Are you sure you don't want to come to London with me?"

"I'm dizzy."

"Stop playing it. Before you got dizzy you were going at it beautifully."

"I told you before, I don't want to." I was getting irritated with him chasing me with the idea.

"You prefer to teach ballet at this little community theatre?"

"Right now I do, an maybe after I'll return but for now I'm here. Not like I'm wasting away."

SS

Chris came home dragged in by one of his friends. I could have sworn he was my father's twin but a bit younger and with a fatter rounder belly. Chris was laughing loudly as Cod put him on the bed.

"Eliza, he got a bit drunk."

"I can see that, Cod."

"He just needs to rest now. I wouldn't worry myself over him."

"Thank you." I really did not want to know what happened to him. I just wanted Cod to go.

"No problem. I better get going."

"Thanks again," I said trying to smile and breathe it off as being normal. Chris coming home like this all pissed as I sit and wait. This was normal. Completely normal. Cod left and I stared at Chris who turned over smiling at me. The upper part of his shirt was damp.

"Eliza, Eliza, I just couldn't believe it."

"Believe what?" He kissed my legs.

"I came this close." He indicated the closeness with his fingers. "This close."

"This close for what?"

"God, I'm fucking sick. Where's Cod?"

"He went home."

"Oh. I just need to sleep. Eliza, let me kiss you?" I came towards him smelling in that thick drunken breath. I quickly avoided his lips and I left him to his needed sleep.

Later, I went back to see him sleeping in his clothes and slobbering over his shirt. I undressed him as he lay there still and warm, once in a while chopping his lips together as if to pick up the saliva.

The next morning, I woke to him throwing up and hearing him bang into the shower stall. I got up and made coffee as he came in grabbing his head. Nothing was said, he was too busy cradling his head. He took a glass of water with him.

"Do you want anything?" I yelled after him.

"No." His voice was small and pained.

I enjoyed hearing his pain. He came back and sat down, squeezing his temples.

"How are you feeling?" I sat there observing his red eyes.

"Alright."

"I saw Cod last night."

"He brought me home, right?"

"Yeah."

"I was pretty smashed last night because I came up a winner."

"Oh." Oh was all I could say. I just preferred to ignore him. And then it clicked—he won fucking money. "Wait, Chris, you gambled?"

"Just a bit and I won back double. Not really much but I didn't lose."

"Why, do you usually gamble?" I shouldn't have asked because I knew he'd lie.

"No, I'm not a big time gambler."

"I thought you had night school?"

"I did and I needed a break."

"Oh."

"Eliza, I wouldn't have gambled if I thought I was going to lose."

"I didn't doubt it, Chris."

"You never doubt anything, do you?"

"No, I don't."

"Get off it. I know how you feel about this gambling. Look, I didn't do anything. I didn't lose and I don't do it every bloody day."

"You don't have to tell me. Remember, you're the one who came home drunk."

He sat there as I sat across looking at him, both of us catching each other's nasty stares. It came back to reality, this was our first little fight. I laughed.

"What are you laughing about?"

"You know, Chris, this is our first fight."

"First fight?" His red eyes opened wide.

"You still want to go at it, don't you?"

"I don't know. I have a headache. Plus, my head is spinning. It's been like this since last night."

"Go lie down."

He left the room as I sat there. I turned the dull pages of the newspaper. It was weird now, I sat there knowing that he gambled and I forgave him, not even the thought of what he did recycling into my mind. I was jolly, floating up in my chair, sipping coffee and casually with no interest flipping the newspaper page to land on the comics.

Later on that day we walked together to St. Maurice Park. His arms were around me, kissing my head as we entered the worn down forest path looking for that green shaved grass where the picnic tables loomed about.

"Eliza, did I ever tell you I love your name?"

"Yes, you did."

He pulled me in. "What would you say to making love? Since we've had our first fight. I was a little bit sore before, but now I'm ready to go, baby."

"Right now?"

He nodded his head. "Come on, like fucking animals. I'm mad about you." He whispered.

We entered the bushy forest where you could see evidence of the productive sales of sex residue scattered around and squished into the mud.

We took our clothes off and pulled down into doggy-style. I thought it suited the nature of the whole day. As soon as we fucked it all out we quickly dressed, concerned about the lurking perverts. We jumped out of the woods and into the path of a smelly jogger, huffing like he was working really hard.

"Sorry, there," the jogger said for almost running into us.

"Fucking piece of shit," Chris said under his breath.

"Tell me about last night."

"What?"

"Don't worry. Tell me, I'm curious."

"After work when I should've been heading for school, I took off with Cod. He really is swell. But anyways, we went to a local pub and started out with a couple drinks and both of us ended up betting, just a bit, cause you know I'm not a gambler."

"For some reason, I don't believe that."

"I know, that's why I said it, to stir you up, love."

"You didn't succeed, did you?"

"We won. And I met some of Cod's boys and we bought one or two rounds of beer. I forget, but it was a good night."

"I see."

"Do you really see?"

"Yeah, I do."

"Eliza, I really don't want you to worry. I really mean it, I'm not a gambler."

"I know, I know Chris." With him he always meant everything, always. "You're a hall-marker!"

"I know when you say it, you mean it as a compliment."

"Carry me," I told him as I jumped up on him. We found our way out of the path and into the main section as I searched for Amanda's family barbecue. I spotted Kel and Amanda both talking under the shade of a tree. Although meant for romance, it didn't look that way.

I tapped Chris on the head. "They're over there."

"Kel!" He didn't respond. "Brother!" He screamed it out. Kel finally looked up.

"Chris!" he screamed back.

Chris ran with me on his back almost dropping me a couple of times.

"Hi, Eliza!" She came over all excited giving me a hug. "We're just taking a break right now. My little cousins are running amok and you want to know why?"

"Why?"

"Because my family left Kel in charge."

"They left me in charge because you were off with your aunts and I know they were testing me to see what type of father I'd be."

"Where did you get that beer from?" Chris asked eyeing it out.

"Amanda, can you get them some beer?"

She left.

"This is Amanda's annual family picnic. You name it they

have it! Pork sausages, beef sausages, chips and potatoes."

"Every year Kel attends this function."

"Yeah, and this is the first time you've been!"

"Well, I have Eliza with me if any of Amanda's family want to talk they can go through her."

"Ah, that was thoughtful!"

"Yeah, I pretty much try to be."

"Since I've become the bouncer for Chris, I guess we'll be enjoying the picnic from out here."

"I spend most of my time out here, so does Amanda. Her family is full of small children. It really is fucking unreal. Ah, here is my love." Kel took the two drinks from Amanda and handed them to us.

"What are you talking about?"

"The family picnic."

"You know, I really enjoyed it when I was a small girl, but it's completely crazy. Did you tell them about the older relatives?"

"No."

"Well, most of them sit on the bench staring at the children. They sit there and talk, yelling once in a while at the kids to shut up. But they talk about the gossip in the family. What was funny today—"

"Yeah, you found it funny."

"It was funny. When me and Kel arrived, my family, they're all talking to my mum asking her when I'm going to marry Kel. That was a blast because when we walked in they looked up. All silent. And the men relatives, except my dad, were looking at Kel for some sort of tribute to their chatter. Instead, he just gives a nice wave hello. It was absolutely brilliant."

"I wasn't about to ask you for your hand right there and then."

"If you did, I would've said no."

"That's why I love you!"

"Sure it is, Kel! Are you hungry?"

"Yeah."
"What do you want?"
"Surprise us!"
"Come on, Kel!"
They went towards the picnic.
"They are really made for each other!"
"Yeah I know. When he's sober he's someone else completely. Understanding, loveable, kind and gentle!"
"That's right, an what about you?"
"Acidic!"
"Loveable!"
"Am I?" He asked innocently.

Mr. Jamison

We were waiting at a nice little dining table in Wolston with Chris wearing his suit which he saved for special occasions with his parents. We both sat there silently touching the silverware waiting for his father.

"There he is!"

Chris's father was a tall and well built man. He still had hair which he gelled to one side. Behind his father came a woman. Her short frosted blond hair framed her cheery red suit which complimented her bright red smile. The image of her stuck in my mind: the red suit, perky short hair and the award winning smile.

"Those are plugs," Chris whispered to me.
"Hi, Dad."
"Hi, Chris. How are you?"
"Good, and you?"
"Fantastic."
"Hi, Chris," said the woman poking her head through.
"Cheryl. How are you?"
"Good."

Good was definitely good to say.

"Dad and Cheryl, this is Eliza."

"Hi," we all said smiling and shaking hands. After the greeting, we all sat down and looked at the menus. Chris sat at the edge of his seat as he pulled at his black tie. I put my hand on his thigh. I adored this little boy who wanted to be anyplace but here.

"How is night school coming?"

"Good, no complaints, Dad." He grinned.

"Eliza, Chris was saying you're a ballet dancer and that you teach ballet?"

Here came the resumé talk: "Yes, I'm teaching ballet up at St. Maurice Theatre. I used to be in a dance company before moving back to Wolston. Travelled the world for a bit. I might go back but for now I like teaching the little children."

"Interesting. I understand that you are living together?"

"Yes," Chris replied as he played with his tie, gulped his wine and stared at his father.

We ordered after that.

"I own Brown Real Estate," said Cheryl. "You might have seen our red signs posted here and there. When I was younger..."

The resumé talk went on and it clicked that I'd seen her in the ads. I watched Chris sipping his wine as his father observed him attentively to make sure that he was behaving.

"Chris, what is going on with the workers?"

"What do you mean by that?" The wine was settling in because now he was smirking from the corner of his mouth as he talked.

"How are they working? Any reports, in other words?"

"Na. None really. They're doing just fine. Cod helped me a lot in learning that whole department."

"He should know because he's been there for a while now. He still has two children and his wife is still Doris?"

"We have reached the testing hour, eh Dad?" The whole table fell silent. I was ready to burst because the tension was high on everything that was Chris. He sat there soaking it up as he guzzled the wine. "Beautiful, eh!" He winked at me.

"What about Cod?" asked his dad chewing hard on the steak. Cheryl chewed on her food like their discussion was not even going on.

"Cod has one more child, and his wife is still Doris. She really is a lovely bitch! Loves to holler, that one!"

"Chris!"

"But she does, just ask Cod. He talks about her all the time!"

"Tell me, Eliza, how can you live with that?"

All eyes were on me now. I swallowed the piece of meat in my mouth which humbly went down followed by that hard to bite laughter.

"Usually, he's more agreeable!"

"Hear that, dad, I'm usually more agreeable. So proper and with such elegance my dear Eliza delivers the truth."

I didn't know what to say. I was on the spot.

"I think that's enough out of you, Chris!" he said dryly as he wiped his lips with the cloth napkin.

"Too bad it wasn't that easy!" He tugged at his tie again. He examined Cheryl who was sipping, no, drinking down her wine. Her blue eyes caught Chris's blue eyes. "Sorry Cheryl, that you had to see this! Dad doesn't mean what he does. He is a genuine man."

"That he is." She smiled, adoring Chris's father who tried to put a grin on his face. "Let us make a toast to Chris's father, Charles Jamison, for being a genuine man."

We all raised our glasses.

"Cheers!" she said.

"Cheers!" Everyone followed, making Cheryl happy while Chris's dad placed on a trying grin.

The excitement ended as we drank down the wine.

"So, what are you two doing tonight?" asked Mr. Jamison as he tucked his credit card in his wallet.

"We're going up to my old place because Kel is having a

party."

We all got up and Chris put his arm around me.

"Thank you, Mr. Jamison."

"You're welcome, Eliza, and I want to thank you in advance for taking my son. I don't see how you did it."

"Real funny, Dad."

"Good night!"

We left the place entering the dark atmosphere of the night. Chris lit two cigarettes and placed his arm around me as we walked up to the train back to St. Maurice Bay.

"What do you think of my dad?"

"He's nice."

"Yeah, and Cheryl, she literally is a poster girl."

"How long have they been going out for?"

"About a month now. They met at some sort of conference. I can't stand how she laughs at everything, and my father just sits there across from me ready to kill me. I love that part of it. I don't see how he can stand her. Laughing and doing that toast."

"He doesn't seem to mind."

"Because the old man doesn't want to be alone."

Kel's place was booming with music and people shouting and laughing. Chris took off his tie, jacket and shirt and wore his little white t-shirt. He went directly to the fridge and grabbed the beers as I threw my jacket with Chris's stuff in the closet. Everyone was jumping all around, dancing hard to the house music which was booming past the limit. Drew came up to me.

"Hey baby, come on and push that groove thing," he said taking my hand and dancing with me. He noticed Chris getting two beers. "Yo, Chris, give me one!"

Roses

When I got home, the quiet darkness greeted me. I flicked on the lights room by room and hunted for surprise attackers. I poked my head into the bedroom and saw the bed sheets scattered around the bed as if he had fought them to get out of bed. The kitchen was bare. First, I turned the stereo on and from there, with no dangers lurking about, I went into the washroom and took a shower.

Chris was at school by now or if he didn't come home before midnight he had skipped his classes and went with Cod, his new-found soul mate. I was Chris's soul mate on the weekends.

I relaxed on the couch and waited to hear the door unlock as the news flashed by the hour.

The door clicked into the unlocked position and I heard Chris step through, slamming and locking the door. He came in carrying red roses.

"Who are those for?" I happily asked.

"For you!" he said grinning away.

"What for?" I replied, holding them cautiously and smelling the faint, faint fragrance of cut stems soaked in water.

"Because." He held me in his arms and kissed me. "Because I love you."

"Don't give me that!" He took the roses and put them on the table. "What are you doing?"

"Come with me." He put me over his shoulder and carried me to the bedroom where he plopped me on the bed.

"Now," he said unbuttoning his shirt. "Those roses are to tell you that I won big this time."

"How much?" I took him up on the game and watched his eyes jut out further from their sockets. "How much?" He fluttered his eyelashes at me.

"Close your eyes."

I shut them and smiled up at him. "Now, tell me how much."

He put his soft rough hand over my closed eyes. "Keep them closed." He waited for a moment. "Listen to this."

I heard the endless flipping of bills whisking against my ear. I pleasantly opened my eyes to Chris's winnings.

"It's beautiful, isn't it?" He took off his shirt, t-shirt and undid his jeans. "It was all because of Silver. At the beginning all the others were right behind biting his ass, and I take a sip of my ale and look up thinking that I lost. Crying there in my own self pity over the loss—" Chris feasted his storytelling eyes on me. "So, there I am sniffling over my little loss and Cod starts nudging me and telling me to look up and soon it changes into, 'Fucking Christ Silver!' He shouts. Wooooo! It was fucking unbelievable. It was a piece of God's great work. Silver made the leap of faith. And here is my winnings love." He slid off his jeans and stood there in his white boxers holding the thick set of bills. "Eliza, I did this all for you! Wooooo!" He tossed the money.

I pulled him on top of me. The money fluttered all around us. "Do you want to show me how it is to be a winner?" I asked as I kissed his neck.

He struggled at tearing off my clothes. I ripped off his boxers which tore easily but the elastic part snapped back and unfortunately it happened to be the area of Chris's enjoyment.

"You're okay?" I asked all mother-like. The laughter rose as the elastic part hung there along with his penis. The hidden pain of his expression was completely hilarious.

"Yeah. They were just new ones, that's all." He shrugged it off as he stepped out of the elastic band.

"Good to know."

He grabbed me from behind patting me on my ass. "Tonight, you'll be my little French poodle." He hit me hard to make me tremble underneath his hand.

"An what are you?"

"A fat bulldog," he replied pinching my nipple as the other hand found its way into my creamy clitoris. I leaned back as he gave me a good dog's fuck.

"Ruff, ruff!" I pounced around with my tongue huffing out.

He howled, chasing me on all fours on the bed until we slammed into each other. Chris fell off the bed.

"What are you doing down there?" I asked turning my head

in a questionable way.

"My bitch pushed me." He jumped back up and tackled me down.

My moans were as high as his were low and deep and grunting underneath it all. I leaned back, tearing at his hair as we ended in a sweaty splat.

Both of us lay there on the flattened, crumpled, rosy-blue-green paper money.

I stared at the bright ceiling thinking of the amount of money that came spraying down and feeling the sweating money glued to my skin. I didn't know what to think. I lay there listening to him move from his heavy breathing into a thick snore.

I got up and placed the roses in a vase. The roses, stiff and closed and crowded, stood there in the soaking water, and I couldn't look away, I couldn't help feeling like Chris's lucky charm.

I smiled as I heard Chris collecting his money. I crawled on the bed, passing him a couple of bills that were under the sheets.

After he put the money away and came to bed, he clapped off the lights which happened to be one of his new items.

Days
Days became normal days where he asked me for money. I didn't think much of it because it was normal—we shared everything, it became part of the custom of being a couple living together. And it was love. We became a huge number one. Chris meant Eliza and Eliza meant Chris.

I heard keys drop on the tiled floor from outside. I opened the door and Cod was there holding up a beaten-up version of Chris. Right away, my mother's skills took over. I helped Cod pull him in. Chris kept spitting up blood.

"Chris, you're home now." Cod told him to make him stop spitting carelessly.

Chris squinted up. His eyes were black and puffy. He tried to smile but it made his lip bleed. His finger held his bleeding lip.

Instead, he said my name underneath the build-up of saliva that was mixed with blood. He swallowed hard after that trying to hold down whatever seemed to be coming up when he coughed into his hand or shirt.

Me and Cod dragged him onto the bed. He lay there in pain not moving but wanting to move as he jerked his head around.

"Eliza, love, it was fucking unreal, tell her Cod." I got a face cloth and put it on his lips and his rough-skinned hand took over.

"Stop talking."

"I don't think she wants to know." Cod peeked at me with his bruised cheek. "Do you?" he asked realizing I might be different from his wife.

"I just don't want him to talk because he's fucking bleeding all over the place."

"What else can't I do?"

I ignored Chris and left the room to get the nursing kit.

"Shut up," I heard Cod whisper to Chris. "Are you getting ice?"

"Yeah, I'll get everything."

I returned and Cod helped put Chris together. I washed the dry blood and placed the ice over the bruises that were forming into bumps.

"What happened?" I asked placing an ice pack over Chris's eye.

Cod's eyes flashed up followed by Chris's other eye watching to see if my face was as calm as my voice.

"We were at the pub an I placed a couple of bets in. These pricks came in an basically it started from there. First, there was a lot of shouting an then it happened. A fight broke out. Me an Chris made it out pretty well, mind you, it looks a lot worse than it is."

Cod observed me as he broke out a grin. A lifetime of lies and he hadn't stopped yet. I looked down at Chris.

"Are you feeling better?" I stroked his head.

"A bit," he mumbled.

I loved him all bruised up. I was lost in his blown out of position face. One eye scanned around and he closed his lips wanting to rest underneath all the bruises and the puffiness.

"I should get going," said Cod. I was about to get up. Instead, I sat there staring at the fat bastard. It was like watching a mini-series of my father playing out through Cod. I swear, there must've been a book of sayings for bastards. They always had the same advice: Smile, be relatively well mannered with Hellos, Goodbyes, Thank yous and once in a while say please but not too much otherwise you might be considered a fag. The dos and don'ts of being a fat bastard. I got up and followed him out the bedroom.

He turned around in the hallway. "Should I let myself out?"

"Yeah, if you don't mind."

"Take care."

Cod left. I waited to hear the door slam and returned my attention to Chris who was trying to stand up.

"Can you help me?" He tried swallowing his thick saliva that wouldn't give any air of release.

"What are you doing?"

"I want to get up."

"What for?"

"To undress." He stuck his hands in his pockets. "Look at that, they fucking robbed me, fucking pricks." He almost spun over.

I took off his clothes that were drenched in blood and beer. He lay there stiff on the bed in his boxer shorts. I pulled the sheet over him as he rested there with one eye closed and the other soaking under the dripping ice. I turned off the light and went into the kitchen and sat down thinking about the fight. The fight that was over nothing and left Chris beaten and Cod with one bruise on his cheek.

By the time I went to bed, Chris's body was sprawled out over the bed. I shoved him aside and he groaned a bit thinking that I was trying to steal his sheet, which he tugged absent-mindedly under his arm.

In the late afternoon, he dragged himself in with a grunt.

"You look better." He wasn't as bloody and ghoul-like as last night.

"I fucking hurt. I took such a beating last night. Did Cod tell you anything about last night?" His one black eye and one blue eye tried to read my response of good or bad.

"Not really."

His eyes lit up because he had an adventure to tell me.

"Cod placed his bet and this time he lost and it wasn't a big deal or anything. I was ready to go. Cod wanted to watch the next races and of course, the horse that he bet on came first. And these assholes came in all obnoxious, and me and Cod were getting ready to go. And Cod looks over at the loud group and says, 'Keep it down.' And then they start talking back and from there a tiny fight breaks out."

"I don't believe you."

"What?"

"I don't believe you, I think—" I said flipping through the classifieds.

"Oh right. You tell me what went on that night. Why I got all fucked up by jocks? What could it possibly be, Eliza?" He glared at me waiting for an answer so he could back all the other shit he was already thinking about.

"I don't know. You want to tell me?" I said.

"Playing a sweet little school girl. Is that what you're doing? So you're going to be wrapping your little legs around my neck asking or rather begging me to tell, to tell you the fucking truth you want to hear. Which is, yes, I lost a fair amount at gambling, basically, I lost all my money that night. I didn't even have enough for a beer, smokes or a train. After that I decided to get in a fight so you could feel sorry for me. That was my whole plan. I wanted to lose the fight too so I could look as good as I do now."

"That was my money you lost?"

"Fucking right, well what do you want now, Eliza?"

"I don't want anything from you."

"You don't want the truth anymore?"

"I do if you're going to tell me."

He got up. "You want to know what fucking happened. I was sitting, I lost all my, I mean your money and that money I really borrowed was to pay them back for what I already lost. And they beat me up fairly good. Is that better, Eliza? And you know, I still owe them money."

I sat there as he went back to bed. I had heard all this before, "bad bets broken necks," my mother would tell her friends about my father's normal troubles. She'd give it a nice melody.

I left to go to the theatre but I really wanted to be gone.

I came back at night and followed his laughter to the living room. I wanted to make him cry. I simply smiled at the thought of it as he tried hard to smile back in that cocky way of his. It didn't last long because it made his lip bleed. His finger held in the blood.

"Nice weather out there?" he asked, his eyes bruised and wide.

"Feeling better?"

He laughed loudly at the TV and glimpsed at me.

"I'm still a bit sore. I haven't been this beaten before. I thought you should know, Doctor Mum. And you should know that they were trying to kill me, about three of them were doing me in at the same time. It was fucking incredible. I mean, here's me and Cod right? And six jocks and I'm singled out and two others gang up on me. Both of them holding me up and pounding the shit out of me. The other bastards watched the scene and finally decided to break it up. It was fucking unreal."

I came over obediently, leaving behind me the closed door, closed and locked. I came over to him and kissed his cut lips as I put my arms around him. Holding him.

Together we laughed at the comedy.

Conveniently

Conveniently, St. Maurice Theatre closed down to renovate, so I was out of a job. My pocket money kept disappearing and the roses when he won piled up stale and dead on the windowsill.

Conveniently, I was searching for something, I forget what, but I found Matthew's little postcards instead. Neither of us being good writers ever wrote much. I read the first postcard. I noticed the address and he begged me to come, guaranteeing me a part in the ballet. The next postcard, the company named, 'Exposure' had their opening performance. He wanted me to come out and be a part of Exposure. This time he left a phone number and his new address. And it closed off, *I hope I will be seeing you! Lots of Love Matthew—Waiting!*

The third card was after the opening show, and it said plainly in quick handwriting: *make a visit out of it, Eliza.*

I took all three postcards, folded them, and placed them inside my coat.

All of a sudden, out of great convenience, I took out a small suitcase because that was all I needed. And I packed. I avoided looking at Chris's things. I wasn't going to give my misdirected feelings the pleasure of breaking down into a flow of tears, or throw my sappy face onto a pillow because all that love I felt, the warm-tingling feeling—the pleasure I got when he was happy—it wasn't anything supernatural I debated in my head. I replaced it with the times of Matthew and sometimes Ashley where I felt the repeatable moments of warm tingles. It wasn't anything new or special. And with those thoughts I zipped up my suitcase and put it beside the door. I went back to the kitchen and wondered if I should leave a note. A note with all the words I couldn't form. I tore a piece of newspaper and got a pen. I stood there terrified that I had heard the click of him coming through the door but I knew he was still at work. I didn't want him to see me leaving, or better yet, stop me.

I wrote in big letters: *Chris, love, dear fucking soul mate, I left. XOXO!*

I had to be mean. I clapped the lights off. I opened the door and I scanned to see if Chris had come home sooner than he should have. I shut the door, locking it and left.

I took the train down to my mum's home. She opened the door and once again I was pulled into a hug. But she noticed, holding me tightly, that only one hand was responding and she pulled away holding my shoulders in her hands. Her eyes went heavy upon the suitcase and they turned up at me with questions: She was leaving and where to? Or was she moving back in?

She stepped aside, letting me in.

"Are you moving back?" she asked, smiling with hope.

"No, I'm going to London. I came here to say goodbye."

"When are you going to be back?"

"I don't know right now."

She sat down on the couch as I followed.

"I'm making some tea, do you want some?"

At first I was going to say no but my lips answered, "Yes." She went to the kitchen.

"Is Paul still at work?"

"Yeah. Are you going to be performing up there in London?"

"I think so. I'm going back again. I have no choice. The Theatre is closing down to renovate. I'll be meeting up with Matthew. We danced together at school and in the company."

"Oh." She entered with two teas. "What about Chris? Is he going with you?"

"No, he's staying at my old place. I decided to go because it was performing or going back to the grocer."

"It just makes sense. Maybe we'll come up an see you perform when Paul gets time off."

"That would be great. So, what's new?"

"Nothing much. That's the thing, nothing really changes. The kitchen is still the same. Too many decisions even though it is just one decision. Even the gossip in Saber is pretty dull. Oh wait, Frankie's parents are actually moving to Bury."

"Frankie, my old friend?"

"Yeah, she married Carl but that didn't work. During the divorce she was supposedly seeing her next gentleman that was paying her way. An that is why her parents are moving to Bury. I was amazed myself. I knew the marriage wasn't working out because she had a separate place an she was working an she still is working in the centre of the Wolston business area. I forget the business she's working for. But her new husband works there. Always a happy ending in Saber."

"Did you ever talk to her?"

"No, not even her parents. Me an your father weren't that close with them. Living up in Bury, I can't believe it."

"Why did she marry Carl?"

"I don't know."

"Where's he?"

"He's still around. To tell you the truth, Eliza, I can't believe you're going again."

"You thought that this was the last stage for me?"

"No, it just seems too soon." She gave me a hug and it felt good to fall into her arms.

"I'll miss you too, Mum." It was the first time I felt it.

Closed in each other's arms, we let go and I wrote down where I was staying followed by my number.

I left on the train heading out to the ferry. There I was again sitting on a different plastic seat and I thought about Chris coming home and seeing the note. Imagining what he would do: Maybe break down but that would be too flattering of a thought. More than likely he'd toss it out.

I didn't know and I left it at that as I sat there watching the darkness lapse into the lights of the docks.

Landed again. I was travelling back into something different. I took the train into London and sat in the back with books. One was a trashy romance and the other was a horror to keep me awake. I hadn't opened either one yet.

I stared outside at the passing green fields until my eyes were dry for sleep.

The dreams I had were of familiar faces passing by at a quick speed. And it turned into a performance where everything was going as normal until for some reason I was backstage watching them and crying. The crying took a turn into Chris's orgasmic fingertips as the audience did an applause of masturbation.

In London, I walked because I was sick of sitting. I walked through the streets searching for Matthew's address.

Finally with sore feet and exhausted eyes, I found it. I pressed the bell. No answer. I pressed it again. Matthew appeared in his pyjamas. He was wiping his tired eyes. He stopped when he noticed me through the intricate white gated door. He opened the door.

"Eliza?" A question followed by an immediate answer of a hug.

"Hi, Matthew."

"I can't believe you're here and this early." Matthew held the door open as I came in. I followed him upstairs to the next door. "You took the ferry?"

"Yeah."

"Okay, you can sleep in the extra bedroom because I have a slight situation in my bed."

"Oh, you thought you had to put out right away."

"Well."

"Shut up."

He showed me to the guest room and leaned against the door, scratching his head.

"We'll talk later?"

"Yeah. Thanks, Matthew."

He gave me a hug and a kiss.

I sat on the bed sinking my head onto the pillow. Feeling awkward here, again. Lying in a new bed, in a new home. At one toss of the bed, I faced the window with white blinds, some of them bent at the ends. Thinking of my deserted bed. I turned around to the dark wall where nothing resembled it at all. I fell asleep, only to find myself facing the bent blinds with the sun creaking in and crossing over my face.

Winnings

My winnings came to me nice and full. Eliza was happy with it. It was well earned money and school definitely paid off with the lectures on statistics. But in all great winnings, one night can take it all away.

Me and Cod were sitting there discussing who to place our final bet on. At that particular deciding moment we were already down.

The front doors of the pub opened to reveal Brian and Carl. They came over eagerly seeing the loss in our faces.

"How's it going?"

"What do you think?" I asked him. I was sick of this fucking wide cunt.

"I think you boys need a little help. Now tell me, what do you think about that?"

"We'll take it, Brian."

"That's my boy, Cod, an Chrissy here. What will it be?"

We placed the bets down. All my money passed through and I couldn't have had a better feeling, positively knowing that I was going to make the money back. After they gathered the money, they walked back to their table and we watched the monitors sipping ceremoniously at our pints.

Good trust-worthy Coal already broke through the pack. I sucked on my smoke long and hard yelling under my breath: "Come on, come on." Out of nowhere two other horses were gaining on Coal. They were keeping it tight. As it got closer to the finishing line, Coal died down. Completely died away. The whole race seemed to be staged.

We sat there seeing the money go straight down the shithole. I could already feel Brian laughing at me. Cod didn't bet as much as me this time. I finished my beer and Cod went up getting two more.

"That's got to hurt now." Carl observed me with a grin.

"Not for you," I told him.

"I guess not."

Cod came back and handed me my pint. I chugged it down trying to ignore the cunt's ugly face examining my every move.

"So, Chrissy boy, you owe a whole lot."

"Thank you, right, I know that. And I know too to give it to you next week or is there any other surprises?"

"You're a little smart, aren't you? I do you a favour, an you get all pissy about it. Where's that old Chris, the one that was scared of gangsters like us?"

That drew the line for me. Each sip Cod took kept reminding me to remain calm. His blood shot eyes pleading with me.

"Remember, next paycheque, unless little Chrissy boy wants to talk about it some more." He bent his head close to mine breathing hard as he normally did. I couldn't help it, I punched him in the jaw and he swaggered a bit. Then Carl, his business associate, tried to seize me as I fought to push him away.

"Hey, hey!" Neil shouted as Carl pinned my arms behind me and Brian was feeling his jaw. "Take it out!"

"Look, boys!" Cod was shouting. "He didn't mean a thing."

"Oh, look your mummy is crying for you." He pulled my hair so my face was right up against his face.

I spat on him and he backed away as if I punched him in the eye. "Fucking fairy, I'm—" He took an opportunity to smack me hard as Carl was struggling with me to get me out. My face was warm with his hit and the beer in me kept me above. "Is that the best you can do, you fucking fairy!" He fucking squared me with the boot and I went down. God, that fucking hurt, the fucking pussy went for the cheap shot. "Fuck, fuck."

Now Carl had no problem taking me outside and he pinned my arms even further back trying to straighten me out for Brian.

"Now tell me, what the fuck was that about?" Brian screamed and spat out each word.

"I love you, you dumb pussy," I told him under my laughter and he pounded me.

My one eye throbbed and I could feel blood dripping from my lip as my eye blinked at him for the next move.

I saw Cod in the distance smoking as he glanced around to see if anyone was coming and I knew he couldn't do a thing. We owed them money.

"I'll give you a little free advice. In gambling, you can't be a poor loser. An Chrissy, that is what you are. You're a fucking little squirmy pussy." He punched me in the stomach causing me to slouch. "A fucking poor loser." He punched me in the other side of my stomach and then he pounded my head. All I could think about was the money I had lost. It was ten paycheques worth.

Carl released me and I fell to the ground, which didn't do me any good.

Brian kneeled down. "You want to be friends now?" he asked as he searched my pockets and took my smokes and the rest of my money. "Cheers." Both of them gave me one last good boot.

Cod came over and helped me up. I wiped the blood from my broken lip with my shirt and I walked myself to Cod's car, every step emphasizing the bruises. We got into the car. The car roughly jolted on the gravel which vibrated through my body and continued to gnaw at my head.

"You need help?" Cod asked as he parked the car.

"Na." I shook my head. I pushed the door open. Out of nowhere, it started dumping rain. I stuck out my legs and my feet landed in an ankle deep puddle. I shoved myself up. I slammed the door because that was the only way it would shut which caused me to fall in the puddle. "Fuck." More blood squirted from my lip.

Cod helped me up each step and I painfully vomited and started spitting because the blood was coming on thick. Cod knocked on the door.

"Chris, Chris you're home." Cod tried to remind me so that I would stop spitting all over the place.

There was Eliza. I tried to give her a grin and another gush of blood dripped onto my shirt. I held my lip. "Eliza." I coughed it up as I raised my shirt to catch the thick substance from the back of my throat. I stared at Eliza and tried to come forward to show her I was a bit better but that didn't help too much. Both Eliza and Cod caught me.

They dragged me awkwardly onto the bed. I moved my head around and I found both of them partially in the hallway with the light behind them. They seemed like two angels watching over me. I smiled feeling the blood dripping and I caught Eliza's glistening eyes.

"Eliza, it was fucking unreal. I mean—" She left and returned with a face cloth. "Eliza—"

"Shut up." She dabbed at my lip.

Cod came closer into view. "I don't think she wants to know." Eliza glanced back at Cod. "Do you?"

"I don't want him to talk because he's fucking bleeding all over the fucking bloody place."

"What else don't you want me to do, Eliza?"

She left and I wasn't too sure if she would return.

"You shut up or you'll be on the street." His voice turned from his wise whispers to his shout. "Are you getting ice?"

"Yeah, yeah I'll get everything."

Eliza came back with a small bucket of ice and the first aid kit. They both sat on the bed fussing over me. The bruises stung with perfect accuracy. My one eye burned under the ice pack.

"What happened?" I watched Cod who glanced down at me and back at Eliza.

And Cod's story began:

"We were at the pub an I placed a couple of bets. These pricks came in an basically it started from there. First, there was a lot of shouting an then it happened. A fight broke out. Me an Chris made it out pretty well. Mind you, it looks a lot worse than it is. Eliza, I was amazed they even could after I pounded the shit out of them. Pardon my French. But nothing happened out of the usual. A little fight, that's all." He looked thoughtfully at her and down at me.

Old Cod came through. Eliza peered at me gently with all her care as she ran her fingers through my hair.

"Are you feeling better?"

"A bit," I muttered trying not to disturb the cut's crust. I shut my eyes and relaxed under Eliza's massaging fingers. I fell asleep until I heard the door bang and I opened my eyes feeling the cool dampness of my shirt. "Can you help me?"

"What are you doing?"

"I want to get up."

"What for?"

"Undress." I sat up and tried to plunge my hands in my pockets and they couldn't fit and I tried to stand. I stood there digging my hands into my pockets checking for money and there was nothing. I noticed Eliza who was spotting me to see if I'd fall. "Look at that, they fucking robbed me those fucking cunts." I struggled with my shirt that wouldn't let go of my chest and that's when I fell onto the bed. Eliza came over and undressed me. I could hear her throwing the clothes on the floor as I lay there in my boxers trying to relax. She carefully placed the sheet over me. All I kept thinking about was how much I loved her and from all that thinking I got hard and I could do nothing about it. She had already left the bedroom and all I could do was sleep.

That night I felt that I did it to her. That made her leave, besides me trying to get money out of her to pay off my debt. I had to tell her it was for my books or groceries. I knew she didn't believe me, especially when I came home late but I knew not to be dragged in by Cod. Some nights we'd argue about my gambling and I'd tell her, I would never gamble her off. I was better than her father. But then it just happened. Everything was going great. I was a bit smarter with my money when it came to gambling. I bet less that was all.

I came home after class on a Friday. The apartment was dark and I flicked on the lights thinking that she had gone out. I went to the kitchen, clapping on the lights and I saw the note on the counter in thick blue ink on a torn piece of newspaper. *Chris, love, dear fucking soul mate I left. XOXO!*

I stood there. I couldn't fucking believe it. She had left me. I went to the bedroom to see if she had really gone. I clapped on the lights. Most of her clothes were gone.

"That fucking bitch!" I kept mumbling as I rushed outside into the rain to search for her, even though I knew I wouldn't find her.

First, I went to St. Maurice Theatre but it was closed for renovation. I sat around under the theatre's canopy having a smoke trying to think of another place she'd be and I couldn't think of any. I would give her mum a call. I was stuck, I was broke and my girlfriend, my fucking love or fucking soul mate is how she saw me, was fucking gone. I knew it was my fault, my gambling had driven her away but I thought honestly that I was getting better. I was betting less, I kept going over it in my head. Thinking about it and getting soaked, I headed up to Kel's place. Amanda was gone for the weekend.

"Hey."

"You're fucking soaked!"

"Yeah."

"I tried calling you. Drew's coming down and it will be a boy's night. You're staying?"

"Yeah." I took out a beer.

"What's the matter with you?"

"Eliza left."

"You, she left you?"

I couldn't handle it. "No, she left to do her ballet."

"When is she coming back?"

"She's not too sure."

"Ah, that sucks."

That night I sat there drinking and puffing away and I ended up sleeping on the couch knowing between my sleep and the hours of the sun breaking through my lids that Eliza wasn't home.

I woke up, and I caught the last couple of minutes of the sun before that dark cloud declared another grey day.

From the Dead

Matthew and two other people discussed where I was going. I stood there in my black tights and tutu, ballet shoes edged out with my arms crossed. Once in a while I let go to feel the hardened hair-sprayed bun in the back of my head.

I watched them look over and back at me with shaking heads as their hands held their chins. Matthew came up to me.

"Welcome, friend," Matthew said giving me a hug like I had accomplished a lot out of this audition. "Eliza, you're in. All I have to say to you is, that if you would've been here sooner you would've got something better. I'm sorry, but we have to put you in the corps. So, are you going to stay?" He put his arm around me, edging his ear out waiting for a response like he was a big director waiting for the star to speak. To make sure everything was okay.

"Yes, Matthew, I will stay." I gave him a kiss on the cheek.

"That's my girl."

"An Matthew, dear, darling all I have to say is after this ballet, I will get to pick my part," I told him wagging my finger at him.

He playfully bit my finger. "A princess, are you?"

"More than that!" I walked away.

"Be back for two!"

I was back before two. I studied the lead Charlie perform her part as the serpent in *Mama*. She was good. The steps were simple and flowed through her body. There were no extra flourishes like in the Metro. The faint music flowed easily over her and it came to an end as she crawled into a ball followed by my group entering the stage. My group, we were the earth worms.

We waited for Matthew to come as I twirled my ankles. We followed Matthew's directions which wasn't easy because the simpler it looked the harder it was to form the body into the new form of simplicity.

At one part we all lay on the floor, squirming slightly as the violin's whining went into a strong booming. We grew into the music.

"Feel out the air!" Matthew screamed as he stretched out his arms and hands.

We followed him. Everyone's hands searched through the air in different directions. We crushed to the ground, feeling out the ground and the music turned back to the whiny violin and we pulled our bodies in.

At home, I was introduced to Charlie again and we talked about the ballet as Matthew discussed what he was trying to do and Charlie would argue at her point as a dancer. I managed to disappear into my room and from there Charlie's insanity took over eventually accusing Matthew of cheating on her, giving one ballerina more attention than the other and the door slammed.

Someone knocked on my door. I put down the romance novel I had just started. Matthew came in. "Sounds like I'm done for?"

"Yeah."

"I bought you a beer because I need one."

"Did you cheat on her?"

"No." He opened up the bottles. "Do you have any

cigarettes?"

I went under my bed and pulled out a wrapped pack. I was trying to quit because now I was performing.

"I've been trying to quit, but I mean she makes me, you know?"

"Yeah, I know, because both of you make me. So did you cheat on her?"

He took a drag. "No, let me tell you something about her. In a couple of her last relationships both men have cheated on her more than once. And she told me this because it is one of her insecurities in life. She told me this before we got serious. And I guess I got more attracted because I took it as a challenge and to tell you the truth, I love it when she gets jealous. She actually believes that I'm screwing everyone. Except for you."

"Why is that? Does she think I'm a freak or something?"

"No, because I told her, you're in a relationship. Remember Chris?"

"Slightly, yes I do," I replied grinning with the assurance of my yellow teeth.

"You're with Chris still. It's unbelievable but you know I love it too. I really think if she weren't like this I would cheat on her. Because I love her passion and what's even funnier when she'll get back I comfort her with sex or love, mind you that's what she calls it. She's all the opposites of me Eliza, and I love it. I really do, and deep down inside of me I know I can help her get past that jealous stage. Honestly, I don't know if I want too."

"Because you're fucking sick."

"Maybe I'm in love."

"What's the difference?"

"Such a romantic. Did you learn that from—" He picked up the book. "From *Fantasy of View*?"

"Yeah. I find it very knowledgeable an extremely thought provoking."

"You like Charlie?"

"Yeah, she's nice." I didn't know how to respond.

"What happened with Chris?" he asked searching me for some sort of answer.

"Nothing much." I didn't want to talk about it so I could relate it to him. Besides there was nothing happening with me and Chris. He was back in Wolston.

"When you left, did you say goodbye to him?"

"Yes, I did this time. If that's what you're getting at."

"I'm happy for you."

"I like the ballet." The door opened and Charlie entered my room.

"What are you talking about?" She entered grinning.

"About the ballet," Matthew responded not looking at her but out the window.

"It is really good," she responded and he returned to her like they had both said I forgive you. Grinning happily at both ends.

And again we discussed the ballet with her interludes of it. They left my room and I returned to my book.

"I'm sorry." She broke down outside my door.

"I'm sorry, too."

They obviously were used to these terms because both of them responded with 'I'm trying'. I was starting to think that they were twins because they had exactly the same responses to everything. I listened to them in between the words of the romance novel. They sounded like parents reasoning their side of the argument. I never heard Matthew respond so calmly. I never heard him talk like this before. That's when I left. I went outside to find a newspaper to see if I could afford my own place. The sounds of I'm sorry kisses still pecked in my mind. Their calming words.

I searched the paper, but nothing seemed reasonable except having a stranger for a roommate. I didn't need that. I headed home again. When I got there it was empty. They were gone. I sat there holding the novel, wondering out of pure curiosity if that is what me and Chris sounded like after we fought, so therapeutically enlightened and in love again. The thought dried out into the teasing seduction of the young virgin underneath the castle's stairs.

Up There

One night during the third week of their show *Mama*, Matthew pulled me aside and held onto my arms like I was about to run away.

"What?" I asked checking my bun. It crunched under my hand.

"I need you to do Charlie's part, she's sick. Can you do it?"

"Yeah. How can she be sick?"

"Don't ask now just get ready."

He pushed me back into the dressing room and I took Charlie's hanging red tutu. I was going to play the serpent. I took off the brown tutu and put the red one on. I stepped out of the dressing room into a new excitement.

"Eliza, you do know it?" Matthew's serious puffy face intensely examined my eyes making sure I wasn't lying.

"Yes, Matthew, I do. You did make me the understudy."

He dragged me into a space in the back.

"I want you to show me, scene two in act two."

I twirled and stretched upon right-now the make believe tree and carefully fell to the ground.

"Good, just stretch out more when you're climbing the tree. I want to see those hands crawling."

I showed him again, stretching each finger apart to crawl on the airy tree.

He pushed me to the side of the stage and I watched what was supposed to be my part take place on the stage. Matthew kept his hand on my back as if getting ready to push me onto the stage. The audience was a mesh of faces watching the scene unfold and it was my turn. The music changed and I went on. My mind went blank as I went into the Charlie's steps. They were much smoother as I slithered through my part and to the tree where I met my partner the blue bird. It was really Thompson one of the male dancers. He pushed me away from the hanging glittering pomegranate and I dramatically fell. I glared at the audience and then, I whipped back to the fluttering Thompson. Creeping to a stand, I reached for Thompson to hold me up as the worms tried to retain me. I let my body collapse over Thompson as he held me up. He did his little well known run off the stage. And off stage he let me down.

"Beautiful." Matthew took me aside. "How are you feeling?"

"Good, how did I do?"

"Beautiful, I really mean it. That's the best I've seen." He kissed me because everything was going good so far. From backstage, I observed the audience who seemed so small in front of me. The serpent swarming in me and waiting urgently for my turn. It was my turn again with Matthew getting ready to push me.

I performed with the disgusting sensuality and sexuality of the serpent. Killing the blue bird in the end with my love. And the bird lay there as I slithered off the stage and the worms swallowed the bird.

The curtains were drawn and the clapping began as I came out, followed by the main cast. They clapped and I bowed. Each face grinned with approval of what they'd seen. I was excited and hot under the lights. I bowed two more times to the ongoing claps.

The curtains closed, the clapping died and we left the stage. Matthew gave me a hug and a kiss.

"God, I love you Eliza." He looked at me. "I didn't tell you that there was a critic in the audience."

"That's fine." I was too happy about my performance and I didn't care what the writer wrote.

I changed out of my costume as the thought of the critic nagged at me and made my skin crawl at the possibility of my performance being reviewed.

Before I could head into the night, Matthew grabbed me. "We're going out!"

We headed to a local bar where we sat huddled in the back with special cocktails. Both of us played with the straws, swirling the ice.

"So when Charlie gets better, will she be taking her part back?"

"No and for that matter she's not going to get better."

"What, she's dying?"

"No, nothing like that. Charlie's pregnant with my kid." His eyes flushed all hot with the liquor he kept twirling around in his glass. "She was going to do the performance but she felt sick, so I took her off it. And right now she's back in Wolston."

"You two broke up?"

"No, she felt she needed room to make the right decisions and she went to Wolston yesterday."

"I don't know if you want me to congratulate you or console you."

"I don't know either. I was hoping that you'd just pick."

"Congratulations, an I'm sorry."

"Beautiful, cheers."

"Cheers."

We clicked our glasses and it hit me that Matthew had really changed; he was slightly more mature.

He kept chasing his ice around drunkenly and sipping the remaining watered-down drink. "I'm breaking with her tomorrow."

"What for?"

"Because I can't take this conservative crap, it's been killing me. I mean, I think she should have the baby. Being a father won't be that bad. But living with her and being a father would be bad."

"I thought I was losing you there."

"Maybe for a while until you realized what you missed. Let's forget this."

That night we sat there drinking and forgetting about everything as the dark atmosphere of the stylish little bar took over. Matthew blabbed on like his usual self and I fell under the table holding onto the table's centre leg.

Matthew was still going on when we left. I carried him home and gently tried pushing him onto the bed instead of falling on me. He fell on the bed, bouncing once.

"God, this feels good. Come on Eliza." He tried grabbing me and I pulled away. "I'm going to bed." He turned over with his face smashed between the pillows.

Review

Before going into work I stopped to look at the review. I found the article and raced down from the simplicity of the sets to where my name was: *"Elizabeth Fellows is a promising dancer for the future. She's the sort of dancer you never take your eye off of for a second for fear of missing some fantastic moment that will never come again. However, her acting skills are too dramatic and she seems to forget her partner David Thompson who plays the Blue Bird. Thompson is a remarkable dancer."* And it went on.

There was nothing I could do. I really didn't know what to think. Instead, I walked to the theatre thinking of good things to say about the article. I had never felt so retarded as this when I stepped in the theatre. Everyone was flipping through the paper.

Pity was in their eyes and the pity was beginning to form as I walked in. With that I raised my head and did an excellent performance of security. I went into the dressing room and changed into my costume and entered the stage and performed. After the clapping, I came out alright. I felt good and better standing there, knowing inside my head that I forgot about the audience. Even when I was bowing I didn't look at them. I focused on my used-up slippers and listened to the waves of clapping followed by the curtains crushing over.

Stardom

At the backstage entrance stood two little girls in pink dresses twirling two pink roses. They gazed up and smiled with their pink glossy lips as they pulled at their daddy and pointed to me.

They screamed, "Daddy!" as he groped them in his arms.

He watched me as he whispered in his daughters' ears. He let them down gently and they came over to me.

"This is for you." They held out the roses and bowed like they were on the stage.

"Thank you," I replied taking the two roses.

The father broke between the two smiling girls. "Hello, Miss Fellows. I'm Ted Buckley."

"Teddy daddy, Teddy daddy," both of them said.

"I thought you gave a beautiful performance and as you can see, my daughters really thought you were terrific."

"Thank you. Do they take ballet?"

"Yes they do. This is Mildred and Maxine."

They gave me another bow and shook my hand.

"Their mother used to take them to the ballet all the time and now I do it."

"Where is she tonight?" I asked twirling the roses as the girls spun around me.

"She passed away."

"I'm sorry."

"But I wanted the girls to meet you. And girls—" he gathered them in his huge arms crushing their puffy dresses, "do you think Miss Fellows is absolutely enchanting?"

"Yes, Daddy."

"I'm hungry."

He stood up and tried charmingly to say, "Ah, you really are."

"Thank you. It was nice meeting you an nice meeting you two, Mildred an Maxine."

"I was wondering if you could join us for dessert. It would be great if you had some ballet stories for the girls you could share."

He kneeled down to the girls and whispered in their ears brushing away the stiff curls.

"Please, Miss Fellows, will you come with us for dessert?" the pinkest girl asked fluttering her eyelashes.

And for some reason I stared at all three and my lips lashed out, "Yes."

He squeezed my neck, taking full advantage to bring his lips to my earlobe to whisper, "Thank you for making my girls happy." He wore a big grin as he released my neck.

I felt horrible leaving the theatre to suddenly be on the street. The pit of my stomach gave me an uncontrollable fit of the giggles. My smile, not wearing thin, only grew more and more until my teeth became my lips.

His scent made me sick. His scent lingered around everything he touched. Even the roses exuded his scent. There I was walking as if I was the madly in love mother and wife that he had lost. Next stop would be to join hands. I pulled away from them. The thought of hands, mother, wife and too many daughters left me somewhere in there.

We entered the café which was small and deserted except for two people behind the counter. The girls picked a seat.

"Me and Miss Fellows are going to order. What would you two like?" he asked with two fists on the table, leaning over to hear their answers with great consideration.

"Chocolate."

"Okay."

He put his hand on my back as we walked to the dessert tray. The two workers crowded behind the cooler waiting for us to make a choice.

"You can call me Teddy. And I wanted to tell you that besides making the girls happy, I'm very happy you came too. I find you enchanting Miss Fellows, to say the very least."

I smiled politely. "I'll have the brownie an a tea." I swallowed hard.

"Okay." He gave me his little girl smile.

"I'll be right back." I went to the back where the washrooms were. I kept on walking to the kitchen. It was small and empty, and I headed out the back door where I ran and ran past all the people who were out, people who were curious and wanting to help because I was running. I got up to the flat, unlocked the door and sank into the darkness. Matthew was out. I lay there on the floor, holding my head with salty tears stinging my dry skin. I couldn't stop. I stared at the blurry darkness around me. Nothing feeling good. I went to the washroom and stripped down. I had a hot shower with the lights low. I didn't want to see anything. I just needed the water coming down, washing away the sweat. I heard the door open. I wrapped a towel around myself and kicked my clothes into my room where I met Matthew. I smiled, feeling normal. He was so happy with the performance.

The sweat came through my pyjamas, and the sheets were knotted around my body. My eyes opened, shocked from the darkness of my room because I thought it would've been daylight.

Slight shadows formed under the darkness. The mirror across from me glommed back in different shades of black. I couldn't take my eyes off the dark shiny version of me. She was huffing and her hand wiped away the tangled strands of hair stuck to her face.

The images of my dream were still fresh and flashing through me with the feeling of fear crushing over me. I don't know if I was standing there or if I was the naked pink fleshed child or maybe I was the all around narrator.

The naked child lay there on a sheet with her firm plump bum shining like two small moons. A man's face, I couldn't remember whose, but the feel of his rough face scarred the smooth surface of the new bum. He kissed it hungrily, breaking it in with his face until the images moved to his soiled hands grabbing, tearing at the little un-pressed bum. Tearing and penetrating the smoothness of the tiny bottom which was so small under his two gigantic hands.

Helpless, I sat there seeing the images pass like history except this one had all the moving animation leaving me hopeless. The images turned and turned in my head. I sat there stupidly petrified not knowing where he might be hiding.

I wiped away the tears that fell over my clammy skin. My eyes observed my darker self lurking and waiting for me to look away and I knew she would then crawl onto my bed and kill me. I got up, stubbing my toe. Now I was limping and trying to massage the warm rush of blood. I flicked on the light getting rid of it all, the dream and her and him.

I opened the door and went into the washroom. I bent over the sink and sprayed cold water over my face, washing away the sticky residue. I looked at myself, mad in the mirror with water drops sticking to my skin. I flicked off the light seeing the dark side of myself and I flicked it on seeing the light side. I made a couple of ugly faces at the mirror.

I heard Matthew opening his door and I greeted him.

He felt good and happy under my arms and under the smooch of my lips for a kiss good night. He didn't take that too lightly.

I got up from Matthew's bed. He was already passed out. I changed back into my pyjamas and picked up my panties. I shut off the lights and crawled into the cool sheets of my bed.

Found

I stopped reading the romance novel because the hot seductions became fluttering hearts of making love where the mysterious cruel man fell deeply in love with the virgin dove. Their first night of passion he gently treated her with careful thoughts of feminine touch. I was thinking the writer must have been a nun, or better yet a man who thought he was writing about what women wanted. I picked up the horror book. Porn and horror made a beautiful couple.

The bell rang. I got up and opened the door, expecting more than likely one of Matthew's little rendezvous'. I found Chris there with his blue, blue eyes gaping at me. I stood there stunned, staring at him. I didn't know what to think or how to respond. All

I knew was that it was return of the dead for either side.

"What are you doing here?" I asked trying to hide the smile that kept trying to peek through.

"I miss you." Before I could respond, he reached in and kissed me. He pushed me inside with his weight banging me against the wall as I slammed the door, locking it. I directed our rolling and banging into my room.

Both of us fell onto the bed, bouncing as we ripped each other's clothes off. I kissed his body missing his cheap cologne and his gelled gooey sleepy-head.

He sucked hard on my skin as I clawed him with my nails. The scratches and blotched areas were how we stamped each other with the scars of love. The excitement died down because the bed couldn't be pushed into the wall anymore.

Chris turned to me almost out of breath and kissed me. We lay there staring at the ceiling as our heads rested overtop of each other.

The front door slammed as Matthew returned from grocery shopping.

"Who's that?" Chris asked getting up.

"Matthew." I pulled up the sheet. "How did you find me?"

"I went to your mum's house and she told me everything. I was surprised because I thought you would've told her that you left me. And I knew from there that you didn't mean too." Chris glanced over at me for a response. Nothing came. He put his jacket on. "I came."

"An what are you doing now?" I asked not understanding why he stood glaring with an unlit smoke hanging from his lips.

"I'm leaving now." He lit his smoke and opened the door. I was about to call his name out but I wasn't going to fall for it. The bastard was getting me back. He came back in the room and stood in front of the bed and pulled out his wallet, holding out a wad of cash. "This is your money. No hard feelings, I hope." He shrugged his shoulders. "Good night, Eliza." He threw it on the bed.

I sat there eyeing him, knowing not to cry and knowing not to say one word to him. Not to show anything to that bastard. I was ready to kill him.

He ran into Matthew.

"Are you back?"

"No, I just came to pay her my debt."

"Oh."

The door shut. One fucking sweet bastard. I dressed, practically running through my clothes to get to the front door. He was up the street walking with that satisfied look. I ran up to him, tapping him on the shoulder. He turned around casually smirking with that same smoke hanging between his lips. I punched him in the face. I stood back as he grabbed his face in shock.

I was so pissed off at him. "You like that, you fucking bastard?" I laughed at the bastard.

He laughed. "Oh God, fucking God this hurts, my love. I missed you too, Eliza."

I held his face and examined his red cheek all concerned. "It wasn't that bad." Once he straightened up with me under his arms I asked, "What was all that back there?"

"Getting back at you and I did a pretty good job of it."

Chris came on the weekends and waited around for me at the backstage door or in front of my flat. He knew how to find me and when Monday rolled around he was gone. Sometimes I gave him money to pay for my share but I knew once I gave it to him, I could see that his little mind was seeing it all put into one bet. And seeing him calling up Cod to consult which horse would come in first.

Most of the time before he left, we'd fight and then he'd sneak out, but Chris always returned.

An Idea

I went over to Eliza's mum's house, hoping she went there after taking off on me.

I could hear the television blaring through the screen door about some news with gunshots and helicopters hissing in the back. I carefully straightened myself out, taking out a stick of mint gum and chewed it down quickly. I knocked on the door, making it rattle. Paul peeked over from the couch and he got up pulling his lanky body forward.

"Hi, Paul."

"Hey, Chris."

"Who's there?" I heard her mum shout in the back.

"Chris!" I shouted back at her.

"Lovely." Her voice rang through.

Paul opened the door. "Do you want something to drink? Beer?"

Eliza's mum came in. "Want tea?"

"No thanks, a beer would be nice."

"I'll get it," said Paul.

"How are you doing?" She hugged me. "Eliza's off again."

"Yeah." Paul passed me a beer. "Thanks. I've been alright. Except last night I had the worst night. Somebody stole my scooter." In reality, I needed money so I had to sell it.

"But you're alright?"

"Nothing happened to me. I was at a pub and I went out and it was gone and Eliza's gone too."

"Horrible. I know it is a bit lonely without her. But she's doing her dancing again which I think is fabulous."

"It is better than working at the grocer. She wasn't too happy with that."

"No."

"How's everything here?"

"Great."

We all sat down on the couch with the television off as the conversation carried on and I waited for the right time to ask for Eliza's new address. I found the perfect timing with the last sip of my beer.

"Could I have Eliza's address? Somehow I lost it. Probably last night."

"Sure, just let me get it." Her mum got up and returned with a piece of paper with Eliza's new address. I folded the paper gently getting a glimpse of Eliza's new address in London.

"Thanks. I should get going, I have to meet my dad."

"Alright, Chris dear." She gave me a hug. "Take care now."

"You too."

"Do you need a drive?" Paul asked as he picked up the television remote-control.

"No thanks. Bye."

I was out with the mission accomplished. Someday I was going to give Eliza a surprise; it was just a matter of when.

A long tireless month passed and I was ready to go and see Eliza. I was ready with money to pay her back. I thought that hopefully it would shut her up. I took the fastest transportation, airplane and it couldn't go fast enough. I arrived early on a Friday morning. I took the train to her address, which didn't take too long.

I knocked on the door, nice and loud to make sure she heard it. The door opened and there she was looking beautiful with her big eyes shocked at seeing me.

I felt her fat wad of money in my pocket and I wanted her lips to say something. She tried to smile but the poor thing was confused. She actually thought that she got away.

"What are you doing here?" she asked.

I looked down at first and then up at her with complete sorrow in my eyes. "I, I missed you." I grabbed her quickly and kissed her hard, pushing her inside and crushing her body against mine. I could feel her body opening up to me as she pushed me onto the bed. I fucked her. Once I got my lovely fill of her, I relaxed on the bed. I heard the front door open and I got up and dressed. "Who's that?"

"Matthew. How did you find me?"

"I went to your mum's. I was surprised she welcomed me so openly after you broke up with me. But her and Paul were quite welcoming. And from there I asked for your address and that is it." I looked at her confused eyes. "I came."

"An what are you doing now? You're not leaving?"

I took a smoke and lit it looking straight into her little teary-eyed face. "I'm leaving." I took out my fat wallet and pulled out the bills. "This is your money. No hard feelings, I hope. Good night, Eliza." I tossed it at her and the bills scattered over the bed. I gave her a nice gentle grin and left. I opened her bedroom door and ran into Matthew who looked surprised at seeing me.

"Are you back?" he asked all too happy to see me, the fag.

"Perhaps." I gave him a smile and walked past him hearing his little sorrow sigh. I left knowing that she'd be right behind me, more than likely screaming for an explanation. Down on the street by myself I felt her gentle love tap on my shoulder and I turned around giving her a big grin and she slugged at me. Holy fuck did that hurt.

"You like that, you fucking bastard?"

"Holy fuck, Eliza, this fucking hurts." I rubbed my cheek. "Love, I missed you too, Eliza."

She placed her hand on my sore cheek and told me, "It wasn't so bad," under her little voice and I knew she was back.

"What was all that back there?"

"Getting back at you and I obviously did a pretty good job of it."

I took her underneath my arms and kissed her reassuringly. I took her out to a café that was right up from the street.

"What have you been doing?"

"The usual, school is almost done. And yeah, I've been going to my classes. I haven't gambled, if that is what you're so concerned about. I've been quite good."

"Right." She ignored me and I knew that was on her mind most of the time. "You kept the apartment?"

"Yeah." She sipped at her drink glancing about. "Look, Eliza, I'm sorry for hurting you. For gambling. Just everything, I'm absolutely sorry. The last thing I wanted to do was to hurt you, and I'm sorry if I did."

"Fine."

I gave her a smile that always made her smile back.

My stay with her would be the same: My apologies were never ending, and each trip I tired endlessly to please her before I had to say goodbye to return to Wolston.

The Ballet Experience

After work on Friday, I headed up to London. I bought myself a ticket with the last of my winnings and took the tube to go see Eliza perform. She had sent me a ticket and explained happily over the phone that she was playing the lead. I was excited for her.

Once I arrived in London, I went to her place and changed into my black suit. I took the last of the change from her little glass jar to add to the rest, which were crumpled in my pocket. I had just enough for flowers and the tube.

I arrived at the theatre. I sat there with groups of old people all dolled up for the ballet.

I watched carefully the tragic romantic storyline trying to keep pace with the slow moving dancers followed by the put-me-to-sleep music. But I watched Eliza for the first time doing her performance and of course, that's what kept my first ballet experience awake and alive for me. From the distance, her little figure jumped and bounced on that fairy prick of a man that held her high and graceful to the audience. That concluded part one. I headed outside for a smoke and a sip from my little canister of whiskey.

After a few gulps of whiskey, I headed back in and took my seat. I waited for the seniors to return from the dawdling lines for the washroom. I took another swig and smelled the old perfumed broad followed by her ancient popper in his Hush Puppies.

"Excuse us." Her crimson-lipstick gave me a grin for a young man.

I stood up gracefully telling them under my hot breath, "No problem."

"Thank you," she said, her wrist jingling with hot jewels.

I gave her a smile and sat down. The lights came down and the curtains rose and my Eliza came rushing in followed by the fairy man rushing his little body towards her. I sat there still and still until that was it. I clapped nice and loud for Eliza.

"Wooooo! Eliza, Wooooo!" I shouted out to her, hoping that she would hear my cheer amongst the applause of the crowd. The old people glanced back not knowing what to make of it and they turned back to concentrate on their clapping.

I loosened my tie as I exited the theatre. I bought her three red roses.

She came around the corner in her pretty tight black dress.

"You were fantastic, gorgeous, a beautiful doll on the stage. And for such a lovely lady that's the least I could say and this is the least I can do." I gave her a kiss and the roses.

"Right, Chris." She took the roses. "Are you hungry or thirsty?"

"First, let's make up."

After a good romp, we got dressed and got something to eat. I'd get all the questions that Eliza was concerned about.

She pulled on a pair of jeans. "Are you still gambling?"

"No." I kissed her as I finished buttoning my shirt. "I've been at school. Been a good boy." That was the truth because I'd been losing most of the time. My unfortunate streak deterred me from gambling as much. And I was doing better as a person.

"Glad to hear it." She ruffled my hair.

After having a final parting lay and both of us getting dressed, I had to find the appropriate time to ask her for money.

"Baby, love." I grabbed her, hugging her as both of us stared at the roses that were on the night-table. "You were fantastic on Friday. Absolutely."

"Yeah, love, an how many times did you tell me that?" She broke away and sat on the bed. And I feared what she was going to say next. "What do you want?" she asked placing her hair in a ponytail.

"Nothing." I looked away, looking right at the three roses that were starting to droop. I had practised this quite well. "I just need a little bit of money to get by, that's all." That's when I gravitated to Eliza.

"I can't keep doing this, Chris." Her eyes averted down to the ground to avoid mine. "You come here an always after you need money for fucking what? You fuck me an it's as if I'm paying you to fuck me. What the fuck do you need the money for? Why don't you ask your father? He owns a fucking factory!"

I picked up her chin. "Look, I'm not gambling, so you can stop worrying about that. I swear to you that I gave it up."

"What do you need it for?" She leered at me with her eyes turning ugly.

"I need some to get me past the week."

"Why can't you stop lying to me?"

"Fine. Eliza, I need the money because I need it to gamble because you know I can't fucking keep away from it!"

"I'm not some stupid whore. You fuck me over an over again, always coming back for a fuck an then you go back to spend my money on fucking what I don't know."

"I fucking just told you, to get through the week. I just finished paying off Brian."

"One of your jolly old debts."

"Yeah, what about it? You knew I would be paying this off. So why are you acting all surprised like this just came out of the fucking blue? You fucking well knew about it. That was the last time I ever played, and now I'm paying it off. And you're still blaming me. I've told you how many times I'm fucking sorry. And you know, too, that it costs fucking money to come out and see you. Paying off my debt and coming to see you, you add all that up and that means I am fucking low on cash." I shoved my clothes into my bag.

"Fuck off! Don't you dare make me feel guilty for your mistake. I'm not your fucking mother, Chris."

This was the part where I brought it down. "Eliza, look, I swear to you that I'm not gambling, alright? I just finished off—"

"Alright." She went to her night-table and pulled out some bills placing them into a nice roll and gave it to me. I held onto her hand. "Let me fucking go." I let her go. "I really mean it. Let me go."

"I love you."

"Chris, I just can't do this with you anymore. You can't keep coming down every time you're low on money. I can't do this. You understand?"

"You know it's not like that. I come down because I miss you."

She stood there with her lips pressed tightly together as if she held my world between them with her eyes glaring coldly into mine.

"Chris." She shook her head as I held her hand. "Just go."

I kissed her, her lips loosening up. "Trust me. I'm trying hard to be a better man. And I need you."

"For what?"

"Your love." I kissed her again. My head painfully searched for reassuring words. "Eliza, I'm not going to give up. And you know that. Trust me, that's what I need from you. I'm sorry for the pain in the past but I don't gamble. Alright?" I gave her another kiss.

She glared away from my eyes but I knew she was mine still. "Chris, you should get going." She stepped away and picked up my jacket.

I took my jacket and I opened the front door. "I love you."

"Right, bye Chris."

I kissed her goodbye.

On the plane, I indulged in the view of the thick rosy glow of London. The view was nice from the sky and so magical with Eliza at the centre of it. Her pleas and arguments filled my head and left me feeling guilty for leaving her alone, and attached to an asshole, me. I was flying back with her money, nice and secure in my pocket and I was thinking how to apply my next bet and the losses that faced me in Wolston. I felt like an asshole but I was in love and I didn't want to hurt her. That was important.

Closing

Thompson lifted me high and above. It was a beautiful part in the ballet where I reached high and declined slithering down him.

High above, my body under his straining arms, I felt a quick wobble. He tried with the skills of a dancer to balance me as his face remained solid in character, his hands attempted to find that trained balance.

He dropped me. Splat. Broken, I lay there on the stage floor. I couldn't feel anything. I was stuck staring at the strong wires that held up the ballet's white backdrop.

Matthew's face floated over me. His lips spelled out my name as his eyes lucidly observed me. He lifted me up and the recorded music continued playing. I finished off the ballet, seeing the steps but not feeling my body move.

I raised my head to find the performance. I was in Matthew's arms. I watched his lips quickly move and his eyes sank into mine as he waved his hand in front of my face. I lay there staring back, feeling the pain in my back and it all turned to black.

I was being eaten under the state of blackness because of

the pain in my bones. I felt the pressure of being crushed and displaced in the mixture of my muscles. All of it dissolved into a vibrating hot pain.

The white ceiling greeted me and I knew I was dreaming. I was happy glaring at the white ceiling, knowing that my performing career didn't end in such a blur.

I closed my eyes, stretching my body, and my body sprung into a tension of pain. It wouldn't stretch out, instead my foot was wrapped, shaped and stiffened and my lower back splintered in agony. I lay down, still feeling the pressure of pain receding back into its pocket.

I opened my eyes again this time noticing the vases of flowers surrounding my head. I don't think I'm dead was one conclusion I came to. That and I wasn't home. Instead, I was in a cosy hospital room with piss-like lighting. I sat up feeling a stabbing pain from my back shooting up. A nurse came rushing in to see how I was doing. She pressed a button and the bed moved into a sitting position.

"How's that, Miss Fellows?"

She wanted to hear better although that was not her job but with that smile of hers I couldn't resist saying, "Better."

"Good. And how are you feeling today?" She was fixing the pillows poorly so as not to disrupt or start any pain.

"Sore," I replied silently. I didn't want her red jolly lips to turn upside down.

"Expected."

"What happened?"

"Your ankle is broken and your lower back is bruised. So you won't be going anywhere." She picked up a clipboard hanging from the foot of the bed. "And how is your head?"

"Pounding."

She handed me some pills. I took them down wanting her to leave as soon as possible but she kept grinning and drew her attention to the flowers surrounding me.

"Looks like someone is loved." Happiness sprung through her from nowhere. Maybe that's why the friendly nurses wore white. The white gave them that pure highness of a happy being that a doctor with expensive garlic breath and cold sticky fingers couldn't do.

I smiled.

Matthew came in and saw me grinning. He grinned too. The nurse headed towards him. They exchanged concerns on my behalf. Nodding heads with dull hurried replies of yes.

Matthew gave me a hug and a kiss.

"How are you feeling?"

"Fine, still in pain."

"Do you remember anything?" He sat on the edge of the bed.

My memory being a thought out dream, I replied, "Yes, Thompson dropped me." I tried hard to swallow and to catch new breath.

"He sent you some get well flowers." Matthew pointed above my head.

"Tell him thanks."

Matthew read Thompson's card, "I'm sorry. Lots of love and hope to see you on your feet again soon. Soon is underlined. Thompson."

"That is sweet of him." I couldn't be angry in front of Matthew. I couldn't be anything lying here.

"When do I get to go home?"

"Soon, maybe today but you'll have to stay off your feet. And the doctors want to do a couple of checks to make sure everything is alright."

"Matthew, does Chris or my mum know about this?"

"No, I don't have their numbers. Did you want me to—"

"No thanks."

"Do you want to talk about anything?"

"No, I think I'll rest before the doctors come." He pressed the button and the bed reclined down. Back to the holey ceiling and the pissy light giving a feel of stained piss hanging above me. I fell asleep hoping to wake up someplace and someone else. The pain in all active movements gave a lucid memory of the fall. The drop and the sounding thump, thump of my bones and body coming to a splat.

My mind slipped into Thompson's accidental death. Thompson's tragic fall. The images of every possible physical tragedy happening to him passed through me. Behind his devastating end I would ask innocent little helpful questions of wonder: Whoops, did that fall on you? Whoops, was that a bus?

How much I wanted to push, gently push. Wish after wish after wish. Hoping with crossed fingers that when I saw Matthew again I'd hear of Thompson's tragic end. He ran in front of a bus. Oh my God, how sad. I would grab my heart out of love for pure drama.

The doctors peeked at me with great big shakes and nods agreeing on the situation. Checking out each wound with their shaky cold fingers. Wanting to know when they pressed the painful spots.

"Any questions?" the younger doctor asked me while he took off his glasses. He gave me a slight smile.

Dreading the worst, I spoke the worst. "I won't be able to dance?"

"You should be fine but not like how you used to be." He grinned brightly.

"What do you mean?"

"You more than likely shouldn't perform pro-fess-ion-ally." He sounded that one out, giving a long drawl on the L. "But I hope you prove me wrong. On the brighter side, it will be fine but like all broken things they're never perfect again. However, you are young. So if you work really hard, you just might be able to perform and it never hurts to try."

I sat there looking at them stupidly. On the brighter side I would be fine—that was great, really great but not the same.

"I'm sure, Miss Fellows, it comes as a shock. We have excellent therapy."

"I'll do it back home in Wolston. I'll be fine," I assured the doctors with a healthy grin.

"The good news is that you're fine to go home. How does that sound?"

"Good news."

They left and I picked up the vase from Thompson and I was ready to toss it out the window.

Fortunately, Matthew came in and helped me get ready and set me up with a new set of crutches. I swung my way out of the cheery hospital.

Back

I took good care of the cast because I didn't spend all my time in bed waiting for this piece of cement to come off.

I would bathe with a plastic bag over it and wash my toes carefully. After, I would clip my nails and choose a matching nail polish.

I got very possessive and obsessive with my toes. I thought about wearing socks since my toes would freeze. Usually I had to put cream on them because they were so dry that even the nail polish was crumbling off. I scoured for huge pairs of socks. I always carried an extra pair just in case it rained.

Besides the uncomfortable bathing activities with my bagged foot, I got a lot of privileges, like more leg room. People even pushed me first through the lines. I didn't need to fake the look of agony. I leaned over my crutches and they all stepped aside. And with that I gave them all a pleasurable, "thank you."

Matthew took me to the airport. He carried my small bag that I had when I arrived. We had our ceremonious goodbye and I left.

I would be back in Wolston soon. I didn't tell anyone I was

coming back. I thought I'd give them a surprise because ringing them up and telling them my little sob story was too much for me to handle. I preferred to show them. Showing them that everything was fine.

I sat there on the plane and watched England's green disappear into the regular fog where I couldn't see anything at all. Always the same experience when I went home. The fucking fog blocked the view to show me what I was missing. The fog kept the city bottled up where I had to go on memory.

Soon enough, the plane made a bumpy landing. The only problem was that I was the last to get off. Once off with my small bag, people outside helped me get a taxi.

I hopped inside my dark home, I went to the bedroom to make sure Chris's things were looming about and they still were. I sat down, taking off the sock seeing the toes with blue sparkles gleaming in the light. I opened my bag and pulled out my foot cream. I dabbed a bit on my hand and massaged my dry toes; the blue sparkles, sparkled onto the palm of my hand.

I heard the door unlock, open and slam shut. I heard Chris walk up to the bedroom where he remembered leaving the lights off. His head popped into the bedroom and he found me rubbing cream in between my toes. He was speechless.

"Hi, Chris, I'm home." I opened my arms to him.

He came over noticing the cast and gave me an anxious kiss. Not too long because he wanted to ask, "What's with that?" He touched the hard surface in response.

"I had an accident on the stage. Thompson dropped me an you can see that's why I'm home."

"You're okay though?"

"Yeah, it happened a while ago. I wanted to surprise you. Wait till my mum sees it." The thought excited me.

He kissed me gently as if I was wounded for life. "What does that mean?"

"That means that I can teach ballet. Look, I don't want to

discuss this right now. I'm fine. Aren't you happy to see me?"

"Yeah, I'm surprised."

He sat there and I was getting irritated by it. The pity looks and talk were too much.

"Why are you wearing a suit?"

"I had dinner with my mum."

"Ah."

Sitting in silence, still and breathing, we went back to our nice normal activity on the bed.

Mum's Greece

The rain was drying up, school was over and summer holidays were starting. At the time, I kept trying to convince my dad to buy me a car instead of another scooter and still no reply came.

My mum was getting ready for her annual getaway to Greece's fine beaches and she wanted to go out for dinner and catch up.

I was sitting in my suit, pulling at my tie waiting for my mum to join me at this fancy restaurant which was close to her place.

She showed up wearing a sheer ivory summer dress; she just couldn't wait to get back out there. We greeted each other with a good hug and she gave her little boy two kisses on the cheek.

"How are you?"

"Good. You're tanned. When did you go for that?"

"That was from my recent trip out to Greece. I was out there a week ago. I had a fantastic time. Always do." She picked up the menu and ordered the wine. "How is Eliza?"

"She's performing in London."

"That's great. You know, Chris, I would love to meet her sometime."

"When she gets back from London, I'll introduce you."

"Yes, and school's done, right?"

"Yeah."

Her blue eyes glimpsed up at me and returned to the menu and then back at me.

"Chris, dear, I need to tell you something. It's good news."

"What?"

The waiter interrupted and we ordered.

"What is it?" I asked as she took a big gulp of wine and held out her pointy finger.

"Chris, I've made some lovely friends in Greece which explains why I want to go back so suddenly." She paused and smiled. "I bought this dress in Greece. It's lovely, right?"

"Yeah."

She took a deep breath filled with wine. "Chris, I've met somebody and he's going to come back with me this time." The words rapidly came out as she took a massive sip of wine, dabbing the corner of her mouth with the napkin. Her lips were getting ready to talk again.

"He's Greek?" I asked. I thought I should show some concern.

"Yes, and he's also a lawyer. He lives out there for the summer holidays."

"When did you meet him?"

"A while ago," she told me trying to avoid my eyes as she concentrated intensely on tearing the bread apart and finishing her wine.

I didn't know what to say to her. "That's great," I responded and she smiled. I guess she thought I would react badly to her having a boyfriend, but I assumed that when they got a divorce that was one of the intentions.

"Look mum." I held her hand as the other one poured the wine. "Why are you acting so nervous? What I'm trying to say is that you and dad got a divorce and that means you're going to be seeing other people. You don't have to act all nervous about it. For fucks sakes, Mum, I didn't think you divorced dad to become a nun."

She laughed at this. "Chris, you're right. Just that, forget it, you just watch your mouth."

"Sorry."

After dinner, I walked her back home and she slipped me money for a taxi.

In the taxi I couldn't wait to get home with all my attention on my stomach that was filled with wine and too much rare steak.

When I got home, my stomach concern switched to surprise. Eliza was on the bed with her leg in a cast and looking absolutely angelic with her toes waving at me.

She was back. I had a feeling from that heavy cast that she wouldn't be taking off too soon.

Our short talk and concern led us to the main point and we fucked each other senseless that night.

A Great Man

The last day I saw him, we were at the bar waging a small bet. We both won back the little amount and decided to call it a night. He was going to drive me home.

"Cod!" a woman shouted. She ran over in plastic shoes which made her fat body wobble. She dropped her white fringed purse and bent over, showing thick brown roots pushing out the blond which she brushed away from her heavy blue eyeshadow. She gave a short wave.

"That's my niece, Sharon." He gave her a nice gentle wave.

She came over. "Hello."

Cod stepped right in. "Chris, this is my niece, Sharon."

"Hi, Chris. Uncle has told me a lot about you. But he didn't say how cute you were. Are you still going out with that Saber chick?" She glanced past me and gave Cod a nice big red-lipstick grin with her jumbo tongue resting between her teeth.

I didn't want to encourage her and being a bit under the bevy, "Thinking about marrying her."

"Ah."

And Cod cut in. "I'm going to give Chris a drive home. You want to come?"

"Yeah, because Auntie Dor wanted to make sure that you're staying out of trouble. An Uncle, are you staying out of trouble?"

I got in the backseat as Sharon sat down.

"Shut up, Sharon, dear."

"Could I have a smoke, Uncle?" she asked.

He took out his pack and handed her one.

"Thank you. So, did you two win?"

"A little bit."

"That's good, cause Auntie doesn't like any losers, isn't that right Uncle?" She nudged him with her plastic fingernail.

"Sharon, please shut up."

She giggled loudly under the cigarette as she tried tuning the radio but all she got was static and she turned it off. The car jerked into the parking gear.

"See you on Monday," he reminded me.

"Bye, Chris." His niece gave me a wave and a kiss. He pushed her back in the seat. "If she says no, I'll take you."

"Ah, shut up."

She giggled and Cod took off.

When I arrived at work on Monday I received the unfortunate news that Cod had died of a heart attack. I stood there with the other workers hearing the announcement. I was shocked because I didn't understand what had happened to him. He seemed healthy, fine and normal. I went to see Debbie.

"Ah, Chris." She hugged me.

"Did you talk to Doris?"

"Yeah I did. It's horrible, isn't it? Doris calls me an, an she asks after me an I after her. An from that she tells me that Cody is dead. An I told her, she, that, that I was sorry an she was crying all an that, an told me she had to go." Debbie brought the blue tissue to her nose.

"I feel so sorry for her with those children. But I'm going to give her a ring later. I think she needs as many friends as possible right now. You worked with Cody. Maybe you could ring her up too."

"Yeah."

The phone rang and I took my leave and headed back to work.

As the day grew on the gossip around Cod's death became the main topic during the breaks. I went back to Debbie and her eyes lit up as she saw me.

She blew her nose. "Chris," she said under the blue tissue as her other hand reached out and fell onto the desk. "Doris called back, she's still feeling rough an all, that poor girl. The funeral will be on Friday. An Cody, the old boy, died of a heart attack. It is really horrible. Truly is." She rubbed her nose. "Also keep this just here now. Between us. Cody had a girlfriend an she found him stone cold in her bed. I couldn't believe it. An Doris is completely shaken up with the whole ordeal. It's absolutely horrible." She blew her nose. "Anyways, you better get back to work." She scooped her tears with a fresh blue tissue and headed up the stairs.

"Debbie, who was she?"

"Sharon, she didn't give me her last name. I don't even know if she knows it."

I punched out early because I told my dad I would contact Doris and comfort her for a bit.

I tried calling Doris's number but it was busy every time I rang and I decided to just give up on the whole event of comforting her. I don't think she would much appreciate my comforting words of Cod and she might even yell at me. Besides, I was completely taken aback that Cod had a girlfriend; he had never mentioned her at all. I never would have guessed.

At the funeral, Cod's co-workers stood with their wives as I joined them with Eliza.

One of them nudged me. "Where's Jamison?"

"He had to go away." I didn't tell them that my dad already had a trip planned out with sweet old Cheryl. "On business." I responded to him.

"Never rests, does he?"

"Unfortunately."

The immediate family, Margaret and May, stood on the sides of their mum as little Marvin stood in front trying to grab the coffin. In between sobs Doris had to keep dragging Marvin away from the coffin. Then came the priest and on the other side was Sharon crying just as hard as Doris. The one rose Sharon held lost its petals with each exploding blow of her nose into the white tissue.

The bible shut and he crossed and everyone followed with amen. The coffin was cautiously lowered and Doris pushed her children to wave goodbye to their daddy. Suddenly, a single red rose was thrown in. The rose's petals left a small floating trail to the coffin. Doris glared at that young hussy who was wiping a very steady flow of mascara tears.

"You!" she screamed and her children stepped behind her. "You, stay away from my husband!"

"I have every right to be here. He did die in my bed!"

Doris was unleashed. "That doesn't give you any right! That only means that you, you killed him you fucking slut! If only you knew how to fuck properly. An another thing, Miss Slut, if he really loved you why didn't he leave me for you?" Cod always said that she was one smart bitch.

"He was in my bed and it was after we made love, not little babies!" She pointed at the children with her snotty rag. "Anyways, he referred to you as the Bitch an I—"

The priest gladly moved out of the way and hugged the bible to watch these two women fight over a dead jolly man. God, right there, I would miss my times with Cod. Only this could be Cod's funeral.

One good slug of Doris's fist was caught by Sharon and then they tumbled down. Screaming, cursing, pulling at each other's hair as their dresses rolled up to show that big hot hussy's black panties and Doris's white slip prepared for these unfortunate occasions.

The three children cheered their mum on.

Enough screaming entertainment passed and two of Cod's co-workers took a brave step in to separate the two. One of them got smacked accidentally by Doris who quickly placed her aim a little bit more to the right where she finally punched Sharon in the jaw.

"Cod taught me that, you fucking little slut!"

"Bitch!" Sharon kept shouting. She struggled in the man's arms as her legs kicked spastically in Doris's direction.

The other man let go of Doris who was straightening out her dress like a lady and the children surrounded her, giving her a group hug.

Cod's fresh tart lowered her spandex dress. He let her go and she walked off trying to set her torn peroxide hair.

The funeral convened with the rest of us throwing our flowers into the grave. I stood by the edge, holding one red carnation which I threw down. And in that hole I could hear Cod laughing. He must've died a happy man.

He was lying in that white satin bed lecturing me: *I have a beautiful family with a lovely an concerned wife. A man should always have a bed that is more than welcome to him. An that is Sharon, she's always ready to go. It's always those young ones that have had young men who don't know one hole from the other an treat it as such. An Sharon saw that Cody boy knows how to make a big pussy nicely moist. An with that you're guaranteed a ride always.*

Cod was a great wise man. I smiled down at the coffin and walked over to Doris who was dabbing her eyes as she watched Cod's co-workers drop flowers.

"Doris."

"Chris," she said softly.

"This is from the boys from work. We're all going to miss him."

She took the card. "Thank you so much, Chris. Thank you." She held my hand for a minute and released it taking her hand back to the corner of her eyes.

I said a couple of words to the others as we made our way to our loved ones standing there in black.

The thunder roared, the rain poured and I joined up with Eliza who snapped the umbrella open and we walked away. I looked back to see if Doris was still there at the grave but she was already shoving her children in the car with her mouth moving incessantly.

Cod and Mum

After Cod's funeral, we walked to my mum's house. The lights were on giving a yellow glow to the windows. The door opened and this time it was Paul. At first he didn't seem to recognize us.

"Hi, Paul," I said.
"Ah, Chris an Eliza."
"Who's there?" my mother screamed.
"Chris an Eliza."

My mum pushed Paul aside and gave me a kaleidoscope of a hug. She pulled away, examining me up and down and she noticed the big black sock and the two wooden crutches holding me up.

"Eliza, my God what happened?"
She opened the door and I hopped in followed by Chris.
"On stage, at my last performance, my partner dropped me by accident an I've been in crutches since."
"Why didn't you call?"
"Yeah, that's what I still want to know." Commented Chris.
"I don't know. I wanted to give everyone a surprise."
"You're alright? What about your ballet?"

"I can teach but to perform on the stage as a career wouldn't be best unless the ballet was about someone who kept falling. I could handle that much."

Chris and Paul moved to the couch.

"What are you doing in Saber?"

"Besides visiting you, Chris had a funeral to go to. One of the workers died of a heart attack."

"Common in Saber, I'll say that much. How long have you been back for?"

"Two days about. I was going to come earlier an call."

"No need for it."

She pulled out a chair for me at the kitchen table and sat down lighting a cigarette and blowing the smoke above into the pool-table kitchen light.

She looked back at me as if I was reading her thoughts. "So, what else is new?"

"Nothing much, except this cast. After it's off I'll start looking for a teaching job. St. Maurice is still renovating."

"I hope you're not thinking of the grocer." She needed to lecture now.

"No. What have you been up to?"

"Besides deciding on the wallpaper for the kitchen, not too much."

"Paul isn't losing yet?" I asked looking over at Chris, knowing that he was still betting.

"No, I don't have to worry about that. He's godsent." My mum replied winking at me.

"I wish Chris was." I said reluctantly.

"What do you mean?" My mother asked touching my hand.

"He gambles a bit." I told my mother smiling like it was okay.

"Chris can afford too. Unlike your father, he gambled like he was a rich man. You know when he died I had to pay off his debts."

"Why didn't you say anything to me?"

"Don't worry Eliza, Paul helped me. You don't have to worry about Chris, his father owns a factory."

"Right." I burned my tongue on the hot tea.

"The tea's hot. His gambling isn't bad, right?" My mother blew over her tea.

I gave her a big smile. "No mum, it's fine. He plays like a gentleman."

"That's what I thought. Chris is a good boy. I really like him and you know he would never hurt you. He's an honest man."

"Yes Mum." I said rolling my eyes.

"I know you don't believe me but when you get older you can tell the assholes from the real men. Real men don't hurt the ones they love." My mother took a sip of her tea. "I saw this really nice sunflower pattern for the kitchen."

Greece and Beyond

"My mum's back," Chris told me as he handed me a cup of tea. I was watching the silent news on the television.

"Oh." I sipped at my tea and speculated the newscaster's words as the pictures of an airplane crash filled the TV. Cops and blabbing sorrowful relatives who blew their noses in between their words.

"She wants to know if tonight is okay."

"Yeah, that's fine." Back to the newscaster giving her summary of the crash.

"She has a boyfriend."

"Greek?" I asked taking interest. The news took a turn for the worse and went to the reviews of current dramas and comedies.

"Probably, she didn't say. She said she was bringing a special guest that she wanted me to meet."

"Does she know about me?"

"Yeah. We'll be meeting her at the same restaurant."

"Does your dad know that your mum is back?"

"I don't think so. They really don't communicate. Once they signed the papers everything was over between them. When I was living at home with my dad, I came home once and found the trash full of pictures of him with my mum. He threw them all out."

I wore a simple black dress and one sandal to show the matching gold glittered painted toenails. I sat down on the bed and watched Chris getting into the same black suit. He buttoned his collar and started knotting the tie.

"Come here," I told him.

He pulled the knotted tie up to his neck. "What?" He asked looking down.

I pulled at his tie and brought him down. "I like you like this." I kissed him on the cheek missing his lips. He took my face in his hands and forced me to kiss him. He pushed me down and unbuttoned my dress. Then he pulled off my black panties which curled around his finger.

"Do we have time?" he whispered between his teeth as he bit me and tossed my panties.

I lay back down and watched with anticipation as he pulled out his penis and sunk lovingly into me.

In the restaurant, Chris pointed out his tanned mother. She wore a cool blue dress that was too summery.

Chris's mum squeezed him, as her gentleman friend shook my hand introducing himself as Joseph, with a thick Greek accent. His black hair kept flicking into his eyes and he'd move it back in place. I wondered if it was a wig because the hair kept flicking back in his eyes every time he moved his head, and when he patted his hair back it shifted to one side.

Chris introduced me to his mum who shook my hand and smiled with her smooth shade of pink-lipstick.

Chris's introduction to Joseph was followed by, "I heard a lot about you." He grinned with white teeth.

Chris replied with a stern smile.

We all sat down picking up the menus. Once we ordered his mum's attention went towards Chris.

"What have you been up to?"

"I'm done with school."

"Is he still paying for it?" She gave him a concerned stare.

"Yeah, and I'm still working at the factory."

"And how is that going?"

"The same. One of my friends, a co-worker, died. Cod. On the brighter side Mum, tell us about Joseph."

Joseph sat straight up. Again his hair was shaking as he swept away the ones which got loose. He was trying to look presentable.

"I met Joseph on the beach. I was jogging and all of a sudden we ran into each other."

"Actually, I have to admit that I had spotted your mother before. She's absolutely stunning, Chris."

"Joe." Carole blushed, wanting to keep focus in front of Chris. She gently tapped Joe's hand.

"Anyway, it all started from there." Joseph stroked Carole's hand. His darkness made Carole's tanned skin appear paler.

"What do you do, Joseph?"

"I'm a lawyer like your mother."

Chris lost interest in the lawyer bit.

"And what are you doing back, Mum?"

"I wanted to see you and I wanted you to see Joseph. I missed you and I thought it was important." She tried hard to find the right words and offer her motherly caring look into Chris's eyes. She watched anxiously for a good response to Joseph.

"Ah." He swallowed a piece of steak. "You've got something to tell me?" He took another piece not even looking at his mum.

She took a sip of her wine. Joseph tore at the bread making little balls.

"I'm deciding whether or not to move to Greece permanently." She took another sip and watched Chris nod his head knowing that he was listening to her. "How would you feel about it? You could come and visit me anytime you wanted."

Chris glanced up and took a sip of his wine. "I'm fine with it, Mum. Whatever you want."

She stretched over with her hand across his, "Chris—"

"Mum, whatever you decide I'll be happy with it." He shrugged his shoulders, cutting off a piece of steak. He remained expressionless.

"What do you mean?" she asked, carefully removing her hand back to cut another piece of steak.

"I'm fine with it in other words." He sipped his wine. He placed it down and took the napkin to wipe off his mouth. "That means that you won't be here when Eliza has your grandchild."

"What?" both me and his mum responded simultaneously.

"I don't know. Just go."

"Carole, I'm not pregnant." I replied with serious eyes and she reclined in her seat again. Both of us took a big gulp.

Joseph excused himself to the washroom.

"What do you think of Joseph?" his mum asked.

"He's nice, doesn't say too much and you know, Mum, he's wearing a piece?"

"He thought coming out here would be better for you."

"Right."

"What I like about Joseph is he tries hard to impress me but not too much. And not too little. He's trying hard, Chris, to be perfect for you."

"What about you?"

"Don't turn this around. I'm happy, can't you tell? I don't want to argue. I want to tell you that he asked me to marry him. I told him that I had to think about it. That's why I came out here."

"And I thought you missed me, Mum."

"I do miss you."

Joseph returned as Carole finished off her wine and Chris continued playing with his silverware. They turned their attention to me and I told them all about my pitiful downfall. After the bill came we departed.

Chris's mum gave him a tight squeeze, and me my first hug.

"Chris, let's go out for lunch, okay? Maybe tomorrow?" she asked putting on that I want to make you happy face.

"Great." He gave her a tight grin.

Baby

I took the train to meet Matthew and his baby girl. Matthew was up in Bury staying at his mum's house which was close to the hospital.

Huge gardens with double garages passed by. The atmosphere got fantastically repetitive. Every house had a different coat of paint and it was a twin of the one beside it.

I took the card out from its tight brown paper bag. I stared at the baby.

The cast had finally come off but I had this sensation to touch my ankle making sure I felt the bone in the right place.

I took my pen writing out MATTHEW underneath Congratulations. I sat there staring at Bury trying to form a set of wise words but nothing came except the ending. Lot's of Love to the new daddy, Eliza.

Last Night

"KEL'S LAST NIGHT TO LIVE!" greeted Eliza, Kel and me above Drew's entrance. Inside Drew's loft he had changed his cosy spacious living quarters into a club-land where there was a DJ and a crowd of strangers.

Somebody in the crowd shouted, "Kel's here!" Drew stood up on a chair holding a drink as somebody handed us our beers.

"Kel the Man is here!" Drew paused to point him out as people followed his point with cheers.

"Now everyone, this is Kel's last night before he marries his beloved. Let's not talk about her, let's show Kel the best night of his life. And let's start it off with a toast. Kel, may you remember this night as the best night of your life. Cheers!"

We chugged down our beers.

"Alright, will the honoured guest please join me in the back room?" He said it quickly and the music commenced as we made it to the back. The back was Drew's room.

There was the classic table with all the varieties of Drew's druggie treats and behind the closet's door was Kel's little nibbling fleshy treats before his, 'I do' made it illegal.

"Chris, you do the honours."

"Kel." I got up. "We both got you something so that you'd remember your boys in good humour." I stepped by the closet. "Me and Drew." I wiped my eyes to create an emotional atmosphere and Drew picked up on it.

"That's right, man." Drew wiped his eyes as he continued to cut the cocaine.

"Me and Drew want to tell you that we love you. And I can't go on anymore." I threw my hands up. "Kel, here it is." I opened the door and two lovely ladies came in, blond and big breasted and paid very well to give all their passionate services to Kel. Kel opened his arms and they rushed over to him in their squeezed-tight dresses.

"Thanks." They pushed him down onto the bed. "Holy fuck, thanks a lot."

I observed Eliza to make sure she didn't mind. I had already told her. She didn't care. She was already by Drew, snorting up the white powder through a rolled up bill. She passed me the bill and I joined them. Kel lay down on the bed enjoying the ladies' attention as they laughed, removing his clothes. We took the drugs, leaving an accommodating amount for Kel as he lived out his bachelor fantasy.

Eliza was great. As soon as she got out she was dancing her way through the crowd. I grabbed her, pumping her from the back and holding her tightly. Her body jerked me in the right spot.

This is where it all was for me. Me and Eliza. That was it.

The Wedding

Drinks bubbled high over as the bride and groom finished their dance only to be interrupted by their in-laws. The music bounced off the wooden floor to the fake-wooden-plastic walls.

Chris sat beside me with his bottled beer in one hand as his thumb tapped the back of my neck. He was talking in grand detail to an old man, the lush of Kel's family, about his promotion to manager at his father's factory. Chris's blue eyes looked at me each time the genuine lush took the chance to share some of his big time managing advice.

Chris took my hand. "I'm going to have a dance with my girl."

"I'll have a go with her." He slapped Chris's shoulder.

"Better watch yourself, old man."

The old man's cackle followed us onto the dance floor. Chris held me tightly as we danced too slow for the slow song.

"Chris!" Kel shouted.

We watched the tipsy newlyweds.

"What?"

"Switch!" Kel demanded as he twirled Amanda off his arms.

Chris spun me out of his arms as I passed Amanda's gathering gown and fell into Kel's arms.

Kel held me closely. "I should've married you, Eliza." He whispered into my ear as he gave me a surprise dip.

I looked over to Amanda and Chris. Chris was holding her far away. He glanced over to me and quickly nodded at his wasted friend who was getting ready to whisper more of his delicacies.

"Switch!" Chris shouted.

I spun back into Chris's arms and we ended with a nice lavish dip.

The slow music switched to a disco track. Chris took this time to straighten out his tie and tuck his shirt in for another speech. He snatched a bottle of beer from a black and white waiter as he walked on the make-shift stage. He swayed a bit as his finger tapped the head of the microphone.

"Beautiful ladies and drunk gentlemen. Being the best man and all, I want to congratulate this fun little festive couple. I hope Kel and Amanda have many years of happiness and in Amanda's case plenty of children. I will down this for you, man, for old and plenty of new times. Cheers!"

The sound of manly hollers supported Chris as he chugged his beer. Chris being a performer at heart did a dramatic jump kick onto the floor.

"My lucky girl." Chris gathered me in his arms and gave me a nice drunken kiss. "Did you want to go to our room?"

Before I could answer Amanda tore me out of Chris's loving arms.

"Eliza, do you remember?"

Amanda lifted up her dress. She clicked the heels of her shoes on the floor followed by small jumps. I crossed my arm through Amanda's arm, and we did the dance that every child would have learned during some point of their life in gym class. We slapped our high-heeled shoes on the floor, kicked high and threw each other into a dizzy circle. Chris and Kel joined in, tossing us from each other. Soon under exhaustion we all fell. We lay there letting the air catch up which was the smell of beer mixed with the rich scent of wedding champagne.

Unfortunately, the dance floor was getting too crowded with the disco tracks encouraging the hustle. We got up, stole-found an empty round table and watched the drunken relatives spill their drinks as they danced. I sat down on Chris and tugged at his tie. Amanda placed her dirty white-stockinged feet on Kel's cock. The newlyweds both laughed and guzzled down their champagne.

"God, I can already feel the pounds laying in." She patted her stomach.

"You look beautiful." He kissed her dirty foot.

"You're fucking pissed, my dear husband."

"And I say drink to that. Being pissed with a fat beautiful wife."

"Cheers!" We all drank, laughing with the liquor pouring down and rising at high points.

The camera man came, followed by a collection of family picture-takers. The wedded couple cuddled and smiled as each flash fell over them.

"That's enough! Come on husband!" Amanda dragged her husband out of the room.

"What about you two?" The camera man asked as he steadied a camera.

I glanced at Chris and he winked in his dreamy drunken way. We kissed passionately for the photo. After the flash, we sank lovingly under the table.

It ended after our libidinous descent, a kiss and then a sudden rush of coma. I woke up in our hotel room with my dress flung someplace and Chris snoring beside me. I got up feeling extra sore with my ankle killing me as the rest of my body weighed on it. The whole scene of the night played over in my head. The crawling, the attempted fucking and at moments feeling ghastly sick, but we did make it back to our room.

I found Chris's crumpled shirt and put it on. I massaged my ankle as I sat there staring at the fun mess and knowing that once I made it to the toilet I'd be throwing up.

An orange curtain-glow filled the room, warning me that the maid would be interrupting soon. Chris rolled off the bed. His body made a heavy thump on the carpeted floor.

ISBN 142510381-2